Two men came out f

One carried a shotgun, the other had an automatic pistol in his hand. Harry and the gray-haired man scrambled into the rear of the Caddy, the accountant expertly gunning the car out of the parking lot and around the curve. Through the rear window, Harry and the gray-haired man watched as the two from the cruiser ran to the parking lot, firing at the rapidly receding Cadillac.

"You called that one right," said the gray-haired man. "What tipped you off?"

"Didn't fit," said Harry. "That's just not the kind of boat you expect to see at a crummy dock like this."

"Is somebody gonna tell me what's goin' on here?" the accountant asked over his shoulder.

"Later," said Harry.

Also by Alan Cullimore
published by Tor Books

A GOOD PLACE TO HIDE

ALAN CULLIMORE

A BAD DAY IN THE BAHAMAS

TOR

A TOM DOHERTY ASSOCIATES BOOK
NEW YORK

A BAD DAY IN THE BAHAMAS

Copyright © 1989 by Alan Cullimore

A TOR Book
Published by Tom Doherty Associates, Inc.
49 West 24 Street
New York, NY 10010

ISBN: 0-812-50143-8   Can. ISBN: 0-812-50144-6

Library of Congress Catalog Card Number: 88-50992

First edition: January 1989

Printed in the United States of America

0 9 8 7 6 5 4 3 2 1

ONE

Harry Foster sat on the almost deserted beach, idly pitching pebbles into the clear, calm waters.

Harry Foster, proprietor of an apartment motel on South Florida's Gold Coast, owner of an old thirty-eight foot Hatteras in its slip at the Belle Mar Marina had a little money in the bank, not a real care in the world except that he was bored out of his goddam mind.

There had been a time, back in the old New Jersey days, back when he was marketing manager of a paper-box company and when his wife had walked out on him leaving him deep in debt, that the thought of being in his present circumstances would have seemed an unattainable heaven.

Of course, that was before his name was Harry Foster; it used to be Harry-Something-Else. But that was before he'd left his old life behind—left everything behind, including his name. That was before he'd drifted down to South Florida and got lucky. At least, he'd thought he'd got lucky at the time; now, he wasn't so sure.

Sighing, Harry pitched one last pebble into the water, climbed to his feet and reluctantly made his way back up the beach to his motel, the Balmy Breezes. Corny name, but long established, no point in changing it. Fourteen apartments ranging from one-room efficiencies to two-bedroom suites. Good middle class trade. Solid. People who came back year after year.

The season was over, only four apartments rented. Business was slack everywhere in July. He walked up the steps from the beach to the wooden-decked patio, automatically noting a lounger that needed fixing, a rip in a beach umbrella, a potted palm that should be watered. Old Mr. and Mrs. Steinmetz were on the deck in their usual morning spot, out of the sun, playing gin rummy. The Johnsons and their two kids sat at a round table in the lobby, sorting over the seashells they'd collected when the tide went out. Frank Obelinsky, paunch hanging over his baggy swimming trunks, was on his way out to the beach, loaded down with blankets, towels, a cooler, radio, suntan lotion and the *Wall Street Journal*. Ahead of him flounced a tanned, white-bikinied young beauty, latest in the line of Frank Obelinsky's young beauties. Harry hoped he would be that lucky when he was pushing seventy-five.

John Chambers, bags packed, waited for Harry outside the office.

"Sorry if I kept you waiting, Mr. Chambers," Harry

said, "I was down on the beach."

"No hurry . . . no hurry."

Harry slid open the glass door to his office, went in, got Chambers' account from the files. Chambers followed him, sat in the visitor's chair by Harry's desk, took his checkbook and gold pen from the inside pocket of his outdated, tan linen Palm Beach suit.

"Any phone calls this morning, Mr. Chambers?"

"No, I didn't make any calls this morning."

Harry passed the totaled bill across the desk. Chambers wrote out a check, Harry stamped the bill Paid, and tucked the check under a corner of his blotter. "Hope you enjoyed your stay, Mr. Chambers."

"Always do. Always enjoy my stays here. Look forward to them."

Three times a year John Chambers came for a week at Balmy Breezes. Always alone, always the same one-room efficiency on the second floor overlooking the ocean. Every January, June, and October he came for the first week of the month. Never had visitors. Walked along the beach by himself, went out for dinner by himself, came back by himself. A thin, trim, white-haired, white-moustached little man of around sixty-five who wore old-fashioned Palm Beach suits and Panama hats, and who was in exports/imports. That's what it said on his business card: John J. Chambers, Globus Enterprises. Exports-Imports. A Miami address.

Export and import of what, Harry had no idea, but whatever it was that came in and went out, it paid well. The thin gold Piaget watch, the two-carat diamond pinky ring, the gray Mercedes 450SL sedan all testified to that.

Chambers folded the receipted bill, tucked it into

3

his wallet. "Got me booked in for October, Mr. Foster?"

"Number eight, as usual."

"Good, good." Chambers got to his feet. Harry stood, held out his hand. He was almost a foot taller than Chambers, but at six-two and a bit, Harry was taller than most men. "See you in October then, Mr. Chambers."

Chambers shook Harry's hand. "I'd like to see you before then. Got something I want to talk to you about. Not now, next week. Think you could come by my office one day next week?"

"Sure. Can you give me an idea of what you want to talk to me about?"

Chambers waved a hand, dismissing the matter as of little importance. "Oh, just a thought. How would next Tuesday suit you?"

Harry went through the motions of checking his calendar. "Looks okay. In the morning?"

"In the morning, around ten, say."

"Next Tuesday. 10 A.M. Your office." Harry made a note on his calendar. "Shall I call before I come?"

"No need. I'll be there." Chambers picked up his soft pigskin grip and matching garment bag. "I'll be expecting you, Mr. Foster."

Harry watched Chambers walk the length of the lobby and out to the parking lot, heard the Mercedes start up and drive off. What the devil did Chambers have in mind? Why couldn't he have told him while he was in the office? Harry shrugged; at least it was something to plan for, something to break the monotony.

Through the office window Harry watched Frank Obelinsky's girl run down to the ocean, long blond hair flying, breasts bouncing, bottom jiggling. Maybe that's what he needed, a jiggling, bouncing, nineteen-year-old. Like hell that's what he needed, he'd been married to one. Eight years the marriage had lasted. Eight years of paying the mortgage on a big house he hated, eight years of paying bills his wife ran up as if there were no tomorrow, eight years of suspecting she was sharing her pampered body with an uncounted number of other men. No woman, no matter how great, was worth what she'd put him through. He'd put up with her total, demanding selfishness for eight long years: he must have been out of his mind.

On the day before his thirty-eighth birthday she'd told Harry she was leaving him and an hour later packed her expensive clothes into her Italian luggage, got in her Corvette, and took off. Harry never saw her again, never heard from her except via demanding letters from her lawyer. So Harry walked out of the whole New Jersey mess, walked away from the job he hated, the mortgage on a house he no longer wanted to live in, and from his wife, who won an uncontested divorce from him.

He'd run away from it all to South Florida, changed his name and started again, started a whole new life from scratch. He'd made some money, quite a lot of money. To be honest, he hadn't really *made* the money, not by the proverbial sweat of his brow; he'd literally fallen into it, had it handed to him on a plate, a totally unexpected windfall that had been enough to let him take over Balmy Breezes. And he did that because he met a woman and had ended up married to her. A woman very different from his first wife. A woman of cool intelligence, a woman of discriminating tastes, a women with whom he'd believed he could share a good life. A woman who, like himself, was going through the process of warily recovering from the hurt and disillusionment of an unsuccessful first marriage. This time it would be different, they said. This time it would be forever.

But it didn't work out that way. Twelve months later, defying all logic, she left him and went back to her ex-husband who'd treated her so badly. Harry was stuck with Balmy Breezes—which he'd really bought only because she'd wanted it and at that point he would have done anything to make her happy.

This irony finished marriage for Harry Foster. No way was he going to go through that emotional turmoil a third time. He now kept his relationships with women down to basics: dinner and bed; a ride in his boat, picnic, and bed. Variations on a theme that ended with good-bye the next morning. No woman shared Harry's bed for two consecutive nights. It was a rule of the house.

Tuesday finally arrived. Harry drove the thirty-odd miles south into Miami for his mysterious appointment with John Chambers.

Globus Enterprises Inc. proved to be located in an ugly old six-story brick building in a run-down part of the city, an old business section that had seen better days when Miami had been a slow-paced, peaceable town. That was before it was enshrined in the Hall of Ill-Fame as one of the major crime centers of America. A toy manufacturer, a cloak-and-suit wholesaler, two mail-order houses, and a restaurant supply company were listed as sharing the low-rent space with Globus.

An ornate, vandalized, cage-type elevator creakily carried Harry up to the third floor. Globus was housed at the far end of a dingy corridor, the company name lettered in chipped gold-leaf on the frosted glass panel of an ancient, scarred, oak door. Harry went in to what was obviously the fusty domain of the secretary-receptionist. A name plate on the littered government-surplus wooden desk said this was Mrs. Rose Cellini.

Mrs. Rose Cellini, an elderly, bad-tempered-looking woman in an unflattering black dress, sat behind a vintage Underwood manual typewriter hammering out an invoice. Her uniformly jet-black hair was fashioned in a lacquered and unshakable beehive. A hint of a moustache shadowed her upper lip. She looked up suspiciously as Harry entered.

"Yes? What do you want?"

"I have an appointment with Mr. Chambers, my name is Foster."

She picked her intercom phone. "There's a Mr. Foster here, says he has an appointment. Shall I send him in?" A pause, she hung up, said to Harry, "He says you can go in."

Opening off the reception area was another frosted-glass paneled door. Mrs. Cellini pointed to it. Harry heard the buzz and click of an electric lock release, then went through the door into Chambers' office. A sparsely furnished office. A couple of green metal file cabinets, a wooden table, a metal desk with a wooden swivel chair behind it in which John Chambers now sat. A straight-backed wooden chair for visitors. No family photographs, no personal mementos on the desk top. An in-and-out tray, a stack of file folders, a standard marble-base pen set and two black dial telephones.

"Ah, so you made it," Chambers said. "Good, good." He pointed to the visitor's chair. "Sit down, sit down Mr. Foster."

Harry sat on the hard, vinyl-seated wooden chair.

"Would you like some coffee?" Chambers asked.

"Sure, I'd like some coffee."

Chambers picked up the intercom. "Mrs. Cellini,

bring us some coffee." He turned to Harry. "How do you take yours?"

"Black," said Harry.

"That'll be black for Mr. Foster, and you know how I take mine, or you should after twenty years." Chambers waited while Mrs. Cellini said something, then shouted into the phone, "Of course you've got time, don't be ridiculous." Angrily he slammed down the receiver. "One of these days I'm going to get rid of that woman and get myself some good-looking young girl who won't answer back when I tell her to do something." He smiled at Harry. "Now, let's get down to the business at hand."

He leaned forward, rested his elbows on the desk. Today, John Chambers wore a banker's gray three-piece suit, custom-made by a good tailor many years ago, and an immaculate white shirt with a starched collar, the kind that used to be featured in Arrow ads. His tie was pale gray with a diamond stickpin in it. A precise, fussy little man of the old school.

"I must say you've got me curious," said Harry. "What's this all about?"

"Got you curious, have I?" Chambers chuckled, bobbing his white-haired head. "That's good, that's good. I hope my proposition takes your fancy." He tidied up the file folders on his desk, moved them to one side, straightened the in-and-out tray. "We'll just wait till that woman brings us our coffee and then I'll get down to details."

His office door opened. Mrs. Cellini came in carrying a tin tray with two paper cups of coffee on it. Heavy-footed, her face tight with disapproval, she banged the tray down on Chambers' desk, spilling some of the coffee, then wordlessly turned and walked out.

Chambers watched her go, shaking his head. "She

can open my door without me pushing my buzzer. I've got to find out how she does that." He passed a paper cup of black coffee to Harry, tasted his own, grimaced. "I keep telling that woman to buy a coffee maker so I can have a decent cup of coffee, but will she . . . ? No, she gets this sludge from a machine down the hall. For herself, she makes tea."

Harry sipped his coffee. It was awful.

"Now," said Chambers, "what I want you to do for me as a favor is deliver a package to a friend of mine."

Harry took time to digest this. Chambers waited. Conversationally, Harry said, "Can I ask a few questions?"

Chambers smiled paternally. "Ask away. You don't learn anything if you don't ask questions, I always say."

"This package. Where do you want it delivered? Who to? And just so there aren't any unpleasant surprises, what's in this package? But the real question is, why me? There are plenty of courier services that'll deliver a package. What's so special about this one?"

Chambers tipped back in his chair, steepled his fingers. "All very reasonable questions, Mr. Foster, but I couldn't give this job to a courier service, it's much too important for that. And why you? Because I consider myself a good judge of character and believe you can be trusted. Because you own a boat, which is essential to this assignment, and because I think you'll find my proposed compensation for your time and trouble hard to resist." He leaned forward, folded his hands on the desk top. "To answer your questions in order, I want this package delivered to Haiti. I will tell you who it's going to a little later on if you agree to help me. And in the package will be one million dollars in cash."

9

Harry choked on his coffee. "One million dollars . . . ?"

"That's right, so you can see why I need someone I can trust." Again Chambers smiled. "It goes without saying that I would make this very worthwhile to you. I wouldn't expect you to do something like this for nothing. I hope you won't take offense at that."

"Hold on, you're moving a bit too fast for me," said Harry. "To begin with, I've got a motel to run. I can't just pick up and take off for Haiti, even if I wanted to."

"Oh, come now," said Chambers. "Admit you're intrigued by the idea. I told you I consider myself a good judge of character, and if I read you right, you'd welcome a chance of getting away from that motel of yours for a while. I think you're thoroughly bored by it. It doesn't seem at all the sort of thing a man like you should be doing. I know you—you like running around in that boat of yours—and I want this package delivered by boat."

Harry took another sip of his coffee. "By boat? To Haiti? That's a long trip."

"So it is, but a very pleasant one. Just cruise down through the islands and cut across. Marvelous trip, only wish I could go with you."

"Now just one damn minute, Mr. Chambers, I haven't said I'll make this crazy run. I've got a lot more questions—this whole thing sounds just the least bit suspicious. Nobody delivers packages to Haiti with a million dollars in them, not unless it involves something illegal. Does this involve anything illegal? Because if it does, I want to know about it."

"Very wise," said Chambers. "Never get involved in something you don't fully understand. That's one of the principles I work by."

"All right, then tell me about it so that I do understand."

"Well, it's like this," said Chambers. I've got a friend, a very good friend, we've done business together for many years—I can vouch for his integrity—and he finds himself in a rather delicate situation. The FBI, God visit a plague on them, wants my friend to testify at one of their hearings up in Washington. Now my friend—who's done nothing wrong, you understand—has good reasons for not wanting to testify. He's a very busy man, and these hearings can go on for weeks. My friend just can't spare the time, which is understandable."

Harry said nothing, but was thinking a lot. The casual mention of the FBI had suddenly put a whole different complexion on this favor John Chambers wanted from him. He waited.

"Besides," Chambers went on, "those dreadful government men are likely to try and pin something on my friend. You know how they operate."

Again Harry waited.

"And it so happens that my friend had also been planning a little well-deserved vacation in Haiti around the time these wretched hearings are to be held. Good place for a vacation, Haiti, now that things have cooled down there. They treat you well, and they've got no extradition."

"You sure about that?"

"No problem," Chambers said with a touch of impatience. "Believe me, in Haiti there are very few problems money won't take care of."

"So that's why you want me to take the million dollars, is it?" Harry asked innocently. "So that your friend can have some spending money when he skips the FBI hearings and takes his little well-deserved vacation. Money I deliver him by boat."

Chambers spread his hands, palms up. "He could hardly be expected to get on a plane and take that much money with him, now could he? I mean, that's not logical. Some nosy customs officer might decide to look in the box and then ask embarrassing questions. Let's be reasonable."

"Oh, by all means let's be reasonable," said Harry. "But would you mind telling me why your friend needs a million dollars for his little vacation in Haiti? A million dollars is a lot of money to spend on a little vacation."

"He might decide to extend his stay," said Chambers. "And he might decide to invest in real estate down there. There are all kinds of opportunities in Haiti, as I understand it, and a million dollars doesn't go as far today as it used to."

"Let's leave that part for the moment," said Harry. "Tell me why you want me to deliver this package in my boat. It's just a sport-fishing boat, nothing elaborate. Would take me a fair amount of time to make that trip in a boat like mine."

"Fits in perfectly with my plan," said Chambers. "Let me tell you what I propose, and you tell me if you can pick any holes in it. Goes like this. Two of my people charter your boat for fishing, a nice two-week charter—they want to do a lot of fishing. You start here, take them across to the Bahamas, to Bimini, say, then you work your way down through the Islands, as was previously mentioned, and when you get to the bottom of the Bahamas, when you get to . . . what's the name of that island right at the end?"

"Great Inagua."

"That's it, Great Inagua. Well, when you get there, what do my friends realize?"

"Let me guess," said Harry. "They realize that it's only a hop, skip, and jump across to Haiti."

Chambers beamed. "My goodness, you grasp

12

things quickly, Mr. Foster. Exactly as you say, they realize it's only a hop, skip, and jump across to Haiti, which is somewhere they've always wanted to visit, and what better time than this?"

"And at the same time, drop off the million dollars to your friend who happens to be there and waiting."

"The perfect opportunity," said Chambers. "What do you think of the plan. Can you see any flaws in it?"

"Several," said Harry, "but no big ones. All very logical, if logic is the right word to use here."

"So, will you do it for me, Mr. Foster? Will you help out me and my friend? I would be very appreciative if you could see your way clear."

Harry pulled his chair close to Chambers' desk. "I'm not saying I will do it, but if I did, just how appreciative would you be, Mr. Chambers? I'm not stupid, and I know you don't really expect me to swallow that story about your innocent friend. I'm quite prepared to believe the part about there being an FBI hearing and that someone intends to skip the country and hole up in Haiti to avoid having to testify. So let's get down to the nitty-gritty. What you want me to do is smuggle in a million dollars in hard cash so that this whoever-it-is won't have to come back here for a long, long time. Isn't that the situation, Mr. Chambers?"

"I suppose you could put that interpretation on it, although we businessmen do have to go to extraordinary lengths these days in certain circumstances."

"And you want me to take all the risk," said Harry, "which puts this affair slightly out of the 'doing you a favor' class. So tell me what's in it for me for taking those risks."

"Ah, the approach direct," said Chambers. "Nothing better than putting all one's cards on the table. What's in it for you, Mr. Foster? A nice all-expenses-paid, two-week fishing charter, a chance to dump the nuisance of running your delightful motel onto someone else while you're gone, and 5 percent of the million dollars when you make the delivery. That's fifty thousand dollars, Mr. Foster, which would make it a very profitable charter for you.''

Harry thought, weighed the pros and cons of the whole improbable proposition. There was an illicit spirit of adventure to the wacky scheme that appealed to him against his better, more reasoned judgment. Why not? It sure as hell beat sitting in that motel, watching his life dribble away one dull day after another. He'd bought the place because he'd married Jane, and now that she'd gone back to her ex-husband most of the reasons for running Balmy Breezes had gone with her. Even at a time like this he thought what a crappy name Balmy Breezes was.

"Half up front, half when I deliver," he said to Chambers.

"You've got a deal." Chambers stood, held out his hand. "I'll want you to leave in a week, can you be ready by then?"

Harry shook Chambers' tiny, manicured hand. "I can be ready. We'd better meet again, say three days from now, and iron out the details of this fishing charter you're hiring me for."

"Very well," said Chambers, "three days from now. Same time?"

"Right."

Chambers reached into his desk drawer, took out a checkbook, wrote out a check for twenty-five thousand dollars, passed it across to Harry. He looked at it, a large, elaborate Globus Enterprises Inc. check with John Chambers' name signed in a flowery, old-fashioned script. It bore today's date.

"Your retainer," said Chambers. "You can cash it

any time you wish, Globus is a very financially sound company."

"I'm sure it is," said Harry, even though he still hadn't the slightest idea of what Globus actually did.

He left. Rose Cellini looked up from her typing as he passed.

"Goodbye, Mrs. Cellini," said Harry. "Thanks for the coffee."

She sniffed, went back to her typing. Shortly after she heard the elevator take Harry back down to the lobby, Mrs. Rose Cellini left her desk, walked along the hallway to a pay phone, and made a brief local call.

TWO

As Harry drove back to Balmy Breezes he tried to analyze the John Chambers proposition, to put it into some kind of perspective. How much of Chambers' story was true? What was the real purpose behind the shipment of a million dollars to Haiti? The first and obvious interpretation was that drugs were involved. With Miami now a key distribution point, vast sums of money routinely changed hands—a million dollars would be considered small change for some of the transactions that fueled the illegal economy of Florida.

And while popular fiction invariably featured Hispanics as the evil figures behind this massive operation, Harry knew only too well that in the shadows were just as likely to be a banker from a respected family or a lawyer of impeccable establishment background. The huge profits to be made from heroin and cocaine proved tempting to the most unlikely people —John Chambers, for example? If he had proof that Chambers was involved in drug trafficking, Harry would give Chambers back his retainer and pull out of the deal, for there was no way he'd let himself become tied into those sordid, despicable dealings. Apart from the morality issue, too many of those caught up in this no-rules game ended up dead.

But until Harry knew the full story he decided to give John Chambers the benefit of the doubt. Until that time he'd go along with the whole preposterous scheme. Chambers had been clever to pinpoint Harry's boredom with life as proprietor of the damn Balmy Breezes. He'd hit on the one approach that would prove irresistible—the prospect of being paid to spend time on his boat. This was about the only thing that kept Harry sane: every moment he could play hooky from the motel he would be on the *Rimshot*, out on the open sea, putting as much distance between himself and the mainland as his limited free time would allow.

And now, out of the blue, had come this chance to spend two whole weeks doing what he enjoyed most. Harry had been hooked the moment Chambers threw that kicker into the pot. He'd have to fix up with Martin Pomeroy to look after Balmy Breezes while he was away. Whenever Harry took off for a day or two, Martin Pomeroy was the one he called in to baby-sit the place. This was something he could do this morning, go see Martin.

The exit signs on the highway told him he was approaching Fort Lauderdale. He hadn't been aware of the miles ticking off; the sweet-running little BMW made short work of the drive. Luckily he hadn't been pulled over by some zealous cop wanting to know

why he was ramming along considerably faster than
the legal limit. Harry turned down Sunrise, made for
the unpretentious apartment building where Martin
Pomeroy lived in somewhat less than luxury. A lot
less.

He found Martin exactly where he expected to find
him, sitting in a canvas chair on his tiny apartment
balcony, sipping a beer, half hidden in the jungle of
flowering vines and tropical plants that hung over it
like a canopy and filled every available inch of space.

Martin waved a languid hand as Harry walked out
onto the balcony from the studio apartment that was
never locked. An all-too-familiar story behind Martin
Pomeroy. Born into a very rich family, he'd inherited
the huge luxury hotel the Pomeroys had owned since
the golden twenties and had drunk the business away
by the time he was thirty-five. That was nearly thirty
years ago. A faded, still elegant figure of great charm,
Martin lived on family handouts and the fifty bucks a
day Harry paid him to baby-sit Balmy Breezes.

"Harry, my dear friend, I'm delighted to see you,
may I get you a cold beer?"

"Thanks, I could use one." Harry sat in the other
canvas chair squeezed in the rainforest of a balcony.
Martin reached into an ice-filled cooler by his side,
came up with a bottle of Carta Blanca, deftly flipped
off the cap, passed it to Harry.

"To what do I owe the pleasure of your visit? Do
you need my expert and superior services at your
establishment? Are you off on another of your little
escapes from the dreary daily routine?"

Harry took a deep draught of the cold Mexican
beer. "Maybe. Depends on you."

Martin raised an eyebrow. "On me? How flattering.
I suspect from your oblique approach this is some-

thing rather different from our usual arrangement. Would I be right?"

"You would. How do you feel about looking after the motel for three weeks?"

"My goodness," said Martin. "Three weeks? It's never been more than three days before. How do I feel about it? I'd be delighted. When would you need me?"

"Starting in about a week."

"Consider it done. Are you treating yourself to a proper vacation or is it business that calls you away?"

"A bit of both," said Harry. "Can I rely on you not to get into trouble, Martin?"

Martin looked pained. "Harry . . . Harry, dear old friend, have I ever let you down in the past?"

"No, but I've never left you alone for this long before."

"Have complete faith," said Martin, reaching down for another beer. "I will be the perfect model of efficiency and propriety."

"How about sobriety," Harry said. "I'm not going to be there looking over your shoulder."

"Not a drop shall pass these lips in your absence," said Martin, flipping the cap of his Carta Blanca. "I shall comport myself with dignity and restraint."

"Word of a gentleman?"

Martin held out his hand. "Word of a gentleman, Harry."

Back at the motel, Harry ran a quick check to see that nothing disastrous had happened in his absence. All was quiet; nobody had missed him. He went into his office, read his mail, then picked up his phone and put a call through to Hog Cay. Guffy Leech was the next man he had to talk to. Whenever Harry wanted company on the *Rimshot* or when he took the boat into unfamiliar waters, he hired Guffy Leech as his mate. Guffy was a native Bahamian who lived on Hog Cay and was generally recognized as the best mate and best fishing guide around. No better man to take with him on the long Haiti junket. At this time of the day Harry could almost be certain of reaching Guffy at Christopher's dock.

The static-laden radio-telephone link was finally made, and Guffy came on the phone. Although Hog Cay was only fifty-five sea miles from the Florida coast, Guffy could have been speaking from the moon.

"Hi, Guffy," Harry shouted, "It's Harry."

"Hi," said Guffy, "you comin' over this way soon?"

"Tomorrow. I'm going to take a run over first thing in the morning, I want to talk to you. You going to be there?"

"I'll be here," Guffy said, "things is kinda slack right now."

"Good, 'cause I need you," Harry said. "See you tomorrow, Guffy."

"Sure thing," said Guffy, and hung up.

Now fired up about the trip, Harry drove down to the marina where he kept the *Rimshot*. The hell with Balmy Breezes, it could look after itself for a while.

The *Rimshot*. His baby. Harry climbed down into the cockpit and, as always, peace and contentment washed over him. All his life he'd been hooked on boats. Power boats, sailing boats, fishing boats, virtually anything that put to sea.

When he was a kid, through most of his teens, the family had lived in Portland, Maine. Harry got to know just about everybody who owned a boat, did odd jobs for them, painted and scraped, scoured and polished, did anything asked of him so long as he could be involved with boats.

Some of the boat owners took a liking to this big, strong boy who accepted any task given him and never expected to get paid for his labors. They started using him as a weekend crew member. Taught him how to handle sail and power, how to read navigation charts, how to use the electronic devices. Before very long they began letting young Harry take the wheel for hours at a stretch, even at night. He was a natural. Goddamit, they said, the boy must have salt water in his veins.

When Vietnam came along, one of the boat owners, a retired navy commander, pulled a few strings and got Harry attached to the Coast Guard. For eighteen months, Harry was in Heaven. The larger issues of the conflict escaped him; he served his time on cutters patrolling home waters. Harry Foster was one man who was sorry when the tragic Vietnam fiasco was ended.

All his adult life Harry had wanted to own a boat, but never, until he'd moved to Florida, and Fate had decreed it was time Harry Foster got a break, never until then had it been possible. And then he'd lucked into unexpected money, enough money to get him established as the owner of Balmy Breezes. Enough to buy him a boat.

He'd shopped around, taken his time, and finally found the *Rimshot*, a thirty-eight-foot sports cruiser owned by a drunk, a guy who hadn't looked after it, a guy with more money than brains. It was a mess. How anybody could treat a boat like that was something Harry couldn't understand. But because it was such a mess, and because the owner wanted to get rid of it, Harry got it cheap.

He worked nights, weekends, every minute he could steal repairing the ravages of ten years of abuse and neglect. In six months, Harry had the *Rimshot* back very close to its original condition. A sweet boat. The main cabin could comfortably sleep four with space forward for a further two passengers who didn't mind using sleeping bags. The galley held a two-plate gas stove, a stainless-steel sink, and an under-the-counter refrigerator. The head boasted the luxury of a full-size, enclosed shower with hot water.

The lower control station had standard instrumentation and full electronics. But much of this was outdated, and Harry was in the process of gradually replacing the old stuff. He decided to install a new depthsounder before he started on the Haiti run. Essential controls were duplicated on the flybridge. The well-planned cockpit was clean and uncluttered. In the stern sat a custom-built fighting chair that to date Harry had never used. Each time he went out with Guffy he promised himself he'd do some game fishing, try for the big stuff, but for various valid reasons he hadn't gotten around to it yet. Maybe this trip of Chambers' would give him his chance to haul in a record breaker.

Power for the *Rimshot*, completely rebuilt twin Chryslers, delivered a top speed of a touch over thirty-two knots. These engines drank a lot of gas, and since Harry sometimes liked to make long, fast runs, he'd put in extra-big reserve tanks.

With four people on board it was going to be mighty cramped. Fine for a casual weekend of fishing and drinking, but two weeks of togetherness could prove to be a different story. Harry hoped the two men Chambers was sending along on the trip were small. He also hoped they were good sailors.

When he was satisfied the *Rimshot* was in shape for the run across to Hog Cay in the morning, Harry walked to a seafood bar where charter boat captains and mates hung out. He met two guys he knew and they swapped a few sea stories, lied a little, drank a few beers, and ate a fair lobster chowder. Harry mentioned he needed a new depthsounder because the one on his boat was ten years old and acting up. One of the guys wrote down the name and address of a man who custom-built the best, said to mention his name and the man would give him a good deal. After a couple more beers, Harry went to see the man and bought himself a beauty of a sounder, a sophisticated job with a big bright digital readout, and a slave unit for the flybridge.

Then, reluctantly, Harry returned to Balmy Breezes and the real world. He suddenly realized that although he'd fixed up with Martin Pomeroy for the upcoming two-week trip, he hadn't made any arrangements for tomorrow's junket to Hog Cay. He'd be gone from the first light of dawn and be away one night at least, too long to leave the place with nobody there to take care of the guests. He called Martin, and Martin said he'd be in early and not to worry. Harry didn't worry. In fact, he didn't give Balmy Breezes another thought.

THREE

The run across to Hog Cay was pure delight: a perfect morning, the lightest of breezes, the ocean well-mannered. Harry kept the *Rimshot* throttled back, in no hurry to get anywhere on a day like this.

Guffy was waiting for him on Christopher's dock, sitting patiently on an upturned box, watching for the *Rimshot* to round the point and make the turn into the narrow, tricky channel that was the only safe approach to Hog Cay. Harry eased the boat in between a battered Boston whaler and a slim, sleek muscle-boat, threw Guffy a line, and killed the engines. He was pleased with himself for a neat bit of boat handling that met even Guffy's critical standards. He reached up a hand and Guffy effortlessly hoisted him onto the dock. A powerful man, five feet ten, 260-odd pounds, a rock of a man. No longer young, his broad black face lined and seamed, his tight-curled black hair almost completely gray. A good man and a good friend.

Harry went through the formality of clearing customs. Percy Smith, the lone customs officer, didn't even bother to ask Harry what was in the box he was carrying under one arm.

In the dark coolness of the Sand Dollar Bar, bottles of Pauli Girl beer in front of them, Harry said to Guffy, "I've got a present for you," and gave him the cardboard box.

Guffy hefted the box and looked suspicious. "What is it?"

"Something useful. A new depthsounder for the *Rimshot.*"

"Glad you didn't buy me nothin' friv'lous," said Guffy. "I s'pose you'll be wantin' me to wire it up for you." He opened the box, examined the sounder. "Hey, man, this is a good piece of stuff. Any special reason you layin' out that kinda money for a new sounder?"

"We need it. We're going on a nice run down to Inagua and across to Haiti."

"Hey, hey, that's a real nice run. Just us goin'?"

"Two more. It's a fishing charter."

Guffy looked up from his beer. "We don't do fishin' charters."

"There's always a first time."

"A fishin' charter to Haiti . . . ?" Guffy asked, the suspicious expression back on his broad, black face. "Man, that's a long haul to catch a few fish. That all there is to it, just a fishin' charter?"

"Maybe a bit more to it,"

"I thought there might be. Apart from fishin', what's the 'bit more' we'll maybe be doin'?"

"Delivering a package to a man in Haiti."

Guffy shot him a glance. "Uh, huh, we not proposin' anythin' that might be agin the law, are we?"

Harry grinned. "You don't think I'd do anything that's against the law, do you?"

Guffy drained his beer, signaled for two more. "People deliverin' some mighty funny stuff to other people these days. Didn't think you was one of 'em."

"I'm not," said Harry. "You know how I feel about that."

"Glad to hear it. Ain't a day goes past that some easy-money man don't come around wavin' a bundle of hundred-dollar bills in my face an' wantin' me to make a quick run from Bimini 'cross to Miami or meet a freighter off Andros. So far I ain't bin tempted —that line a work ain't for me." He grinned. "I ain't sayin' I'm 100 percent pure in thought an' deed, could be I just scare easy."

"We'll need charts," said Harry, "mine don't go down that far."

"I got charts in the house, they should do us, nothin' much changes. Some new radio stations to mark in, but apart from that, nothin' very different from last time I was that way. When we leavin'?"

"Pick up our party next week. Sunday, Monday, maybe. Due in Haiti two weeks after that. Fish on the way down, take a week to come home."

Guffy took a long, slow, contemplative drink of his beer. "I get the distinc' feelin' there's somethin' you haven't told me. Is there? Like what is this merchandise we gonna deliver?"

"A million dollars. In cash."

"Oh my gracious," said Guffy.

"It pays well."

"I reckon." Again he grinned. "These two comin'

with us . . . our fishin' charter people, they gonna be along to watch the money?"

Harry grinned back at him. "That's about the size of it. We drive the stagecoach, they ride shotgun."

"We expectin' any stagecoach robbers on the way?"

"Just kidding," said Harry. "This is just going to be a nice cruise through the islands. I wouldn't want it any other way."

"Me neither," Guffy said, crossing two enormous fingers. "But I don' like them Miami boys, they bring trouble with 'em."

"We won't have any trouble. The man who's hiring us is a businessman, I know him well. He's just doing a friend a favor by delivering him a million bucks without going through a lot of fuss and bother."

"An' breakin' a few currency rules an' regulations along the way, right?"

Harry signaled for another two beers. "I wouldn't be surprised."

"Must say I feel better knowin' all we'll be doin' is a bit of honest smugglin'," said Guffy. "Soon's I've finished this beer I'll git on with wirin' up that sounder."

27

FOUR

Bob Hammersley mooched along the white, coral-graveled road thinking what a godawful place Hog Cay was. A blinding hot day, not a breath of wind to relieve the humid heat, every damn day the same. Nowhere to go, nothing to do except get good and drunk. The liter of Gordon's gin stuck in the pocket of his soiled white linen jacket swung reassuringly against his hip. Get drunk and forget the whole bleedin' place. He considered going down to the beach, but the sand was like an oven. Go to sleep in the sun after a few drinks and he'd wake up with one son-of-a-bitch of a headache. Besides, he wanted company. If he could hitch a ride he'd go and see Mike. Best part of a mile to where Mike docked his boat, and that was too far to walk in this bitching climate.

He found a bit of shade under a scrubby almond tree and took a slug from the gin bottle. Hell, he'd go and see Mike even if it did mean walking, he had a business proposition he wanted to talk over with him. Capping the bottle he jammed it back in his pocket and started off down the road. Christ, one drink and he was sweating like a pig.

Believing as all losers do that a change of scene meant a change of luck, Bob Hammersley's patternless wanderings had led him from New Zealand to England to Canada, working unenthusiastically at any job that came along, drawing on vestiges of skills half-learned in the Army. From Montreal he'd shipped out on a boat to the Bahamas, had been paid off in Nassau, and from there had drifted through the Out Islands, ending up on Hog Cay. From some mysterious source he'd raised enough money to get his hands on a bankrupt marina. He'd failed in that as in everything else. Now he had a two-table pool hall and bar in a particularly unlovely part of Hog Cay. So far he'd managed to keep his head above water with this venture, entirely due to his wife, Sally.

A year ago he'd met Sally, a good-natured, aimless English girl who'd been left stranded on Hog Cay. She'd married Bob, who was some twenty years older than she, without giving it much thought. Sally was cheerful, she worked hard, and the customers liked her. Half an hour ago she and Bob had had a yelling, crying, ugly fight and he'd hit her, grabbed a bottle of gin, and taken off. Which was why he was on his way to see Mike. He stopped for another shot of gin. The island garbage truck came along, so Bob flagged it down with the gin bottle and hitched a ride for the rest of the way.

There was no sign of life on the *Moonglow*, a beautifully proportioned, old two-masted schooner long in need of an overhaul. Its paint chipped, its canvas patched and repatched, its tired old engine shot, the *Moonglow* was theoretically for charter, but less and less often did it put to sea. For the most part it stayed tied up at the Island's cheapest dock space, on which Mike Cholski owed five months' back rent. Mike lived on the *Moonglow*, heating cans of soup and beans on a Coleman stove, bumming cigarettes and booze when he was broke, throwing a party and paying off small bits of his bills when the occasional charter did come along—almost always to end in disaster.

Bob slid back the hatch cover and went below into the darkness, closing the hatch behind him to preserve what little cool air came from the rusty air conditioner. Face flushed, wrapped in an old silk robe, Mike was asleep on a Pullman bed. The cabin was littered with dirty glasses, overflowing ashtray, and empty bottles. On a daybed a girl was also asleep, a crumpled sheet over her, her clothes in a heap on the floor. Bob knew her; she was one of a pair of totally amoral sisters who roamed the Island. This one was Judy; she was seventeen. Her sister, Jill, was a year younger. Their father owned a big Bertram cruiser that he brought over from Lauderdale three or four times a year. The old man was drunk most of the time, no mother was ever around, and the two girls were free to get bedded with impressive single-mindedness.

Bob shook Mike awake. Mike sat up and focused on him.

"What time is it?"

"Nearly half past one."

"Christ," said Mike. He staggered over to the head and urinated. "Oh man, that's better." Fumbling for a cigarette from an almost empty pack of Camels he

30

felt his way back to his bunk and sat down. The cigarette stayed unlit while he searched for a match. Bob struck one for him and held it while Mike steered the cigarette into the flame and took a drag. Through hungover eyes he looked up at Bob. "What the hell you want, anyway?"

Bob hunted through the wreckage for two reasonably clean glasses and settled for a couple that were lipstick-stained but free of butts. He pulled the bottle of Gordon's from his pocket and half filled the glasses. Mike brightened visibly. A big, blond man, blue-eyed, pale lashed, with a broad, tough face now starting to pouch and sag, Mike Cholski looked like an ex-football player or a one-time lifeguard. He'd been both, but not for a long time. But, as Mike said, he wasn't in bad shape for thirty-seven—especially as he was forty three.

He reached for the glass of gin. "Man, that's a happy sight. We had ourselves a party here last night, Christ knows what time it was when everybody left."

Bob nodded in the direction of the sleeping girl. "They didn't all leave by the look of it."

"Oh, her . . ." Mike took a drink of the straight gin, shuddered, and shook his head in wonder. "I've met a few in my time but that one beats the lot. Unreal. Anyway, what d'ya want? Not that I ain't glad to see you and your friend." He raised his glass in salute to the gin bottle.

Bob sprawled out in a canvas chair. "Got something I wanna talk to you about. Chance for us to make some money."

"Let me get rid of that little whore first," said Mike. Painfully he got up and pulled the sheet off the sleeping girl. She sat up, naked, her streaky blond hair falling over her makeup smeared face. "What the fuck you think you're doing?"

"Party's over, time to go home," said Mike.

She took his glass, drank some of the gin, then swung her legs round and sat on the edge of the bed. "Either of you want a quickie before I go?"

Mike picked up her clothes and threw them at her. "Don't you ever get enough?"

Meditatively she scratched her crotch. "That's the trouble with men when they get your age, they poop out. I gotta have a pee." She walked over to the head, sat on the toilet without bothering to close the door, then stood and pushed the flush button. It didn't work.

"Hey," she called, "this thing won't flush."

"It's broken," said Mike, "you gotta pump it by hand."

"Jesus Christ," she complained, gave the handle a couple of halfhearted pumps and then came back into the main cabin. She pulled on her skirt—no panties—and a white T-shirt with It's Better In The Bahamas on it in blue letters. "Anybody got a comb?" Bob found one and she dragged it through her tangled hair. "I hope you don't expect me to clear up this shitty mess?" she said as she looked around the cabin.

Mike took her by the arm. "All I want you to do is get your ass out of here. Bob and me want to talk." He pushed her toward the stairs to the hatch. She turned on her way up to the deck. "Nice party. Ask me next time you have one."

"Bring your sister with you," Mike called as he closed the hatch behind her. He turned back to Bob. "Can you imagine what that little bitch will be like when she grows up?" He reached for the gin bottle. "Now, what was it you wanted to talk to me about?"

* * *

Guffy had the depthsounder wired up in an hour.

"Let's go out and see if it works," said Harry. They took the *Rimshot* out to sea, checking the readings of the shoals, reefs, and dropoffs against their charts.

"Works good," said Guffy.

"We should get the guy who built this to make us a new radar rig," said Harry.

Guffy shook his head. "The one we got's okay. Let's not waste our money."

On the run back to the dock they stood side by side, with Guffy at the wheel. For ten minutes Harry didn't speak.

"What's on your mind?" Guffy finally asked. "This Haiti trip botherin' you?"

"I don't think so. I don't know what the hell's the matter with me these days."

Guffy glanced up from the wheel, started to say something, but changed his mind. Harry caught the look. "Don't get smart," he said. "If there's one thing I can't stand, it's a smart mate."

"Didn't say a word."

"No, but you were thinking smart."

"Me . . . ? Not me. Never catch ole Guffy thinkin' smart."

"And don't Uncle Tom me," said Harry. He left Guffy on the flybridge and went down into the cabin. From a cupboard he took a small gift-wrapped box. His problem was how to give the present to the lady without causing her more trouble than she already had.

The lady—girl, said his conscience—was Sally, and Sally was Bob Hammersley's wife. And Sally was the cause of considerable soul-searching for Harry. The first time he saw her was on his very first trip to Hog Cay. Exploring the Island, he'd wandered down

into the native section and had come across the pool
room at the precise moment when he was in urgent
need of a cold beer. So he went in and sat at the bar
and ordered a Becks. Sally had served him. More or
less automatically he registered that she was a strik-
ingly pretty, sexually attractive young woman, and he
flirted with her in the ritual way men do when they
aren't really serious but are observing the conven-
tions. And Sally made the ritual responses expected
of her, the same responses she'd made countless
times before to countless other men sitting at the bar
and indulging in a little lecherous wishful thinking.

Harry dawdled over his beer, then a second, a
third. The handful of other lunchtime drinkers
drifted off by ones and twos until he was the only
customer left. Sally chatted with him, leaning on the
bar, un-selfconsciously desirable, so close he could
have reached out a hand and touched her. He found
himself not wanting to leave the dismal pool hall
but to stay near this disturbing girl. Then Bob
Hammersley came in, foulmouthed and bad tempered, and Harry realized with disbelief that the
unpleasant, slovenly character was Sally's husband.

Now Harry, an essentially sensible man, made it a
practice to steer clear of situations that involved
husbands, so he finished his beer and walked out,
telling himself that this was one bar he'd avoid in the
future. But he went back the same evening and drank
beer he didn't want, watching Sally's every move as
she opened bottles, poured drinks, made change,
wiped off the bar—bringing youth and vitality to the
shabby, defeated place.

Bob Hammersley did little to help her, just sat by
the cooler, a beer bottle permanently in his hand,
moodily preoccupied by his private, dark thoughts.
Trade was thin; the drinkers were for the most part

native Bahamians with time on their hands and little money in their pockets, a ragtag collection who scraped marginal livings from the Island. No big-time spenders from the luxury cruisers and ocean-going yachts that docked at Hog Cay ever came to the pool hall to throw their freewheeling parties.

For long stretches, Sally wasn't busy, and during these quiet spells she leaned on the bar and talked to Harry, obviously delighted to see a new face in the bar. She asked questions, eager for trivial news of what was happening in the world that lay outside Hog Cay. She never got off the Island, she said. Looking after the pool hall and bar was a full-time, seven-day-a-week job. But one day soon she was going over to Miami to buy herself some new clothes, see a movie, eat at a nice restaurant, maybe go dancing, spend the night at a hotel. She was going to do this as soon as things picked up a little and she could afford to get some help and persuade Bob to take her over for a day and a night. Very soon, she repeated, that's what she was going to do. But she said it wistfully, without any real conviction, a daydream to hold on to.

She asked Harry questions about himself, What did he do? How come he was on Hog Cay? How come he ended up drinking in the pool hall, they didn't see many people there like him. Most visitors ended up in the popular bars down by the dock and marinas. Sally talked a lot to Harry, too much for Bob's liking. Twice he broke up their conversations to put Sally to work on chores he could easily have done himself. But Bob did nothing except sit by the cooler drinking bottle after bottle of beer.

And all this time Harry kept telling himself that none of this was any of his concern. Just how and why this lovely, fey, naive young woman came to wind up married to a morose oaf of a deadbeat like Bob

Hammersley was something he couldn't comprehend, but then he didn't know the improbable circumstances that lay behind this mystery. Could she possibly love this man? Was she prepared to endure the sordid life he provided for her because of some strange chemistry between them that made her willing to waste her young life tied to a bitter, washed-up loser of a man?

He stayed there until the pool-hall bar closed, and as he slowly walked back to the *Rimshot*, although he was no closer to solving the puzzle, he knew that he had to see Sally again. The girl had ingrained herself into his system; he couldn't walk away and forget her, couldn't write her off as just a girl he'd met by chance and who had temporarily aroused in him sexual yearnings that would quickly pass once he was away from her. He couldn't shake himself free of her.

And so, each time he went back to Hog Cay he headed for the pool hall. What he was about to do now was what he'd done a dozen times in the past: go to the crummy pool hall, sit at the bar and watch Sally—always conscious of Bob, sullen and silent in the background, and dream up plans of how to get her out of that place, get her away from her bum of a husband. Buy her expensive clothes, take her to the best restaurants. Spoil her, pamper her. Book a suite at an expensive hotel and enjoy her wonder and pleasure. And make love to her.

But here, the daydream always ended. After all that, then what. Settle down with her? Eventually marry her and raise kids and worry about teeth and taxes and schools and life insurance and retirement savings plans? Maybe at first she wouldn't be concerned about any of these things, but the odds were that later she would want all those codicils to the contract that define and limit conventional marriages, would want all the trappings and trimmings of a normal family life. And Harry wasn't ready to face that, not after two failed marriages; not now, maybe never.

He put the gift box back in the cupboard, started for the door, hesitated, went back again, and once more took the box from the cupboard. The hell with everything, he would give it to Sally.

They got to the dock in the oppressive, sticky heat of late afternoon. Harry was still in a reflective, uncommunicative mood.

"Nuthin' else you want me to do?" Guffy asked as they tied up.

"No. That's it for today."

Slyly, Guffy said, "You goin' up to see Sally?"

"Mind your own goddam business," said Harry, without rancor. "What if I do?"

"Oh, nuthin'," said Guffy, "jest makin' conversation."

"Don't con me," said Harry. "You know what's troubling me, you know the spot I've got myself into. You're too damn smart, that's your trouble."

All innocence, Guffy said, "Me . . . ? Not me. You never find ole Guffy . . ."

"Oh, knock it off," said Harry. "Don't go into your Uncle Tom act again. How's about one quick beer before I go?"

The declining sun of early evening had brought with it a welcome breeze. Harry walked to Sally's place and stopped a couple of times to talk with people who wanted to know how things were going with him and how long he was staying this time and had he been over to Bimini lately and was he going to the barbecue tonight? Hog Cay had a comfortable familiarity for him. He no longer saw its scars and blemishes.

Sergeant Welsh drew up beside him in his Jeep, and Harry leaned on the windshield and gossiped with him for a while. Sergeant Tom Welsh was a native Bahamian. Light-skinned, clipped moustache, British-Army-trained; a tough, cynical forty-seven-year-old pro, chief of Hog Cay's three-man police force. Tom Welsh had one purpose, to keep Hog Cay clean of the drug trafficking that had destroyed the peaceable way of life on so many Out Islands, and this he did, ruthlessly and impartially. The local boys he'd gotten well under control and visiting villains found themselves off the Island before they'd had time to unpack. The sergeant knew that a few of Hog Cay's resident natives took off from time to time and came back with a lot more money than when they left. What the fools did off the Island was no concern of Tom Welsh's. Put one foot wrong on Hog Cay and he'd make them wish they'd never been born.

The sergeant liked Harry, and now and then had a drink with him, but that didn't stop the sergeant from keeping a watchful eye on Harry's comings and goings between Hog Cay and the mainland.

Tom Welsh liked being Hog Cay's chief of police, and he intended to stay chief of police until his next posting and probable promotion to inspector. The promotion was long overdue; some of his methods didn't sit too well with Nassau. But, before he retired, he intended to make inspector. Abruptly, he took off. Harry continued down the Queen's Highway.

Once the personal playground of a few very rich, who, back in the thirties, had come to fish, booze, and brawl in arrogant luxury, Hog Cay, like many a lady of easy virtue and like much overpriced wine, had not improved with age. Lined on one side by half a dozen crumbling two-story hotels, erratically spiked by sagging docks and marinas, cemented together by bars, poolrooms, and a handful of run-down shops and stores, Hog Cay still managed to project an air of bawdy masculinity, an image as vulnerable to close inspection as a Hollywood backlot.

But in spite of the dilapidation, in spite of temporary invasions by tourists and visitors who once would have been denied docking privileges, Hog Cay still beckoned with an inviting if none too clean finger, and remained as faithfully as ever dedicated to the tradition of fishing, boozing, and brawling. For, part in fact, part in legend, Hog Cay provided some of the best game-fishing in the world.

Hemingway had fished and fought with his friends on Hog Cay, but Papa and his gang were long gone, their passions and excesses remembered only in fading photographs behind the lounge bar of the Fish and Game Club. Even those sad shadows were now threatened with final burial under layers of Polaroid snapshots of pale fat men, cigars in mouths and rented fishing rods uneasy in fraternal-order-ringed hands.

Bob and Sally's pool hall didn't rate as one of Hog Cay's tourist attractions. It catered almost exclusively to the local Bahamian trade, and the only whites who drank there were a handful who, like Harry, had been around long enough and often enough to be accepted as part of the scene. The only reason Harry went there was because Sally was there.

One of the two patched pool tables was in use. The jukebox stood silent, a lone, sombre native Bahamian sat at the six-stool bar moodily sipping on a bottle of Beck's. The bar itself was crudely constructed from weathered planks, and the two shelves on the wall behind it held a dozen or so bottles of liquor. There was a big Frigidaire beer-cooler, half a dozen crates of mixers, an assortment of mismatched glasses, and an antique brass cash register.

Sally had made an attempt to cheer up the place with travel posters on the walls and a string of Christmas-tree lights around the frame of the bar. She'd started to paint the grubby walls white, but the paint had run out, and Bob refused to buy more.

The pool players and the man at the bar looked up briefly as Harry entered. One of the players lifted his cue in salute, and the man at the bar half nodded and went back to his beer. Bob wasn't there. Usually he was behind the bar, sitting on a stool by the cooler, a drink in his hand. Sally was checking the meager supply of liquor on the shelves. She turned as Harry sat down at the bar.

A tall, slim girl with a gentle, vulnerable face. Long brown hair pulled back and held with a strand of bright yellow wool. She was wearing a pair of old bleached jeans and a man's white shirt with the tails tied round her waist. No makeup or jewelry. More than ever Harry wanted to take her hand, take her away, have her beside him on his boat.

She smiled, happy to see Harry, but it was a painful smile, and involuntarily she touched one hand to her cheek. As she came closer, Harry could see the cheek was bruised and her eye swollen.

"Harry," she said. "How long are you staying this time? Off again tomorrow, as usual?"

Harry leaned across the bar and held her by the wrist. With his other hand he gently touched her bruised cheek. Sally winced.

"Did Bob do that to you?"

She hesitated, then nodded.

"Why?"

Sally shrugged, not looking at Harry, and made a

token attempt to break away from him. He held her more tightly.

"Money," she said hopelessly. "It's always money. You know how it is, we don't do a big business here but we'd do a lot better if the place wasn't such a dump. I wanted to fix the bar up, it wouldn't cost very much. Just look at it." With her free hand she indicated the whole shabby room. "And I wanted to put in a lunch bar—you know, serve sandwiches and conch chowder and fritters, stuff like that. I could do the cooking, I know how to make a good conch chowder. But Bob wouldn't go along with it, said we couldn't afford it, and he goes on spending money we don't have . . ."

The Bahamian at the bar finished his beer, stood, nodded to Sally and Harry, and went out.

Harry let go of Sally's hand and watched her while she cleared away the man's beer bottle, emptied the tin ashtray, and wiped off the bar. "Where is Bob now?"

She shrugged her thin shoulders. "I don't know. He'll be back when he's ready. He'll go on a drunk till he runs out of money, then he'll be back." Sally leaned on the bar, arms folded. "We've got a bar here and he can drink all he likes, though I wish he wouldn't drink as much as he does, but he still goes off and spends money in the other bars. Usually he takes that Mike Cholski with him, and Mike's never got any money so Bob ends up paying for him too." She breathed a long sigh. "And we can't afford that sort of thing. We're behind on the rent and it's only a matter of time before they cut off our credit at the liquor dealer's. I gave Bob money to pay our electric bill, but he'll blow it, you see if he don't."

Harry slowly shook his head. "Why do you stay with him?"

Sally gave the ghost of a smile. "Oh, Bob's not so bad, not all the time. He's had a lot of hard luck. He was good to me at the start, nobody else would help me, but Bob did. I owe him a lot."

"Did you have to marry him?"

Sally looked reproachfully at Harry. He raised a hand in a gesture of surrender. "Okay . . . okay . . . it's your affair."

"Yes, it is," Sally said, "but thanks for being concerned about me. Now let's talk about something more cheerful."

"I've got a present for you," Harry said, and gave her the gift-wrapped package.

Wonderingly, she took it and impatiently, like a child, tore the ribbons and wrapping from it, then opened the flat box. In it was a roughly hammered silver cross about three inches long, obviously very old, the chiseled design of entwined leaves pitted and eroded. A silver chain coiled round it.

"It's beautiful. Harry, it's lovely." She held the cross in the palm of her hand.

"I bought it from a diver. He found it in a wreck off Turtle Rock. I thought you'd like it."

"It's beautiful," Sally repeated. She undid the clasp of the chain and turned her back for Harry to fasten it at the back of her neck.

"It's not that old," he said, "about 1800." He turned her by the shoulders until she faced him, and touched the cross that now lay between her breasts. "It's Spanish, that's for sure. Not the chain, I had to get a chain for it. The chain's English, probably Victorian."

Sally slowly traced a finger up and down the cross. "I love it. Thank you very much, Harry."

FIVE

The gin was almost finished. Bob's original plan for making money by starting a cannery on the Island had been abandoned, but he had another scheme. Bob always had another scheme.

"Commercial fishin'" he said.

Mike looked at him sadly. "You out of your mind? Where do we get a boat, a crew, the gear? Where do we get the money? You must be outta your head."

Bob poured the last of the gin. "Look, you seen how many Cubans there is round here these days?"

"Fuck the Cubans."

"D'ya realize the bastards have got themselves boats an' are fishin' right here, right off this island? Doin' well, too. One lot's in now, loaded down with bloody fish."

"So what," said Mike.

"So that means they got money. Now take some of 'em who work as crew, lot of 'em would like to go into business for themselves."

"So."

"So what we do is get ten of 'em, say, an' get them to put up five hundred or a thousand bucks each. We form a syndicate. Fix up this tub of yours. They put up the money and do the work, we put up the boat an' run it for them, an' take a piece of the action."

Mike sighed. "This ain't a fishin' boat. An' you need nets and winches and . . . oh Christ, you know what those nets cost? An' where those Cubans gonna get a grand in cash each? Thought Castro took all their money when he kicked 'em out."

"I dunno," said Bob. "But they're like bloody Chinks or Eyetalians. When a Chink or a Wop opens a restaurant the whole bleedin' family kicks in. I dunno how they got their money outta Cuba. Hid it up their arses for all I know. Wouldn't put it past 'em." He waved a finger at Mike. "I tell you, this is a deal where we can't miss."

"Somethin' to think about," said Mike. He reached for the gin bottle. It was empty. "A few cold beers would go down well. Got any money? I'm flat."

"Some. Gotta pay bloody Morgan Scott seventy-three dollars or he's gonna cut off me electric. Shit, you can't move on this damned island without havin' to pay off one of them thievin' Scotts. Bunch of bloody wogs own everything."

"We could always go to your place," Mike said tentatively. "I mean, well, Jesus, you have got a bar."

"Not bloody likely. Me an' Sally had a real fight. Silly bitch, she gets me down sometimes. Anyway, I can't stand the bleedin' place."

"How much money you got, then? I really feel like a few cold beers."

"I got enough for beer," said Bob. "Let's go."

"Gotta have a shave, first," Mike said, rubbing his hand over his face.

"What the hell for?"

"Because I need a shave, that's why." He went to the head, plugged an electric shaver. "Where shall we go?"

"I don't give a shit as long as the beer's cold. How about the Ocean View, that's closest."

"All right." Mike finished shaving and started to scrub his teeth.

"Jeeezus," said Bob. "Let's get goin' for fuck's sake."

Mike came out of the head, pulled on a pair of clean white pants and a denim shirt. Bob headed for the hatchway stairs. "Ready now?"

"Just a minute." Mike was emptying ashtrays and gathering up dead bottles.

"Do that later," said Bob.

Mike began to straighten the beds. Bob shook his head in despair. In the girl's bed Mike found a soiled pair of black panties. He stuffed them in a drawer. Maybe she'd come back for them if she could remember where she left them.

"I'm goin' up on deck," said Bob. "Get a move on."

Mike finished his tidying. He wanted things to look right when he came back, and he had no intention of coming back alone. He'd have to promote some booze; there wasn't a drop on board and you couldn't bring back an overnight guest to a dry ship. For that matter you couldn't bring yourself back to a dry ship. He patted cologne on his face, carefully brushed his stubby hair. Bob peered down through the hatch cover.

"For shit's sake, watcha doin' now?"

Mike went up on deck. "Luvly," said Bob. "A thing of bleedin' beauty."

45

Over-carefully, the two crossed to the dock and headed toward the Ocean View.

Harry was the only customer at Sally's place. Sally stood behind the bar, leaning on her elbows. The silver cross swung between her breasts as she moved.

"Going to be a quiet night," Harry said.

"Oh, it's early. Things'll pick up later on. Would you like another beer?"

"What I'd like is for you to close the place up and let me take you to dinner."

"I couldn't do that," Sally said. "Bob would kill me if he came back and found the place shut up and me not here."

"We could have lobster, a steak, a bottle of wine, coffee, brandy . . ."

". . . and a good cigar?" she giggled.

"If you wanted one. You can have anything you want. If it's on Hog Cay and you want it, you can have it."

"It sounds lovely, Harry, but I better stay here." She straightened up. The heavy silver cross fell back against her breast. She held the cross tightly in one hand, leaned across the bar and lightly kissed Harry on the cheek. "Thank you again for my present, Harry."

He pulled her to him and kissed her hard on her mouth. He felt her lips soften, begin to part, but he pulled away from her and walked out of the pool hall. Unreasoning rage pumped through him. He wanted to find Bob, to beat the shit out of him. He was prepared to kill the son-of-a-bitch. He took three slow breaths; the rage retreated.

Harry realized he was hungry—he'd had nothing to eat since before dawn. Beers, yes. Food, no. He'd go to the Ocean View, they served the best seafood on the Island. Besides, he liked Marcus Marchand, the owner. The Professor, as everyone called him, was always good for a few laughs, and Harry could use a laugh right now.

The wreck of an old, befinned Chrysler taxi was parked outside a native bar down the street. Harry went into the bar, the driver and four other men were playing craps. For five dollars the driver agreed to drive Harry to the Ocean view: in ten minutes he could be back and pick up the dice.

There is only one road on Hog Cay, the narrow, potholed Queen's Highway that follows the south coastline, for it is on the south side that all the bars, hotels, stores, docks, and marinas are jammed together in less than a mile. There are no private cars. At its widest point, Hog Cay is barely a quarter mile from ocean to ocean.

As they drove down the almost deserted road, Harry checked the boats that were docked. Four or five sport fishermen he recognized. Two big-money yachts had arrived. Harry knew their owners and their captains, knew them well enough to be invited aboard these luxurious extravagances for a drink, but their world was not Harry's world. Most of the dock space was empty, but in a few days this would change. The blue marlin tournament started next Monday, and then every inch of dock space would be filled, every hotel and marina jammed, the bars and restaurants packed. And there would be money on the Island, lots of money. During the five days of the tournament and for days after it was over, nonstop parties would turn Hog Cay into Christmas, Mardi Gras, and the World Series rolled up into one giant debauch. Then the Island would go back to bed to recover for the next fishing tournament in six weeks' time.

The cab pulled up in front of the Ocean View. Harry got out and paid the driver, who made a U-turn and gunned the cab back to his crap game.

Most of the drinkers at the big semicircular bar of the Ocean View were regulars and the talk was of boats, fishing, and diving. You could spot the boat people by their deep wind-and-sun settled tans, by their bleached and casually elegant clothes, by their firm handshakes, their easy laughter, their yelled greetings to familiar faces. They talked louder and held their drinks better than most and knew all the verses of the dirty songs. They came in all ages and all sizes and they all looked alike.

The diving, spear-fishing fraternity you knew by the big, multi-dialed, guaranteed-waterproof-to-three-hundred-feet chronometers on their wrists, by the shark-tooth charms and St. Christophers around their necks. They drank less than the others: 120 feet down, breathing metallic air through a frail hose, was no place to throw up last night's excesses.

The tourists were easy to spot, with reddened faces and sunburned arms that met pale flesh under brightly patterned shirts or polyester print dresses. They pointed Instamatic cameras at each other and complained a lot. They all wanted to get away from Hog Cay as soon as possible, back to where they could get a decent hamburger and french fries, where the toilets worked, where there was something to do, for God's sake. Not even a straw market, would you believe it? You can't buy a picture postcard . . ." To overcome their disappointment in Hog Cay they got quickly and nastily drunk.

Marcus Marchand saw Harry come in and beckoned him over to the bar. Harry worked his way through the groups of drinkers, through a nonstop barrage of talk.

From the fishing fraternity:

". . . took it like it was starving. Hadda pour water over the reel to cool it off. Thought the goddam fish would never stop going. Fought the bastard for over half an hour, then he broke off, and I lost him . . ."

". . . just wasn't my day. My mate didn't know a good fishing spot from the hole in his ass . . ."

". . . we shouldda gone to Crooked Rock, that's where the action was. Remember . . . ? That's where I wanted to go in the first place . . ."

From the scuba men, hands tracing the moves:

". . . was down maybe fifty, sixty feet . . . over by Gun Island, you know, where it drops off real deep past the reef. Just havin' a look-see an' I realize I got company . . . 'cuda! Now I've seen some big barracuda, but these mothers I swear to God was longer'n me. Spots on 'em the size a saucers. Lemme tell you, I got outta there fast, went up like a damn cork."

". . . so I let him have it with my bang stick, blew half his head off. Then his pals came by to finish him off. I tell you, couldn't move for goddam sharks."

Marcus Marchand stuck out his hand to Harry.

"Welcome back to the dubious pleasures of Hog Cay, my friend."

A huge, grayhaired and bearded man, six and a half feet tall, barrel-chested, Marcus Marchand looked like a retired all-in wrestler, but in fact had been a full professor of anthropology at a major Canadian university, an idiosyncratic bachelor who had successfully avoided marriage for fifty years. When he hit his fiftieth birthday, Marcus suddenly and without warning resigned, leaving his respected, well-paid and tenured position to open a bar on Hog Cay. Now in his sixties, he was a fixture on the Island, a recognized character.

Harry shook his hand. "Professor, I'm starving and fish is what I want."

"We have grouper and swordfish tonight. I recommend the grouper."

"Grouper sounds good."

"Right, my boy, grouper is what you shall have." The Professor opened the door which led off from the bar to the kitchen, yelled the order to the cook, then turned back to Harry. "Now tell me what's going on in that strange world beyond these parochial shores. . . ."

Bob and Mike were still at their table, several beers drunker. Bob raised his glass, and belched. "I've had as much beer as my gut will hold. I need a couple of good belts." He elbowed his way to the bar, pushed roughly past Harry and put a ten-dollar bill in front of the Professor. "Two large gins," he said. "Gordon's."

Harry moved back to his old position at the bar. Bob again violently shoved him away. "Don't start anything, Bob," Harry said. "Don't start any trouble."

"Fuck off," said Bob, then pushed the ten-dollar bill at the Professor. "You gonna get me my drinks?"

The Professor folded his arm. "No, you've had enough. Go home."

Rage in his eyes, Bob looked from the Professor to Harry, flecks of spittle in the corners of his mouth. "You," he said. "I gotta bone to pick with you. Keep outta my place. I seen the way you hang around Sally. You're after her. I'll break every bone in your bleedin' body if you as much as lay a finger on her."

Harry straightened up. "By the look of Sally's face you've already laid a pretty heavy finger on her."

Bob swung a punch, Harry easily blocked it. The

drinkers close by backed away, glasses raised high. People could get hurt. They could lose their drinks.

"Ease off, Bob," said Harry. "You're drunk."

Bob grabbed a beer glass from the counter, held it by its heavy base and smashed the rim against the edge of the bar, then closed in on Harry, crouched and weaving. The drinkers scrambled in panic to get out of his way. The Professor reached for the billy he kept on a shelf under the bar. Harry backed off and sized up the situation. He had one thing going for him; he was sober. Bob shuffled closer, breathing heavily, the jagged glass held low in front of him. He lunged at Harry's face, a feeler.

Harry was too close to the wall. He sidestepped and moved out into the room, he needed space to maneuver. Bob followed his move, eyes never leaving him, crouched, the broken glass always weaving back and forth. Again he lunged, this time with more purpose. He didn't seem so drunk now, a fixed smile on his face. Harry kept his hands down—put them up and he stood a good chance of getting them slashed. Bob brought the broken glass up low, aiming for Harry's throat.

Bob was left-handed. Drawing on all but forgotten instructions in unarmed combat that had been drilled into him by a rock-hard, bald, and maniacal warrant officer back in his Coast Guard days, Harry acted reflexively. He stepped inside the thrust and jammed the heel of his hand up under Bob's nose. Bob screamed, his face was a bloody mess. Harry went to the bar. "Give me a towel and ice," he said to the Professor. He pushed Bob into a chair and made an icepack. "You better let Nurse Jones take a look, I think it's broken." Harry beckoned to Mike, still sitting at his table. "Take your buddy up to the clinic."

Whitefaced and anxious to please, Mike tried to help Bob out of his chair. Bob pushed him away and stumbled out through the bar door, the bloody towel clutched to his face. Mike followed him.

"Sorry about the mess," Harry said to the Professor.

The Professor shrugged, looked down at the blood on the wooden floor, then back up at Harry. "A bit harder, and you could have killed him, right?"

Harry took a deep breath, he was trembling. The Professor was right. Properly executed, that was a blow designed to kill, to mash splintered bones back into the brain. But his timing had been off, he'd gotten soft since his Coast Guard days, and no fanatical instructor had been there, dancing around and yelling "Kill. Kill the bastard, that's the name of the game." All Bob had suffered was a bloody nose, possibly broken.

Harry's rage had evaporated, the crisis was over. "You're right," he said to the Professor, "I could have killed him. But I didn't. He was lucky."

The Professor poured two shots of whiskey. "I'm tempted to ask why you didn't. That is without doubt the most useless, miserable piece of human garbage I have ever met. He wouldn't be missed. And don't worry about the blood, I'll invent some lurid story for the tourists, they'll believe anything."

Harry slept well, lulled by the gentle motion of the *Rimshot* and cooled by the night breeze. Before he dropped off he ran through the events of the evening. He had to confess to himself a certain juvenile satisfaction in the way he'd handled Bob. And he thought about Sally and hoped that Bob wouldn't work out his anger and resentment on her, wouldn't make her pay for the humiliation he'd suffered at Harry's hands.

So, Bob had sensed his attachment to Sally, had he? Harry didn't think he'd made it that obvious. One thing for sure, he now had an enemy in Bob, a vicious, primitive enemy. He'd better be careful, very, very careful. Although he was sure Bob would be in no fit condition to come looking for revenge tonight, Harry locked and bolted the cabin door, and for the first time in his life slept with a loaded pistol under his pillow. Unneccessary, he knew, but it was a source of great comfort, even though he doubted he'd be able to shoot an intruder in cold blood. But the violence earlier in the bar had awakened in him instincts he didn't know he possessed. For one blinding flash, one red-tinged moment, he had wanted to kill Bob, and that bothered him. And he had felt a gratifying sense of triumph at the sight of his opponent bloodied and defeated. A primitive emotion, quite possibly, but one that no man, if he's honest, is immune to. He'd been tested and had emerged triumphant. Good for the ego. He fell asleep with a smile on his face.

SIX

Harry was up early. He brewed coffee while he shaved, then sat in the fighting chair at the back of the boat and drank his coffee in the peace and quiet.

He decided to see Bob, to make it clear to him that if he ever again hurt Sally then he, Harry Foster, would kill him.

Be a hero, show off for the pretty girl down the street, said an inner voice, but Harry ignored it and walked to the pool hall. In coveralls, her hair wrapped in a scarf, Sally was mopping the floor. She was alone.

"Where's Bob?" Harry asked.

Sally wrung the dirty water from the mop into a pail. "He's gone to Miami. Somebody he knew was taking their boat over first thing, and he hitched a ride."

"How is he?"

"Oh, all right. His nose is sore, Nurse Jones had to put a stitch in it, but he's all right." She managed a smile. "Bob's a bad loser—you hurt his pride more than his nose."

"How was he with you?"

"I kept out of his way last night, and I pretended I was still asleep this morning—he left just after dawn."

She emptied the pail of dirty water into the street, then put the mop and bucket in a closet behind the bar.

"Anything I can do to help?" Harry said.

She sighed. "If you really want to, you can help me load the cooler."

"Sure thing," said Harry.

"The cases of beer are over there . . ." She pointed. "Bring two Pauli Girl, two Beck's and a Heineken, will you?"

Harry fetched the cases of beer and helped her load the bottles into the cooler. "Do you ever get away from here? Do you ever take a day off?"

Sally shook her head. "Not very often. Like I said, somebody's got to be here."

"How much do you take in on an average day?"

She thought. "Oh . . . when there's a tournament on, maybe a hundred and fifty dollars. Otherwise . . ." She shrugged. "Not much."

Harry took a thin roll of money from his pants pocket, peeled off three fifty-dollar bills, and laid them on the top of the cooler. "Okay, there's a hundred and fifty. Put the Closed sign on the door."

As if unsure what to do with it, Sally picked up the

money. "That's silly, I can't just close up, we went through that last night. Anyway, I can't take your money for nothing." She handed the bills back to him. Harry took them from her, went to the bar, rang up No Sale on the cash register, dropped the money in the drawer, and slammed the drawer shut. "Get your swimsuit. We're going over to Gull Island, enjoy a swim, catch some fish, have a picnic. How long since you went on a picnic?"

"I can't, Harry."

He took her hand. "We'll be back in time for your evening trade and Bob will never know."

Sally considered, solemn faced, then nodded. "All right, let's do it. Give me five minutes to get ready." She ran from the bar, and Harry was sadly aware of how young she was.

The living area was roughly partitioned off from the bar. Sally left the flimsy connecting door open and through it Harry could see a heavy, old, sagging velour sofa, an armchair with a throw-rug over it, a folding card table—stained and cigarette-burned—two folding metal chairs, patched linoleum on the floor. He couldn't see into the bedroom, but there was no reason to believe it would be any better. He didn't want Sally to live like this.

She was back in less than five minutes. Under a thin, unbuttoned cotton shift she wore a minimal yellow bikini. On her bare feet, torn white sneakers. The tormenting image of Bob making love to her surfaced in Harry's mind, and he shook his head to clear it.

"What's the matter?" Sally asked.

"Nothing . . . somebody just walked over my grave."

"My grandmother used to say that, and I never did understand what it means." She handed him a makeup purse. "Put that in your pocket, will you? I don't want to bother to take a bag. Is there anything you need? You know, food or beer or anything?"

"Nothing. Lock up and let's go."

Sally took the money from the cash register, went into the bedroom and hid it. "They're honest boys," she said, "but there's no need to put temptation in their way." She hung the Closed sign in the window as they left and pulled the door shut behind her.

"You haven't locked it," said Harry.

"There isn't a key for it. Nobody's going to steal anything. What is there to steal? A few half-bottles of liquor. Beer? The boys might go in for a few free games of pool and they might help themselves to a beer. So what? They'd tell me and pay for it later. They wouldn't cheat me. Most of them wouldn't, anyway."

They walked down the street, side by side, circumspectly, just two people who happened to be going the same way. Harry ached to take her hand, but that would have been foolish. Hog Cay, like all parochial communities, thrived on gossip, and someone would have been sure to make it known to Bob. Why ask for trouble? So they walked side by side, matching paces, like a father and daughter on their way to market or to church. And, like a little girl with her father, Sally kept up a rapid-fire stream of questions. Where was Gull Island . . . ? What was it like? Was there a nice beach? How long did it take to get there?

Guffy was in the cockpit of the *Rimshot*, sorting out fishing tackle. He held out a steadying hand as Sally jumped down from the dock.

"We're going on a picnic," Harry said.

"Are we?" said Guffy. "Where we goin'?"

"Gull Island."

"Want me to drive?"

"No, I'll drive."

They untied the lines, Harry fired up the engines and swung the *Rimshot* out into the channel. Sally stood beside him on the flybridge, enchanted by the whole adventure. For about a quarter of a mile the water was shallow and she could clearly see the clean white sand bottom. Further out, a crescent-shaped line of lazy breakers traced the reef, and in places coral heads stuck up above the surface of the ocean. Until they were safely past the reef, Harry nursed the boat along, the engines ticking over. Then the sea bottom suddenly dropped away and the water was a dark blue-green. Once in the clear, Harry opened the throttles and trimmed the engines until they were contentedly matched. On the calm sea, the *Rimshot* left a clear curling wave behind it that widened out into a vee that stretched back to the reef.

The run to Gull Island took fifteen minutes. Guffy settled his bulk into a canvas chair, tipped a baseball cap over his face, and slept.

At the northern tip of the half-mile-long, uninhabited island, Harry headed into a cove, sheltered from the open sea by a long, wide sandbar. The water became very shallow; he nursed the boat in and anchored some forty feet from shore, then he lowered himself over the side. Sally slid down into his waiting arms, and he carried her through the water to the wide, pink sand beach. As he put her down, she momentarily clung to him, her body pressed tight against him.

Harry abruptly turned, waded back to the boat, and returned with a blanket and a green and yellow striped beach umbrella. Guffy followed him to shore carrying a Styrofoam cooler. On a smooth stretch of the beach, Harry spread the blanket and under one end piled sand to make a raised headrest, then angled the beach umbrella so as to put the blanket in the shade. "Relax," he said to Sally, "we'll go catch lunch."

Sally took off her cotton shift. Harry closed his eyes as she un-selfconsciously hitched her string bikini to make it more comfortable. Obediently, she sat on the blanket, her arms round her knees.

"I'll be good," she said. "I won't be any trouble at all."

Harry and Guffy went back to the boat, put on swim trunks, flippers, masks, and snorkels. From a rack in the cabin they took Hawaiian-sling spear guns. Sally watched as they waded out into the deeper water beyond the sandbar and then swam toward a line of coral heads with only their snorkels showing.

Suddenly, Harry was gone. Guffy followed him down. They were under for less than a minute. Harry broke water, a black grouper of about three pounds impaled on his spear. Guffy came up with nothing, then went down again. His mask pushed up onto the top of his head, the impaled, still flapping fish held aloft, Harry waded to shore. Guffy surfaced with a good-sized fish.

"Lunch," Harry said to Sally. Expertly he skinned and filleted the two fish on the top of the cooler and threw the carcasses to the gulls. While Guffy gathered driftwood for a fire, he went down to the water's edge and scrubbed his hands and the fish knife with wet sand. From the cooler he got two cans of beer, opened one for Sally and one for himself, then sat beside her on the blanket.

"Sooner be back in the pool hall?"

Sally took a slow sip of the beer. "That's not fair, Harry."

"I know. How long are you going to put up with it?"

"Put up with Bob, you mean, don't you?"

"That's what I mean."

"I told you before, I owe Bob. Like I said, he's had a lot of bad luck and I'm not going to walk out on him now."

"What makes you think his luck is going to get any better?"

"It couldn't get any worse."

"How old are you?"

"Twenty . . . nearly."

"And how old is he?"

"What's that got to do with anything? If it comes to that, how old are you?"

Harry winced, and she saw it. "Gotcha," she said triumphantly.

"What did you do before you came to Hog Cay?" he asked.

"Oh, nothing in particular," she said vaguely. "Why all the questions?"

"It's just that I don't know anything about you or how you came to be here."

"You make me feel like a whore," Sally said crossly. "You know, what's a nice girl like you doing in a place like this?"

"Don't be silly," Harry said, "but what *are* you doing in a place like this?"

"You know what I'm doing, I'm trying to run a bar."

"Don't get cute, you know what I mean. How did you end up here married to Bob Hammersley and running his bar?"

"Oh, that's a long story and not very interesting."

"Tell me, just the same."

She shrugged. "What difference does it make?"

"It matters to me."

"Why?"

"Because I want to know more about you. I want to know everything about you."

Again she shrugged. "Nothing much to tell. Where do you want to start?"

"Where were you born?"

"In a dump of a small town in the south of England, nowhere you've ever heard of. Strictly working-class family—when they were working, that is. Most of time my father was on the dole and my mother was pregnant. Five brothers and a sister in a crummy house about the size of a big dog kennel. Fights and arguments all the time, so I got out as soon as I could. Worked as a waitress, any job I could get. Went to London to better myself and ended up in the same rat race. Managed to save enough for a one-way ticket to Canada, ended up in Toronto."

"Things get better there?"

"No education, couldn't type, couldn't do anything that paid a decent wage, but I got by, kept myself respectable, as they say. Made enough to pay the rent on my room and eat regular. I kept off the streets, and that's something."

"How did you get from Toronto to Hog Cay, that's what I want to know."

Sally laughed. "That was really weird, it really was weird. I was working as a cocktail waitress in a hotel out near the airport. A bunch of guys came in one Friday night, spent money like water, ordered champagne, the best. Celebrating some big deal they'd pulled off. At least, that's what they said. I was serving their table. Drunk out of their minds, they were. Older guys. Gold Rolex watches with twenty-four-carat bracelets. Wallets stuffed with hundred-dollar bills. One of them made a pass at me. Nothing unusual in that place, your ass was pinched raw by the time the place closed.

"Anyway, this guy said they were flying to Nassau later that night, in their private plane. Said he wanted to take me with him. Show me a good time, buy me a lot of new dresses and pretty things. Give me money to gamble at the casino. He wanted company he said, wanted a girl like me to keep him company. Just for the weekend. They'd fly me back on Monday in the company plane. It was going to be one big party, he said, I'd have the time of my life. He liked the look of me, I was his kind of girl, so he wanted me to go with him and wouldn't take no for an answer."

"And you did? You went with him?"

Sally nodded. "I'm not proud of what I did. I knew what I was getting into. So it meant sleep with the guy, that was the payoff. Well, it wouldn't be the first time, and the idea of a weekend in Nassau when it's January in Toronto and it's colder than a witch's tit and there's three feet of snow and sludge in the streets seemed too good to turn down, and I was off duty until Monday night, anyway.

"But I didn't think he was serious, thought it was just the booze talking. But it wasn't, he was serious. He stuffed a hundred-dollar bill in my bra, to seal the contract, he said. When the joint closed I changed into my street clothes, half expecting to find the guys gone. But they weren't. The one who'd taken a fancy to me—he seemed the big shot who made the decisions—was waiting for me. There was a big limousine waiting. We all got in and drove to the airport. A private plane flew us to Nassau and it was one big party all the way. How they kept it up, I'll never know. They were all smashed before we started."

"And what happened in Nassau?"

Sally sighed. "What do you think? The guy bought me some clothes. He couldn't take me anywhere in the junk I was wearing. I went with him everywhere he went. To the casino, to fancy restaurants, to big bashes in private mansions. Christ, how the rich live."

"You slept with him?"

Her face set in stubborn lines. "That was the deal, remember? Why does any guy take a girl for a weekend in Nassau? To play Scrabble?" A flicker of humor softened her expression. "Most of the time the fat slob couldn't get it up, he was too drunk, and that made him mad, and when he was mad, he was mean God, he made me sick. I couldn't stand being in the same bed with him, even when he didn't touch me."

Harry persisted. "So we've got you as far as Nassau What happened then?"

She picked up a handful of sand, watched it trickle through her fingers. "What happened then? The bastard dumped me. Monday morning he gave me fifty bucks, told me to go out and buy myself something. When I got back to the hotel, he'd checked out. Gone. Left me stranded. Just went, never even wrote me a good-bye note."

"So what did you do?"

"What choice did I have? The hotel kicked me out. The room rate was two hundred and fifty bucks a night and I had seventy-five dollars to my name. Take my word for it, Nassau's no place to be if you're white, a girl, and broke. So I hitched a ride on a boat to Hog Cay. Somebody told me I could find work here. That was a laugh. You can't work on any of the islands now unless you're a Bahamian or own a business or are married to someone who owns a business."

"And that's why you married Bob Hammersley. Is that how you came to end up where you are?"

"No more questions," said Sally. "Don't ask me any more questions." She handed him her half-empty can of beer and stretched out on the blanket, eyes closed.

Harry tipped the remains of her beer in the sand. He was tempted to grab her, to shake her and make her tell him the rest of the story, to fill in the gaps. But he didn't. Instead, he helped Guffy gather firewood.

Sometime later, Guffy got the fire going. The driftwood crackled and spat out green, red, and yellow sparks from the encrusted seasalt. He stuck the fish fillets on the spears pushed into the sand and angled toward the fire. Harry and Sally sat on the blanket and watched him as Guffy squatted by the fire, drinking beer and waiting for the fish to cook.

Sally put her hand on Harry's arm. "I didn't mean anything by that, you know, about your age."

"Yes you did, you read me loud and clear. You know I'm damn well trying to get you to leave Bob and come with me."

She smiled at him. "I know, but would you marry me?"

Harry hesitated a second too long. Sally made a pistol of her finger and pointed it at him. "Gotcha . . . !"

"Now wait a goddam minute," said Harry. "That's something I'd have to think about. I've been married, twice, and it didn't work."

"You know, Harry, you're as big a phony as the rest. You like the idea of having someone available, someone who'll wait around for you, jump into bed with you whenever you feel like it. But marriage, that's different, that's the old ball and chain.''

Guffy called out, "Okay, let's eat." He brought over paper plates of fish, fresh limes, and chunks of sweet Island bread.

"Aren't you eating?" Sally asked him.

He shook his head. "Not fish. Steak, ribs, I eat. Not fish." He opened a fresh can of beer.

Sally and Harry squeezed fresh lime on the golden grouper fillets and ate with their fingers, and it was good. When they were finished, Sally lay back on the blanket and Harry watched her as she drifted into sleep. He opened two more cans of beer and carried them over to where Guffy was killing the fire.

"Don't say anything," said Harry.

"Oh, I ain't goin' to say nothin', I got enough sense to stay out of trouble."

"Yes," said Harry, "you've got more than I have."

Guffy drained his beer, crumpled the can in his big hand. "Sometimes I think I have."

Sally woke up as smoothly as she'd fallen asleep. The remains of the lunch had been cleared away, the cooler stowed back in the boat. Harry was standing over her, looking down at her. He reached out a hand and helped her to her feet.

"What time is it?" she asked.

"Relax, there's plenty of time."

She looked around the empty beach. "Where's Guffy?"

"On the boat, asleep."

Still holding her hand he picked up the blanket, threw it over his shoulder, then led her up the beach. Sally moved closer and put her arm round his waist.

In from the beach the sand gave way to clumps of wind-bent pine trees and coarse sea grass. Under the sheltering trees, Harry spread the blanket, then held

Sally and kissed her. Gently her lips opened and she pressed tight against him. Still kissing her, he undid the string of her bikini top. It fell away and he buried his head in her breasts, filling his mouth with hard nipple and soft flesh. He tore off the bottom of her bikini and knelt, and tasted the incredible mixture of young sweat and sex. Sally broke away, lay down on the blanket, and held up her arms in invitation.

Slowly he stripped off his shirt and pants, took her hands in his. She pulled him down to her, guided him inside her, wrapped her legs around his waist. For a moment they lay still. Her eyes closed, Sally began to move under him, with him, more and more urgently.

Sally came first, biting his shoulder to stifle her cry. Then they lay side by side, with Harry stroking her hair until they returned to the real world.

On the way back to Hog Cay, Guffy drove the boat, Harry and Sally held hands, and nobody said very much.

He took Sally back to the pool hall. It was as she'd left it, quiet, untouched, and no Bob. She went into the bleak bedroom to change. Harry followed her in, tried to hold her, but she pushed him away.

"No . . . no. Bob might come back." She was frightened. "You better go, honest. If he comes back and you're here, he'll have a fit."

"If he comes back, I'll straighten him out," he said, and was immediately conscious of how stupidly immature he sounded. Showing off to impress the pretty girl down the street . . . Jesus Christ!

Sally raised her clenched fists and shook them in frustration. "Oh, you really are impossible. I don't want you to straighten anything out. You're acting like a bloody kid, Harry."

"Now look . . ." More bravado, more bluster.

"No, Harry, you look. We went on a picnic and you made love to me and it was nice, I enjoyed it, I'd like to do it again sometime. So thank you for taking me on the picnic and please go." She pushed him out of the bedroom. At the door, relenting, she briefly put her head on his shoulder. "It *was* nice, Harry, and I really meant it when I said I'd like us to do it again."

Harry tilted her head, kissed her, and she stood at the bedroom door as he walked through the bar and out into the street.

When Harry got back to the *Rimshot*, Guffy was working on one of the engines. He kept on working as Harry came aboard.

"Say something," said Harry.

"What you want me to say?"

"Tell me I'm crazy. Tell me I should get off Hog Cay and not come back."

"Would you?"

"No."

"Then there ain't much point in me tellin' you."

"I'm double her age, Guffy."

"That you are."

"And she's married."

"That she is."

"So what do I do?"

Guffy reached for an oilcan. "You do whatever you want, if you know what that is."

"I don't know."

"An' you expec' me to tell you what you should do?"

"No."

"Then I won't," said Guffy, and went back to his engine.

SEVEN

Harry decided he didn't want to sleep on the *Rimshot* that night, but would treat himself to the luxury of a bungalow unit at the Fish and Game Club. He got the last one; the Island was filling up for the marlin tournament. A vast, custom-built motor yacht was now tied up at the Club's deep-water dock. An impressive stack of electronics dominated the streamlined superstructure; two motor dinghies hung from davits, a helicopter sat on a pad at the stern. Two bare-chested, barefooted, muscular young men mopped the acres of immaculate deck. They were the only sign of life, but from somewhere in the yacht Harry could hear disco music.

A lot of money, he noted without envy, and briefly wondered who the owner was. He didn't know the boat. It was named the *Persephone* and flew an American flag.

After he'd checked in to the Club, Harry wandered from dock to dock. He watched three boats come in, no one on board he knew, just happy people, here for a good time. Lucky people. Go to the Ocean View and talk to the Professor, that's what he'd do. But the bar was busy, the Professor shorthanded and couldn't spare Harry much time.

At the back of the room was an empty table; Harry carried his drink over to it and sat by himself, thinking. For a long time now he'd lived by the simplistic philosophy of One Day at a Time. Seldom did he make or even contemplate any kind of long-range plan. Eventually, he was going to have to. Harry's table was in a corner, on the wall at right angles to him was a mirror with Enjoy Beck's Beer in gold Germanic script. He looked curiously at his reflection. Someone had once told him he looked like Robert Redford, only heavier. Harry couldn't see it. His reflected image looked back at him without emotion. "It's your problem, so work it out," it silently said. Harry looked away. After this Haiti affair he'd make a complete change. Move to California, maybe.

The Professor came and sat with him. "Sorely troubled, are you not, my friend?"

"Sorely troubled, indeed, Professor."

"There you were thinking you had the world by the balls and now you aren't too sure at all."

"That about sums it up."

"You aren't the first man to face that dilemma, if that's any consolation."

"It isn't."

The Professor scratched his beard. "It's a bitch,

isn't it?'' He put his hands on the table and eased his big body out of the chair, laid a hand on Harry's shoulder, gave him a paternal pat, and lumbered back to the bar.

Harry left when he'd finished the one drink.

In threes and fours, people now wandered down the middle of the Queen's Highway, paper walking-cups of booze in their hands, laughing, singing, arguing. Night had closed down on the Island, and Harry couldn't remember feeling so lonely. Restlessly he walked through the blackness, along the shoddy strip of bars and hotels and down the docks and marinas, irregularly lit by overhanging lamps. Off shore, a second huge yacht had anchored, deckhands still busy under working lights.

In the distance he could hear the yelps and barking of a pack of the Island's half-wild dogs as they tracked down a bitch in heat and fought over her favors.

Women . . . thought Harry, we'd be better off without them.

Sergeant Welsh was making the rounds in his Jeep, exploring every foot of his personal domain. The sergeant never seemed to sleep. He slowed down as Harry walked through a pool of light, identified him, then shot off to investigate a fight that was brewing outside Kid Creech's bar.

Harry was wasting time on Hog Cay, he knew that. He had a morning meeting scheduled in Miami with John Chambers. That meant he'd have to take the early plane over and get Guffy to bring the *Rimshot* across. Apart from his first brief flurry of activity he'd done nothing to prepare for the run to Haiti. Ah, well, it would all get done.

Harry's wanderings took him back to Christopher's dock. He saw that a light in the cabin of the *Rimshot* was on, and this was strange. Guffy seldom worked on the boat at night. He turned down toward the *Rimshot*, and Guffy came up the dock to meet him.

"We got a visitor," Guffy said.

"How do you mean we got a visitor . . . who?"

"She says she's goin' to stay on the boat till you get back."

"Sally . . .?"

"Yes. He came home, beat her up and threw her out. She's escared to go back."

"How bad did he beat her up?"

"Bad enough."

"I said I would kill that SOB, and I will."

"No you won't," said Guffy. "That wouldn't help none."

"Maybe not, but I'd enjoy it. Why did he beat her up?"

"'Cause of you."

Sally was fitfully asleep in Harry's bunk, a blanket pulled over her head. He turned back the blanket and gently brushed the long brown hair from her swollen and tear-streaked face. She whimpered, opened fearful eyes, then clutched Harry's hand. He knelt beside her.

"I'm sorry," he said.

She tried to smile, but it hurt her too much, and she held Harry's hand the harder.

"You can't stay here," Harry said. "You need someone to look after you." He turned to Guffy. "How about Lucy?"

"That's what I was thinkin'. Lucy'll take care of her. I'll get us a taxi."

Harry helped Sally out of the bunk. She clung to him and he held her close and made the comforting sounds that his mother had made to him when he was small and hurt himself. He wrapped the blanket round her shoulders, but she pulled it up and held it so as to hide her face.

Guffy came back with the taxi. Harry carried Sally onto the dock, put her in the back seat and sat with his arm round her. Guffy got up front with the driver.

Lucy's house was a decent white clapboard bungalow set in a quarter acre of thin-soiled land a half mile away from the bars. Guffy had built it for her and Lucy lived there with her two teenaged girls, who accepted Guffy with casual affection. By trade, Lucy was a cook, but she no longer regularly worked. Guffy had removed that need, although she still put on her white smock and white shoes and stockings for the occasional banquet or big party at the Fish and Game Club. Forty-one years old, deeply religious, Lucy was a big, strong, capable woman.

Efficiently and tenderly she took charge of Sally; washed her, undressed her, and put her into one of her daughter's nightdresses, smoothed salve on her battered face, massaged her bruised arms and shoulders with rubbing alcohol, made her a cup of strong tea, and had her in bed, all within fifteen minutes. Harry and Guffy she sent outside. "I don't want you two men hangin' around," she said, "so go away."

They stood outside the house. "I'm going to see him," Harry said.

"Thought you might," said Guffy. "No point in my sayin' don't, is there?"

"No."

"I didn't think there was."

"I'll come by in the morning," Harry said.

"Right. Go easy." Guffy watched Harry walk away, then went back inside the house.

* * *

Bob was behind the bar in the pool hall and he was drunk. Not falling over drunk, but nastily, dangerously drunk. No one was at the bar. A group of young Bahamians, beer bottles in their hands, stood around one of the pool tables, laughing and kidding with four teenage players who were clowning, trying impossible shots, and trading mock-serious punches with the spectators.

Harry sat at the bar. "I want to talk to you."

"Well I don't want to talk to you," said Bob, "so piss off."

"I want to talk to you about Sally."

Bob belched. "Do you, mate? I threw the little bitch out. You want her, you can have 'er. Not that you ain't already had 'er. I dunno where you get off comin' here and playin' the high and mighty with me when you bin screwin' my wife."

"You beat her up."

"Fuckin' right I did, she's my wife. If she goes round droppin' her drawers for every bum off a boat who buys her a present, 'course I'm gonna beat the bitch up. It's me bleedin' right, an' I'll beat her up again if she shows her face here. Like I said, you want 'er, you can 'ave 'er, 'cause I don't want 'er back . . . 'though I gotta admit she's a real juicy fuck."

Harry hit him. Bob fell back off his stool and into a pile of beer cases. His clutching hand brought down the shelves of liquor. The boys around the pool table looked on with interest, the players froze, pool cues in their hands. It wasn't their fight, but it might turn out to be good entertainment.

Harry picked up a beer bottle from the bar, held it by the neck, and waited for Bob. From the mess of boxes and broken bottles, Bob lurched to the bar, ducked down behind it and came up with a shotgun.

Harry slapped the gun barrel with the palm of his hand, knocking it away from him. The blast from the shotgun blew out the poolroom window—the players and their friends dived for cover under the table. Bob pumped another shell into the gun. Harry threw the beer bottle at his head.

For a moment, Bob stood rigid, then collapsed. Harry went round behind the bar and prised the shotgun from Bob's hands. Bob was very still, but he wasn't dead. With the danger over, the boys came out from under the pool table and two of them pantomimed the recent action, one throwing an imaginary beer bottle, the other theatrically falling to the floor.

From the street, people pushed through the door, warily at first, then openly curious. They chattered and pointed, but stayed back from Harry who was still holding the gun.

Sergeant Welsh slammed his Jeep to a stop outside the pool hall and stiff-armed his way through the crowd, his shoulders snapped back, khaki uniform uncreased, steel-tipped, polished Army boots loud on the wooden floor. Harry gave him the shotgun, the sergeant holstered his own .45 pistol, ejected the remaining shotgun shells and put them in his pocket.

"You kill him?" the sergeant asked.

"No, he'll be okay."

The sergeant bent over Bob, helped him to his feet. A lump had started to form on Bob's forehead. Dazedly, he put his fingers to it. The sergeant faced the crowd. "Go home, all of you. Get out of here, there's nothing more to see."

They muttered and drew together, but didn't leave.

The sergeant propped Bob against the bar, strode into the crowd, grabbed two men at random, and heaved them into the street. "Out," he said to the rest. "Get out before I lock up the lot of you." Reluctantly, looking over their shoulders and complaining, they filed out, picking their way through shards of broken window-glass.

When the last one had gone, the sergeant faced Harry and Bob.

"I've been expecting something like this. I'm not interested in the details. Harry, you've got a clean slate here so far, don't spoil it. You . . ." he pointed at Bob, ". . . you've been nothing but trouble since the day you arrived. I'm going to tell the both of you something and I want you to remember it. We run the Bahamas now. Us, the Bahamians. These are our islands—they belong to us. You are visitors. I don't care if you've got a British passport or an American passport or what you've got, if I want to, I'll throw you out and you won't get back. One more bit of trouble, anything, and you're gone." He tugged his starched khaki jacket into place, settled his cap more squarely on his cropped head. "That's all," he said, made a parade-ground turn, and marched out, the shotgun held at his side.

"Who the fuck does he think he is?" said Bob, pouring himself a double shot of vodka.

"One wrong move, that's all," said Harry. "Don't make one more wrong move."

Bob swilled down his vodka. "Piss off," he said, and poured himself another drink.

Down the darkened road from the pool hall, Sergeant Welsh waited in his Jeep. He beckoned to Harry to get in beside him, then drove across the short stretch of the Island to the deserted and rocky north shore. He turned off the Jeep's engine.

"I meant what I said."

"I know,"

The sergeant leaned on the steering wheel; he

looked tired. "I don't like what I see happening. Up in Grand Bahama they got gambling and the Mafia. Bimini and a lot of other islands, they got bad, bad drug problems. On Nassau, our government is full of corruption, they line their pockets and let the Out Islands die. No money for education, for medicine, for roads, or to make employment for the kids, an' all the kids want is big transistor radios, gold bracelets, fancy clothes, booze, and girls. Why should they bother to work as waiters or gardeners or laborers for three dollars an hour when they can pick up five thousand in one night on a drug run?

"I live all my life in the Islands, mun, born on Abaco . . ." The sergeant's Bahamian accent was thickening. ". . . these are my Islands, I want to die peaceful here. People brings us trouble; all the time, more trouble. Don't bring us trouble, Harry, that way we stay friends."

He switched on the engine, put the Jeep in gear and drove Harry to the Fish and Game Club. "'Nother thing . . ." he said as Harry climbed out, ". . . trash like that's not worth being sent to jail for."

In the Club lounge, a dozen people stood or sat at the bar. Harry took the only unoccupied stool. Next to him sat a short, plump, silver-haired man in his late sixties, fastidiously dressed in expensive weekend sailor's clothes—Club-badged blue blazer, impeccable ascot, white ducks, and deck shoes. The man nodded to Harry and went back to talking to the bartender.

One stool over from the silver-haired man perched a deeply tanned woman with white-blond hair. She wore a spaghetti-strap sleeveless black dress calculated to set off her perfect breasts, faultless bare legs, and slim arms. She looked at Harry over the rim of the glass of white wine held in one many-ringed brown hand, her elbows resting on the bar counter. Imperceptibly, she winked at him. The silver-haired man said something to her and patted her arm. Obviously, she belonged to him. The woman smiled, her eyes looking past him at Harry. Behind the man's back she pursed her lips and blew Harry a silent, dirty kiss.

Harry went along with the gag and winked back at her. She put the tip of her tongue between her lips, then once more turned her attention to silver-hair.

Under that black dress is a real grown-up woman, thought Harry. Maybe that's what I need to get my head straight, to get me back on the track. He put his bungalow key on the bar and absently turned the brass tag so that the number four was toward her. She saw it. The bartender excused himself from the silver-haired man and moved to Harry.

"Just a beer," said Harry, "a Beck's."

The silver-haired man turned to Harry. "I'm Frazer Chadlow. Haven't seen you around the Club before, have I?" He was from the South, the Carolinas, possibly.

"Harry Foster," said Harry. "I stay here from time to time, just haven't run into each other, I guess."

The woman leaned across. "My name's Sabina."

"Oh, yes," said Frazer Chadlow, "this is Sabina."

"Glad to know you, Sabina," said Harry.

"You must come and have a drink with us on the boat. That's it, the *Persephone*." Sabina pointed through the bar's wall of glass to the enormous, illuminated yacht.

"Nice boat," said Harry.

Frazer Chadlow turned his head to look at the boat

as if he couldn't quite remember what it looked like. "Bought it off a Greek," he said. "What was the fella's name, Sabina?"

"Skyros something-or-other."

"That was it, Skyros something-or-other, he's getting a much bigger one. Which is your boat?"

"I'm not in that league," said Harry.

Chadlow nodded sympathetically. "You fishing in the tournament, then?"

"No. I'm going to miss it."

"Don't fish, myself," said Chadlow. "Never saw the point of it."

"Now don't forget to come for that drink," said Sabina. "Tomorrow, about five. Frazer usually serves drinks about five."

"I have to go to Chicago tomorrow, remember?"

Sabina put her hand on his arm. "Oh dear, so you do, I'd quite forgotten. It had entirely slipped my mind that you were going off and leaving me all alone tomorrow."

Harry finished his beer and picked up his key. "Good night, Mr. Chadlow . . . Sabina, been a pleasure."

The winding path to his bungalow was poorly lit. Harry picked his way carefully. His bungalow was one of the older ones, smaller and less luxurious than the high-rent ones close to the main Club. Pity he had to go back to Miami in the morning and wouldn't be able to take up Sabina's invitation. She'd made sure he knew that Frazer Chadlow was going to be away in Chicago. Of course, if she wanted to come to him, that was her business.

And Sabina did come to him. He'd been in bed, with the lights out, for about ten minutes when he heard the discreet tap on his door.

"It isn't locked," he called out.

"Don't turn on the lights," said Sabina as she slipped in through the half-opened door.

"Forgive me for not getting up," said Harry, "but I haven't got any clothes on."

"How very thoughtful." She pulled the curtains across the windows. "Now you can put the lights on."

Harry switched on his bedside lamp. Sabina pulled back the one thin sheet that covered him. "You lied," she said, pointing at him, "you've got Jockey shorts on." She slid out of her dress; under it she wore nothing.

"What have you done with Frazer?" Harry said.

"I put him to bed. He gets tired; too much excitement isn't good for him." She looked critically at Harry's body. "Very nice, muscles and everything. I haven't seen real muscles for quite a while." She slid her hand inside Harry's shorts. "Oooh, and that's nice, too . . . and it's getting nicer." She started to massage him with practiced motions. Harry took her hand out of his shorts.

"What's the matter," she asked, "didn't you like that?"

"In these situations," said Harry, "I take the initiative. Is that all right with you?"

Sabina sighed contentedly. "It's just fine by me. I'm so sick of playing nursemaid I could scream." She sat on the bed. "Do you know how long it is since I've been screwed by a real man? Too long. Tonight, when you walked into the bar I said to myself, that's it. Good little Sabina's going to ask that nice man who looks as if he could be a real son of a bitch to take her to bed and fuck the ass off her. So please, pretty please, will you take me to bed and fuck the ass off me."

Harry got up from the bed, picked Sabina up in his

arms, carried her around the room, took her back to the bed, and dumped her onto it. "Like this?" he asked.

When he had finished with her, Sabina lay on her face, not moving; wet with perspiration, her carefully coiffed blond hair a tangled mess. She looked up at Harry, ran her tongue over her lipstick-smeared mouth. "That's what I had in mind."

Harry slapped her bottom. "I thought it might be."

She showered, used Harry's hairbrush, refused coffee. "I must get back to my baby," she said. "If he wakes up and I'm not there he'll throw a tantrum. Are you coming to see me tomorrow?"

"I'm leaving in the morning."

Sabina sighed, "Wouldn't you know." Then she smiled. "Oh my God, that was good."

Harry took her to the door. She kissed him and ran off into the darkness.

EIGHT

Pollack's Inter-Island Air Service handled the Hog Cay to Miami traffic. Harry bought his ticket and sat on the bench outside the wooden shack that was Pollack's office. Sitting in the shade of a scrubby palm tree were the six other passengers for the 8:30 A.M. flight. Four were tourists, happy to be going home, the two others were Bahamian girls who worked at the Ocean View, off for a day's shopping. They waved at Harry and he waved back. Percy Smith, the customs officer, pedaled up on his bicycle, set up shop on a picnic table under another palm, looked at identification, and collected head tax.

The white-haired, shirt-sleeved, middle-aged pilot came out of the office, drinking a can of Coke. He flipped a hand in greeting to Harry.

"Coming with us?"

"Sure, going to take my life in my hands once more."

The pilot pitched the empty Coke can into a trash barrel. "Okay, then, let's get the show on the road."

Followed by the other passengers, Harry and the pilot walked across the blisteringly hot concrete square to the paint-scarred old Grumman amphibian, which sat lumpishly facing the ramp that sloped down into the ocean.

"Wanna ride up front?" the pilot asked.

"Thanks," said Harry.

They climbed the six shaky aluminum steps into the body of the aircraft. The other passengers followed and settled themselves into the thin, torn and patched Leatherette-covered seats bolted to the bare aluminum floor. Harry went with the pilot up the steeply angled aisle of the plane and into what the Pollack brochures euphemistically referred to as "The Flight Deck." He buckled himself into the copilot's seat—there were no copilots on Pollack flights. A boy on the steps closed the plane's door, then wheeled the steps away. The pilot ran through his check, gunned the engines, and the amphibian waddled down the ramp and into the water. He completed his check, then gave the twin engines full throttle.

Laboriously the plane picked up speed, throwing back over the cabin windows waves of sea water that convinced first-time travelers the plane was rapidly sinking. Eventually, the hull was free of the drag of the water and the plane slowly climbed, heavily banked into a shallow turn, then leveled off, like some enormous, aging duck.

They flew low, well below the clouds, and Harry watched the shifting colors of the crystal waters and the sharply defined reefs and coral strands.

"Nice day," yelled the pilot.

Harry raised a circling thumb and forefinger.

Twenty minutes later, the towers and rectangles of the hotels and condominiums of Miami Beach rose improbably above the horizon, and the pilot lined up his approach to Biscayne Bay.

A token customs and immigration check and Harry was cleared. From the customs shed he took a cab to a McDonald's, had breakfast, read the *Herald*, picked up another cab, and was at John Chambers' office three minutes early. Chambers was waiting for him.

"Right on time as usual, Mr. Foster, an admirable quality. Is everything organized?"

"All set," said Harry, which didn't exactly answer John Chamber's question.

"Fine, fine, where do my men meet you, and when?"

"Next Sunday, 7:30 A.M., Al Parson's dock." Harry passed him a hand drawn schematic map. "It's off the beaten track, but they shouldn't have any difficulty in finding it. Don't lose the map."

"I'll have Mrs. Cellini make some copies," said Chambers. "What should they bring with them? Fishing poles or anything?"

Harry closed his eyes. "I've got all the tackle we need. Just clothes—old clothes, deck shoes, sweaters, windbreakers."

Chambers took notes.

"And no booze," said Harry.

Chambers nodded approvingly, "Good, good, no booze."

"And no guns."

Sharply, Chambers looked up from his notes. "No guns . . .?"

Harry raised a hand. "I don't mean we won't have

guns on board. Nobody in his right mind takes a boat through the Bahamas and the Caribbean without being armed, not with the way things are today. Just tell them not to wear guns. Last thing I need is for some cop or customs man to catch one of my party with a fishing rod in his hand and a .357 Magnum under his arm."

"You have a point," said Chambers. "How do we communicate with each other?"

Harry gave him another piece of paper. "This is our route and the stopovers we'll be making for gas and supplies. I've marked the ETAs and departures. Allow twenty-four hours either way. There's a radio-telephone link from each one; I'll call you here, during business hours, and check in. If you want to reach me for any reason, leave a message for me with the operator at the next stop on our itinerary and I'll pick it when we arrive."

"Very simple, very good," said Chambers. "These are the names of my two men who will be going with you." He handed Harry one of his business cards with two names written on the back. "Anything more, Mr. Foster?"

"Not that I can think of right now. If there is, I'll call."

"Fine, fine . . ." Chambers stood, held out his hand. "Have a nice trip, Mr. Foster. Catch lots of fish."

Harry didn't take his hand. "You still haven't told me who I'm delivering your package to . . . or where I find him."

Chambers smiled blandly. "Oh, don't worry about that, Mr. Foster, my men will let you know all in good time."

Harry shook his hand. "Nothing like being careful,

is there, Mr. Chambers."

"Nothing, Mr. Foster."

As Harry passed Rose Cellini's desk in the outer office, where Mrs. Cellini sat entering figures in a big old-fashioned ledger, he bent over and said, "Goodbye, Mrs. Cellini, it's been a pleasure, as always."

Her lips tightened, but she didn't look up. When she heard the elevator take Harry down to the lobby, Mrs. Cellini laid down her pen, got up from her desk, walked along the corridor to a pay phone, and made a brief local call.

Guffy brought the *Rimshot* over from Hog Cay and put it in Harry's slip at the Belle Mar Marina. Harry met him there and they drove to Al Parson's dock. The heavy Saturday morning traffic made this a thirty-minute journey. Early Sunday would see this time cut in half.

Used mainly by retired men who kept small boats there and did a little fishing and shot the breeze and drank a few beers with other retired men, Al Parson's wasn't a fancy dock. A weathered wood-planked T, there were slips for eight boats on each side of the stem. Two fuel pumps were located on the crossbar of the T. Al operated out of a wooden shack at the foot of the dock, and from it he rented boats and tackle and outboard motors, sold bait and six-packs.

Harry parked in the gravel lot that gave access to the dock. To get to the lot from the road meant driving down a narrow, sharply curved stretch that had to be taken slowly.

"Let's take a look around," Harry said to Guffy.

Al Parsons came out of his shack to meet them. "Rent you a boat?" he called.

"We've got a boat," said Harry. "Just looking for dock space, maybe."

"Always room for one more," said Al. "Have a look round, I got 'most everything you need. Gas, diesel, water, bait, tackle, motors . . . look around all you want."

Harry and Guffy walked to the end of the dock.

"Our people will expect us to come in by boat," said Harry. "Now I can't see them standing around on the end of a dock with boxes of money waiting for us to arrive. We could be late, have engine trouble, anything. So what would you do if you were them?"

Guffy looked back toward the parking lot. "I'd wait back there, in the car. Then when I saw the boat come in I'd carry the money to the boat, load it in fast, and get the hell out of here, that's what I'd do."

"I'll go along with that," said Harry. "And say I was someone who knew a million dollars was going to be brought here, and say I was planning on hijacking it, there's two places I'd be. One, back in the parking lot, waiting, and two, in another boat somewhere handy."

"You reckon somebody might be plannin' on hijackin' it?" asked Guffy. "You didn't mention that."

"Just a hunch. Not even a hunch, but as I said to Chambers, you can't be too careful."

"Amen," said Guffy.

They walked back toward the parking lot. Harry said, "I want to be ready so that if somebody does try to get smart, we won't be caught with our pants down. I don't want anyone to jump out waving a gun and saying 'Surprise . . . surprise!'"

"I don' like surprises," Guffy said, "not when they kin get a man killed."

They reached the parking lot. "Tomorrow morning," said Harry, "you drop me off here. I go up to the end of the dock and I stay there, as if I'm waiting for a friend to come and take me fishing. You drive in here, and park, then hang around, look at your watch, get your tackle out, that sort of thing."

"Check."

"This way, anybody we don't like who comes in by boat, I've got them covered. If they come by car, you've got them covered. Got a better idea?"

"Can't think of one. Let's do it your way."

"Odds are I'm looking for trouble that won't happen," said Harry.

"Most likely," said Guffy. "Let's look on the bright side."

Back at the Belle Mar Marina, on the *Rimshot*, Guffy made a pot of coffee and they sat and talked about nothing of any importance for a while. Then Harry left to go to the Balmy Breezes to see what had happened to his motel and his guests during his absence. All was well. Martin Pomeroy was installed in the office, sober and with everything under control. Harry had lunch sent in and he and Martin reviewed all that had to be done while he was away on the Haiti run—bank deposits, petty cash, supplies, paying the maids, and so on. Routine stuff for Martin, who was a very efficient hotel manager as long as he stayed off the booze. Again he promised on his sainted mother's memory that not one drop would pass his lips while Harry was gone. Harry wished he could believe him.

Around seven, Harry took Guffy out for a steak dinner. They went back to the *Rimshot*. Guffy made a pot of coffee and they sat and talked about nothing of any importance for a while, and were in their bunks by ten.

At five o'clock Sunday morning, they were awake.

By a quarter to six they'd had coffee and fried egg sandwiches and cleaned up.

"Okay," said Harry, "time to go." He unlocked a steel chest under his bunk, took out two short-barreled .38 caliber pistols, and gave one to Guffy, who checked it and put it in a pocket of his reefer jacket. Harry put his pistol in the waistband of his jeans and then took from the chest a .30 caliber Enforcer machine pistol and two thirty-shot magazines. One magazine he snapped into the pistol, the other he put in his windbreaker pocket. The machine pistol he wrapped in a towel and stuffed into an army-surplus canvas satchel.

He had no permit for the machine pistol—it's not the sort of toy the law likes to see in the hands of ordinary citizens—but every boat owner was uncomfortably aware of the horror stories of piracy and hijackings on the high seas by drug runners and of the murder of those on board. As a result, many pleasure craft carry a small arsenal of illegal weapons, and who's to blame them.

At six-thirty, Guffy pulled off the road by the turning to Al Parson's dock. Harry got out and set off with fishing tackle and the canvas satchel. Six boats were tied up at the dock; two bassboats with outboards, a homemade houseboat, two aging Chris-Craft runabouts, and a very nice and very fast Glastron cruiser that hadn't been there the day before. The bassboats Harry knew were rentals, the Chris-Craft were zippered up and waiting for their owners.

A pauchy, middle-aged man in his undershirt came through the cabin door of the houseboat, yawned, scratched and stretched. From the general condition of the boat Harry guessed the man probably lived there permanently. That left the Glastron cruiser as an unknown quantity. The curtains were drawn over the cabin windows; no way of telling if anyone was aboard. He'd keep an eye on that one.

At the end of the dock, Harry sat on his tackle box, lit a cigarette, looked at his watch from time to time, paced up and down, and generally put on the act of a man whose fishing companion was late arriving.

Guffy pulled into the parking lot, got fishing tackle from the trunk, put it on display resting against the side of the car, then got back into the driver's seat and listened to the radio.

To vary his routine, Harry went over and chatted with two friendly elderly men who were loading tackle, cushions, rainwear, a Thermos jar, and a Styrofoam cooler into one of the bassboats. They were widowers, they told him, they'd been friends ever since they retired, and they went out most mornings for a half-day's fishing. Harry wished them luck. It was now 7:10 A.M. Harry paced some more. The curtains of the cruiser were still drawn.

At 7:30 exactly, a dark-blue, two-year-old Caddy drove into the parking lot and turned so that it was facing the exit to the road. Harry unfastened the straps of the satchel, rummaged through it, then hooked it over one shoulder. The machine pistol now lay, safety off, on top of the towel. He slowly walked down the dock toward the Caddy. One man got out, a second man sat behind the wheel; the angle of the early sun prevented Harry from clearly seeing him. The man who got out was heavyset, six feet tall, in his late fifties, with a big face, big ears, and a big nose. He wore a white windbreaker with red and blue knitted cuffs and waistband, khaki workpants, and well-worn rubber-soled work boots. His gray hair was cropped, he moved easily. The man unzipped his windbreaker and hooked his thumbs in the waistband of his pants, very casually. If he was carrying a gun, he would now have easy access to it.

The two old retired friends puttered off in their bassboat, waving to Harry. From the houseboat drifted the smell of strong brewing coffee. Still no sign of life on the cruiser. Harry kept walking, raised his hand in greeting to the big gray-haired man in the unzipped windbreaker.

"Hold it there," said the man when Harry was about twenty feet from him. Harry held it.

"I'm Harry Foster," said Harry. "Are you one of the two men I'm supposed to meet?"

"Where's your boat?"

"I changed my mind about loading here," Harry said, slowly walking toward the man, chattering as if they were old friends. "Third slip on your left there's a cruiser, green and white, brown curtains over the windows. See it?"

"I see it. What about it?"

"It bothers me. We're going to take the money in your car to my boat at the Belle Mar Marina. Now, let's not hurry anything . . . act like we got a lot to talk about, but watch that cruiser, okay?"

"Okay."

The driver of the Caddy got out, a short, pudgy, youngish man with thinning black hair and gold-rimmed bifocals. He could have been an accountant. His safari suit was brand new. Under it he wore a yellow sport shirt with leaping sailfish patterned in red. New Adidas running shoes over black dress socks. Harry shook his hand. "Hi there," he prattled, "good to see you, I've heard a lot about you from Jack."

The pudgy young man looked bewildered. "What the hell's goin' down?"

"Smile," said Harry. Guffy joined them and Harry

introduced him with a lot of hand waving and back-slapping. "Now," Harry said, "let's all get in your car when I give the word and let's get out of here. Turn left when you get to the road." He worked his way round so that he could see the cruiser. Someone inside pulled back one of the curtains. The gray-haired man saw it.

"Okay," said Harry, "Let's go."

The accountant got back into the driver's seat—the engine was still running. Guffy went around to the front passenger's side. Harry had his right hand in his satchel, the gray-haired man had his right hand inside his unfastened windbreaker. They opened the Caddy's rear doors.

Two men came out fast from the cabin of the cruiser. One carried a shotgun, the other had an automatic pistol in his hand. Harry and the gray-haired man scrambled into the rear of the Caddy, the accountant expertly gunned the car out of the parking lot and around the curve. Through the rear window, Harry and the gray-haired man watched as the two from the cruiser ran to the parking lot, firing at the rapidly receding Cadillac.

"You called that one right," said the gray-haired man. "What tipped you off?"

"Didn't fit," said Harry. "That's just not the kind of boat you expect to see at a crummy dock like this."

"Is somebody gonna tell me what's goin' on here?" the accountant asked over his shoulder.

"Later," said Harry.

NINE

The pudgy young man who looked like an accountant turned out to be an accountant. His name was Morton Sumway. He said he was a "sort of trouble-shooter" for some of Mr. Chambers' interests, but didn't say what kind of troubles he shot or what those interests were. The gray-haired man's name was Freddie—just Freddie. He offered no information beyond the fact that he'd worked for Mr. Chambers for a long time.

The money was packed into two cartons. One, Tide detergent, the other, Dewar's Scotch Whiskey. Mixed in with the rest of the boxes and cartons of groceries, canned goods, clothes, and tackle, the money cartons attracted no attention.

With everything stowed in double-quick time, Harry headed the *Rimshot* for Hog Cay. The weather was still good but, unpredicted, the wind had freshened slightly, shifted to the northeast, and the Gulf Stream was churned into a broken mess that Harry had to fight to hold course. This didn't bother Freddie, but Morton was seasick and stayed up in the open part of the cockpit to get fresh air. As a result he was thoroughly wet and uncomfortable. But once out of the clutches of the Gulf Stream, and with the seas calm, Morton dried out in the sun and felt a lot better.

"First time I've been to the Bahamas," he said, "not counting Freeport, of course. Been to Freeport lots of time, but just business. Fly in, fly back. Apart from that, never even been to Nassau, let alone to the Out Islands."

"How about you?" Harry asked Freddie.

After a pause, Freddie said, "Oh . . . I know the Islands."

The new depthsounder charted the ocean floor, and with Hog Cay looming up ahead, the big glowing digits rapidly ran back as they approached the reef. Harry confidently threaded the *Rimshot* through the coral barrier. Dead ahead of the boat a young scuba diver suddenly surfaced, saw that the boat was nearly on him, and panicked. But Harry had seen him. He spun the wheel hard over, Morton was thrown across the cockpit, hit his head on a fire extinguisher, lost his glasses and slid to the floor. Freddie and Guffy instinctively grabbed handholds and stayed on their feet.

The *Rimshot* hit the edge of the reef. One propeller struck a submerged coral head and the boat shuddered as the bronze blades bit into the great fossil mass. Harry killed the engines. The scuba diver had gone, seeking anonymity under water—aware that he had floated no warning flag and not wanting to stay around to learn what damage he had caused.

"I'll go down and take a look," Harry said. He peeled down to his shorts and sneakers, lowered himself over the side of the boat, carefully avoiding the razor-sharp coral, adjusted his mask and snorkel, and swam under the boat. He soon surfaced, held up a hand, and Freddie effortlessly pulled him aboard. Harry took off his mask. "One prop's gone, that's no big deal, but I think the shaft's bent. If it is, then we've got a real problem."

"Waddya mean, a problem?" said Morton. His head hurt and he was in a bad mood.

"Because it'll mean getting the boat out of the water and waiting while it's fixed."

"Oh for crissakes," Morton yelped. "How long?"

"A day, two days, maybe longer."

"But we've got a schedule to keep. Mr. Chambers' gonna boil if we don't keep to our schedule."

"What do you expect me to do about it, Morton?" Harry asked reasonably.

"I dunno, but do something. Are we goin' to sit here all day stuck on this damn reef?"

Guffy was on the radio. "Red's comin' out for us," he said to Harry.

"Who the hell's Red?" asked Morton.

"Red's the one who'll fix the boat," said Harry.

"Well I hope the hell he gets it fixed fast. Jeeez, what a way to start off, runnin' aground like a bunch of . . ."

"Shut up, Morton," said Freddie.

They sat and waited and in about twenty minutes Red Garrett arrived in his shallow-draft workboat, threw them a line, and towed them in.

"What now?" asked Morton.

A BAD DAY IN THE BAHAMAS

It was easy to dislike Morton. "What do you mean, what now?" said Harry.

"I mean what do we do while the boat's bein' fixed?"

"We wait, that's what we do."

"And what do we do about them? Morton pointed to the boxes of money.

"We can't leave them on board, that's for sure," said Harry. "The *Rimshot* will have to go into drydock."

"So where do we put them? Where's safe? Where are we gonna stay?"

Harry sighed. "I'm going to do something about that right now. I'll be back as soon as I can." He walked to the Fish and Game Club. Luck was with him,—the bungalow he'd had before was still vacant. Nobody was anxious to rent number Four; it wasn't one of the Club's best, or biggest. Harry went back to the *Rimshot* to tell them the news.

Morton had a hundred questions. "Shut up, Morton," said Freddie. He picked up the money cartons, one in each hand, and they were heavy. "Let's go."

Harry led the way, Freddie and Morton followed. Harry and Morton carried the canvas grips that held their clothes. Guffy piled the rest of the stuff on the dock and then set off to talk to Red about fixing the *Rimshot*.

Morton wasn't happy with the bungalow. "This is no good," he complained. "I mean, you could break into this place with a toothpick. Lookit, the wood's rotten." He prowled around the main room, examining door frames, checking windows and shaking his head.

"Morton," said Harry. "In the morning when the bank people get in from Nassau, I'll have them put

95

the boxes in their vault. They won't ask what's in the boxes, they won't care, they do this sort of thing for people all the time. Meanwhile, you and Freddie can keep watch, take it in shifts."

"I dunno about that," Morton said doubtfully.

Freddie pushed the boxes under one of the high-off-the-floor old beds, unzipped his windbreaker, took a .357 Magnum from its shoulder holster and stretched out on the bed, the gun by his side. Harry remembered his instructions to John Chambers about not wearing guns.

"I'll take first shift," said Freddie.

Harry left the two of them to work things out and caught up with Guffy at Red Garrett's boatyard.

"Red kin take us first thing in the mornin'," said Guffy, "soon's he gets this job finished."

From under the jacked-up hull of an ancient wooden-hulled cruiser Red called out, "You think you got problems? Ain't but one way to fix this tub, an' that's buy a new boat."

"Anything you can to get us out of here fast, I'd appreciate it," said Harry.

Red scrambled out from under the hull. "Do what I can, but you know I don't like hurryin'. I got a reputation. When Red Garrett says a job's done, that means it's done right."

"Sure, Red, I know." Harry tucked two folded twenties into the breast pocket of Red's coveralls. "And I want it done right. Right, but fast."

"Like I said, do what I can. Look by about this time tomorrow, tell you better then, okay?"

"Okay."

Red ducked back under the hull.

Harry and Guffy set off for the Club.

"You ain't asked me much about Sally," said Guffy.

"No, I haven't. Is she still with Lucy?"

"Yes."

"Is she all right?"

"Yes."

"No more trouble? Has he left her alone?"

"So far."

They walked in silence along the hotel and marina strip. On a boat from Shreveport, a promising party was getting into its stride. Back home, the revelers were undoubtedly regarded as responsible members of their community, but right now they weren't back home. Up on the flybridge, a yellow-haired girl in a red bikini and black Greek fisherman's hat happily danced alone to the blasting sounds of Bruce Springsteen. As Harry passed, she threw in a couple of bumps and grinds without missing a beat.

"Things are warming up," said Harry.

And they were. The tournament started the next morning. For the following four days, things would simmer along nicely, and on the final night of the tournament, when the real parties got rolling, the Island would come to a boil. Until that time, everybody got in a little practice. Beside the Government dock a bunch of kids were roasting hot dogs.

"Time we had something to eat," Harry said to Guffy.

"I'm goin' on home, I'll get Lucy to make me something. Want to come back with me?"

Harry wondered if Sally would be there. "No, thanks. I'll get some fried chicken or something and take it back."

"See you in about an hour," said Guffy.

"No hurry, we aren't going anywhere."

Guffy laughed without humor. "An' that's a fact."

Harry got a load of barbecued chicken and two six-packs of beer from the Red Lion. As he carried it

97

out, Sergeant Welsh pulled up beside him in his Jeep.

"Run into some trouble, I hear."

"I hit the reef, chewed up a prop. No way to start a charter, eh?"

"No way at all. How's your party taking it?"

"How would you take it?"

"I wouldn't be too pleased. Be a couple of days before you get away, then?"

"That's up to Red."

"What have you done with your people?"

"We're at the Club."

"I hope they enjoy their stopover," said the sergeant. "You forgot to clear customs when Red towed you in, didn't you?"

"Oh God, so I did."

"Better take care of it, just for the record." The sergeant smiled thinly at Harry and spun the Jeep in a tight U-turn.

Freddie had his pistol pointed at the door when Harry walked into the bungalow.

"Just me," Harry said. "Brought you some lunch."

Morton ate two pieces of chicken and drank half a can of beer. Freddie ate six pieces and drank no beer. Harry ate one piece and drank two beers.

"Why don't you two take a look around the Island," said Harry. "I'll stay here."

Freddie was standing by the window, looking out to sea. "Okay," he said, "I could use a walk."

Morton wiped his face with a paper napkin then polished his glasses. "I don't know. I mean, well, Mr. Chambers made us responsible."

"You can trust me," said Harry. "Mr. Chambers does."

Morton wouldn't let go. "Maybe one of us two should stay. I mean, if there's always one of us here, then that's all right."

"As far as this job is concerned, I'd like you to think of me as one of us."

Freddie picked up his windbreaker and walked to the door. "You comin'?" he asked Morton.

Morton hesitated. "Maybe an hour wouldn't hurt." He followed Freddie to the door, turned to Harry. "You won't go out, will you? You won't go out an' leave the place empty?"

"No. I won't," said Harry.

Reluctantly, Morton left and joined Freddie on the verandah. He was still complaining to Freddie as they walked up the path. When they got to the Queen's Highway, Morton said, "Waddya want to do?"

"Buy a postcard," said Freddie. "I always send a postcard to my grandchildren, everywhere I go. Two of 'em are old enough to read, if I print."

"Maybe I can buy a souvenir for Stella," said Morton. "Piece of jewelry or something. Jewelry's supposed to be cheaper out here, they tell me."

Freddie looked at him sadly. "On Hog Cay all you can buy is booze and junk. Be lucky if they got any postcards less'n twenty years old. Anyways, the walk'll be good for us."

They started down the heat-hazy Queen's Highway toward the cluster of bars and impermanent stores. A huge Bahamian charged past them pushing a wheelbarrow. Sitting in the barrow was a very drunk, pink-faced man wearing a captain's hat and holding an opened bottle of champagne between his legs and a beer mug of the champagne in one hand. With his other hand he slapped the side of the barrow as if whipping a horse, and yelled encouragement to the Bahamian between the shafts. Passing Freddie and Morton, he raised the mug of champagne in greeting and regally bowed from the waist. The barrow pusher stopped at the door of the Red Lion Inn. The captain struggled out of the barrow and weaved his way into the tavern, still holding his mug of champagne.

"You don't see that in Westerfield Heights," said Morton.

Harry sat by the window of the bungalow, sipping on a third beer. When Guffy arrived he would go and see Sally, he'd decided.

Guffy came in, looked around the room. "Where have those two gone?"

"Sightseeing," said Harry. Casually, he asked, "Was Sally there?"

"No. She's gone back to him again."

"I don't understand that girl, Guffy. The man is a drunk, he's a bum, he beats her, and she goes back to him." Harry stood. "You mind the store for a while."

Sitting at a table on the verandah of the Ocean View, Harry pondered on the strange ways of women. His second ex-wife had left him to go back to a husband she'd divorced because she couldn't stand living with him one more day. Now Sally had gone back to Bob Hammersley, the biggest no-good of all times, a man who'd beaten her, thrown her out, and said he would beat her again if she showed her face. It passed his understanding. There had to be deep Freudian implications he couldn't comprehend.

He sat and watched the parade go by, a parade in which there was no place for him. Coming down the street, he saw Bob Hammersley slouching along, a bottle dragging down the pocket of his jacket. Ahead of Bob, four small Bahamian children played a game that involved a lot of hopping on one foot and giggling. Bob roughly pushed through them. They fell back, silent, then getting up courage, jeered at his retreating back. Bob wasn't even aware of them. He turned onto the dock where the *Moonglow* was tied up.

Harry knew that Bob would be with Mike Cholski until the bottle was finished. That gave him time to go and see Sally.

Sally was behind the bar of the poolroom. The shattered window had been fixed by nailing a sheet of plywood over it. She was busy—there was money around and carnival in the air. Some of the regulars had been signed on as mates or helpers; several of them had regular clients who booked them in advance for the tournament. For those whose clients caught big fish, there would be big bonuses; if a record fish was landed, it would be jackpot time. So all the boys were having a few vodkas and milk or scotches or gins in anticipation. Only the tourists drank rum.

The boys were glad to see Sally back, and nobody mentioned her bruised face. Beating your wife wasn't taken too seriously on Hog Cay. Beating someone else's wife, that was different.

Harry stood at the bar and marveled at the recuperative powers of a nineteen-year-old. So far, Sally hadn't seen him, but then she came over with a drink for the man sitting next to him.

"Oh . . . hullo," she said, "didn't expect to see you here."

"And I didn't expect to see you back here."

She fussed around with glasses, not looking at him. "Don't give me a hard time, Harry," she said. "I came back because I wanted to, I'm sorry if it upsets you. I wish you hadn't come, it's asking for trouble."

"Bob's with Mike Cholski, I saw him go on Mike's boat."

"I know. They're cooking up some deal, they always are. You want a drink?"

"No," said Harry, "I want to make you a proposition."

Warily, she said, "What sort of proposition?"

Sally looked along the bar; two customers were holding up their glasses for refills. "I'll be back," she said.

When she came back, Harry beckoned for her to come closer, to bend down so that they wouldn't be overheard. "If you'll get off the Island, leave Bob, I'll set you up in a business. You can have a boutique, a gift shop, whatever you want. In Miami, Nassau, wherever you want to go."

The trace of a smile started on her face. "And you go with it, I suppose?"

Harry didn't smile. "Only if you want it that way. If you don't, the offer still stands."

Sally stopped smiling. "You mean it, don't you?"

"Yes, I mean it."

"Harry dear," she said softly, "we keep going round in circles, keep going over the same thing time and again. I'm married, I believe in marriage. Mine's nothing to boast about, but I'm going to stick it out. That makes no sense to you, I know. It doesn't make much sense to me, but there it is. I've told you over and over . . . can't you get it through your head?"

He took her hand, she let it lie passively in his. "You've told me over and over, and I still don't understand."

"If you don't understand," Sally said impatiently, "I can't explain." She took her hand from his. "Don't be cross with me, Harry."

Bob Hammersley and Mike Cholski sat in frayed canvas chairs in the main cabin of the *Moonglow*, the bottle of gin, now half empty, on the floor between them. They were holding a council of war; the issue was serious Captain Scott trouble.

Captain Scott, a short, tubby, unsmiling, always dark-suited Bahamian of about sixty-five years of age, controlled Hog Cay with a firm and implacable hand, and ruled with feudal authority over his large and surly family.

The Captain's hotels and marinas, the Island freight-boat service, his stores and bars, the electric power-generating company, and the radio-telephone office were all run by his sons and daughters and those unfortunates related to him by marriage. Based on the premise that when he eventually departed this life his family would unworthily inherit the benefits of his fifty years of hard work and rapacity, he kept them, until that time, in total servitude.

A nondrinker and nonsmoker, speculation was that Captain Scott was immortal. It was impossible to imagine Hog Cay without him; he'd always been there and he always would be there. And Captain Scott had put out the word that Bob Hammersley and Mike Cholski had outworn their welcome on Hog Cay and that he intended to speed them on their way. As an opening move, Bob's credit had been chopped off with every supply source on the Island, and he was about to be thrown out of the pool hall for nonpayment of rent.

Mike, who owed five months' of dock fees to Captain Scott's Dock and Marine Services, was without power and fresh water on the *Moonglow* and a mechanic's lien had been placed on his boat. Between them, Bob and Mike owed $2,307. Between them, in cash, they had forty-eight dollars, and forty-two of that was in Bob's pants pocket.

"We gotta do something," said Mike. "Bastard

wouldn't give me a break. Tomorrow the tournament starts, an' I can always pick up a cuppla good charters when a tournament's on. That would get me in the clear, but now I can't even use my own boat. I'm gonna have to sell it."

"Never mind about that," said Bob, "fuckin' Captain Scott wants us off the island. All the other aggravations is just bleedin' window dressing. Speaking personal, I'll·be only too glad to get away from this arsehole place. Question is, how do we get ourselves a stake? And don't give·me that balls about sellin' your boat. Just as well you can't take it out, bloody thing would sink in more'n three feet of water."

Like the owner of an old blind dog, Mike felt the need to defend his sick and decrepit schooner. "Nothin' wrong with this boat a few bucks wouldn't fix."

"Knock it off," said Bob, "the thing's falling apart and you know it—you couldn't give it away. We gotta get our hands on some real money. Make one good score an' we can bugger off an' they can stuff Hog Cay up Captain Scott's jacksie."

"How we·gonna do that?"

"Why do you think we're sittin' here, you prick? To figger out how is why."

Harry left the pool hall telling himself he finally accepted that there was no place for him in Sally's life. He was just a nice older man who'd bought her a present, taken her on a picnic, and been allowed to make love to her. A temporary diversion who'd happened to come along when she needed one, and anything beyond that was his conceit. Okay, he accepted it. He didn't like it, but he'd have to get used to it. Probably a good thing.

As he turned in through the Club gates he saw that the *Persephone* had once again docked its unmistakable bulk. Back for the five-day round of tournament festivities. Back for Frazer Chadlow to flaunt his wealth and play host at lavish parties, with Sabina exhibited as another of his desirable possessions. Sabina, the night-visiting, tied-to-a-rich-old-man Sabina. Sabina of the gorgeous body and appetite of a sexual glutton. A flash of reminiscent lust washed over him.

"I s'pose you went up to the pool hall." said Guffy.

"Yes," said Harry.

"Figgers . . . Oh, while you was gone, that letter or whatever it is came for you . . ." Guffy pointed to the table. A square white envelope was propped against a vase of withered dried flowers. "Young chap in a steward's uniform brought it."

The envelope bore Harry's name in flowing handwritten script. In the top left hand corner was an elaborate crest of nautical flavor and *The Persephone* in raised blue type. Inside was a square of heavy, deckle edged card. It was an invitation and read: "You are cordially invited for cocktails at 5:00 P.M." There was no signature.

"Gonna tell me what it is?" said Guffy.

"An invitation to a cocktail party on the *Persephone*."

"On the *what*?"

"That big yacht tied up at the Club dock, you can't miss the damn thing . . . size of an aircraft carrier."

"Oh my," said Guffy, "we are movin' up in the social world, ain't we. You goin'?"

"Why not?"

"No reason. How come you get an invite? You know them?"

"I met them in the Club bar."

"You better hurry," said Guffy, "it's nearly quarter past five now."

Harry had a quick shower, changed into his one good clean white shirt and the white pants and dark green blazer that were his official guest-greeting outfit at Balmy Breezes. He'd brought it along "just in case."

"Classy," said Guffy.

Harry gave him the finger and went off to his cocktail party.

A steward was waiting at the top of the awning-covered gangway. Harry gave him the invitation. A second steward appeared and escorted Harry across the stretch of gleaming deck, through a metal door, along a broadloomed corridor to an elevator. He pressed the call button.

"Cocktails are being served in the main salon, sir."

Harry got out of the suede-lined elevator after a four-second ride and stepped into an enormous salon that stretched the full width of the boat and was at least fifty feet long. Groups of red, velvet-covered sofas and club armchairs were spaced around glass and brass tables sunk in deep-piled white carpet. Ornate chandeliers hung from the ceiling with smaller versions on the dark-red flock-papered walls. A white, baby-grand piano stood on a low mirrored rostrum.

Sabina, in a scooped and ruffled yellow chiffon cocktail dress, was seated on one of the sofas at the far end of the salon. She was alone. A wheeled trolley of liquor bottles, glasses, and an ice bucket and mix was beside her. She was drinking white wine, the opened bottle in a second ice bucket on the carpet close to her.

"My, don't you look nice," she said, and patted the seat of the sofa. "Come over here and sit by me, I need someone to keep me company. I'd begun to believe you hadn't got the invitation."

Harry sat instead in an armchair across the table from her.

"I got your invitation," said Harry. "Am I the first guest to arrive?"

"Don't be silly," said Sabina, "no one else is coming. Dear Frazer had to go on to New York and won't be back 'til Wednesday. I was on the dock and saw you come out of my favorite bungalow, so I thought, Why not invite that sweet man over for a drink, just for old times' sake."

"Very thoughtful," said Harry.

"Do help yourself to a drink," Sabina said, pouring herself more white wine.

Harry made himself a brandy and soda.

"And what do you think of our little houseboat," said Sabina, taking in the whole salon with a wave of her hand.

"Obscene."

"You should see the rest of it. A perfect example of what you can do with ten million dollars and no taste. This pales beside Frazer's stateroom, straight out of *Playboy*. Awful."

"I believe you."

"Would you like to see my stateroom? I think you'd like that."

"I believe that too, but I'm going to have to say no."

"Say no? Why? We can pick up from last time when I had to leave you in rather a hurry. This time, I'm in no hurry at all."

"That's what I was afraid of," said Harry, "but much as I hate to turn down your kind offer, I can't stay that long. I've got problems, and I've got to get back to take care of them, and I've got to be in good shape for tomorrow."

"You really are a bore," said Sabina. "If you go, I'm not going to pay you another house call, a girl has some pride." She stretched out on the sofa, kicked off her shoes. "In fact, that's the only house call I've ever made."

"I'm flattered," said Harry, "and I promise you it takes a great effort of will to not stay. There's nothing I would enjoy more." A warning voice inside his head told him that if he was going, he'd better go soon. A man's willpower can stand only so much temptation. He stood. "So I'm going now. Thank you for inviting me to your party." He headed for the elevator.

"You're a shit, Harry Foster," Sabina called after him.

He stepped into the waiting elevator. As the door slid closed, Harry had to agree, he was a shit. What is more, he was a stupid shit. The elevator stopped, the doors opened. For a lingering second his finger hovered over the Down button. No . . . not down, out, Harry Foster, before it was too late.

The deck steward materialized and ushered him off the boat. "Good night sir," said the steward, "we hope to see you again."

TEN

N o," said Mike. "Forget it. Count me out. They put you in jail for robbin' banks."

"Only if they fuckin' catch you."

"We'd never get away with it, not a chance."

"Oh yes we would," said Bob, "be a bloody pushover. Like takin' candy from a baby. You know what the bank here's like, it's a joke."

There was only one bank on Hog Cay, a whitepainted, single-story clapboard structure. Every Monday, two bank tellers flew in from Nassau on the morning plane, conducted the bank's business from 10:00 to 4:30, stayed overnight at the Angler's Rest Hotel, opened again on Tuesday morning until noon, then flew back to Nassau, taking with them their satchels and bags of cash and traveler's checks.

"Every bleedin' room on the Island is booked,"

said Bob. "The bars are coinin' it in already and everybody's gonna keep blowin' their dough right through the weekend, an' most of it's gonna be deposited in the bank on Monday, right?"

"Right."

"An' there it's gonna sit until the bank boys take it out on Tuesday an' bugger off back to Nassau with it, right?"

"That's what they always do," said Mike, waiting to see where this was leading.

Bob grinned. "Up until now. We're gonna upset their schedule, 'cause Monday night we're gonna do the bank an' by Tuesday, we'll be out at sea, wavin' farewell to bloody Hog Cay."

"What do we do for a boat? This wouldn't get us very far."

"This . . . ? Jesus H. Christ, you don't think I'd trust this tub, do you? The fuckin' Island's crawlin' with good boats, we can take our pick. Choose a fast bugger with a good cruisin' range. Get four, five hours start, and the sods'll never find us."

Mike let the thought sink in. "How much d'ya think'll be in the bank?"

"How the hell should I know? But it'll be a bloody sight more then we got now."

With that, Mike couldn't argue. "I still don't like it. For one thing, it'll mean bustin' into the bank's safe, won't it?"

"Course it will, you nit. Where else would they keep the money? But you seen their safe, old as God. With a cuttin' torch I could be inside it in ten minutes."

"You could . . . ?"

"Took a course in the army. Weldin' an' cuttin'. Knew it would come in handy some day. Be the only effing thing that ever did."

"We don't have a torch. Where we gonna get a torch?"

"Courtesy Cap'n soddin' Scott's Dock and Marine Service." Bob filled his glass with gin, looked into it as if it were a crystal ball in which he saw a bright and prosperous future. "Gonna work like a charm, me old buddy. Day after tomorrow we'll be headed for the life a Riley, cash in our pockets an' a boat we can flog for a few more grand."

"What boat . . . ?"

"Don't you listen to a fuckin' word I say?" said Bob disgustedly. "The boat we nick, of course. What you think we was gonna do with it when we was through? Give it away, for crissakes?"

Mike shook his head doubtfully. "Not that simple to unload a stolen boat, too damn easy for them to check registration and ownership. I know, I bought an' sold a lot of boats in the past."

"Oh grow up. Where you bin all your life? We cop ourselves a tasty thirty-two, thirty-four footer with lotsa goodies on it, whip across the Gulf to Mexico . . . Puerto Juarez, say, an' unload it for fifteen, twenny grand with no sweat. Them greasers won't ask no questions, crooked as corkscrews, the lot of 'em."

"How come you know so much about Mexico?"

"Was in bleedin' jail there. Vera Cruz. Picked up a lotta useful information in clink. Cost me every penny I could lay me hands on to buy me way out. Like I said, they're a bunch of bloody crooks."

Mike tilted a little gin into his glass. "An' while we're bustin' into the bank safe, what about Sergeant Welsh? That bastard's everywhere."

"Ah . . . our good effing sergeant," said Bob. "Mustn't forget our wog chief of police, must we?" He laid a finger knowingly along the side of his nose. "I got the measure of that sod. Con-bloody-trary to what everybody thinks, the bugger does sleep, an' he's a creature of habit. There's four hours when he ain't around—one in the mornin' till just after five. That big buck constable of his takes over then . . . the one that's as black as the ace a spades . . ."

"Mathews," said Mike.

". . . that's the one, Mathews. Anyways, Constable Mathews waits till he know the Sarge is safely out of the way, shows his face so we all know we're bein' protected by the strong arm a the law, then he fucks off to Maudie Brock's place, you know, by the bakery. He's havin' it off with Maudie. Then he comes back on duty at half past four lookin' like the cat that ate the bloody canary."

"You sure about that . . . ? Every night? How do you know?"

"I make it me business to know these things," Bob said, winking. "Never know when it's gonna come in useful, like now. So, playin' it real safe, we got a cuppla hours, from two till four, to do the bank, nick us a boat, an' fuck off."

"That's another thing," said Mike. "What boat? Which boat we gonna take?"

"Got me eye on three. Thirty-four-foot Uniflite, docks at Brown's. A luv'ly Bertram up at the Club, an' a smashin' new Viking ties up at Christopher's. That's a bit bigger, forty footer, I should reckon. Take our pick. The beauty is, nobody sleeps aboard 'em."

"You should have bin a detective," said Mike, impressed.

"Not dumb enough. But make up your mind, you in or out? With you or without you I'm gonna do the bank. So, are you fuckin' with me, or ain't you?"

Bob took a deep breath, considered the alternatives, reluctantly nodded. "Count me in."

* * *

After Harry left the *Persephone* he sat on the Club dock for a while, smoking a cigarette and assessing the situation. The complexion of this John Chambers assignment had changed considerably since he'd taken it on. He wasn't naive—he'd known from the start that what he was doing was not strictly according to Hoyle—but he had truly thought that all he was involved in was helping Chambers smuggle currency. Not legal, but not a criminal act. And he'd known that carting a million dollars around in cardboard cartons had to involve a certain amount of risk—that's why he'd been so cautious about the transfer arrangements at Al Parson's dock. And although he'd never really anticipated an attempt to hijack the money, it had happened. What's more, Freddie and Morton hadn't seemed unduly surprised, they'd acted as if it was the sort of thing that was to be expected. The big question for Harry was this, did the fact they'd eluded the attempted hijack on Al Parson's dock mean they were now in the clear, or was it possible—or probable—that there would be a further attempt? Somebody had tipped off somebody that Freddie and Morton would be taking a million dollars to Al Parson's dock. Who? It could only be someone at John Chambers' end who knew he was planning to ship out the money. An inside job. What it all came down to was exactly who was John Chambers and what kind of business was he in. Was Globus Exports/Imports just a cover for a strictly illegal operation such as drug handling and distribution? Was John Chambers importing narcotics under the cover of a seemingly small-time operation, the kind that is usually concerned with cheap transistor radios and cotton goods and cameras from Taiwan or Hong Kong or Japan? Harry couldn't answer any one of his own questions, and he didn't think he would get any answers from Freddie or Morton.

Still swirling all this around his mind, Harry walked back to the bungalow.

"That was a short party," said Guffy. "You bin gone all of half an hour."

"It was dull, so I left," said Harry. "Freddie and Morton not back yet?"

"I can see 'em coming up the path now," Guffy said. "Morton looks pretty mad. My, he's a cantankerous young man, don't seem to like anythin'."

Morton was hot, tired, and angry. "This is a crummy island, I mean, there's nuthin' to do, nuthin' to see, nuthin' to buy. Drinkin' an' fishin', drinkin' an' fishin', that's it."

Freddie had his postcard. Standard tourist picture of white sand, waving palm trees, and the evening sun sinking in a colorful blaze of glory. Wherever the picture had been taken it certainly wasn't on Hog Cay. Freddie sat at a bamboo table and happily printed messages to his grandchildren.

"Now they're back, I'm gonna take off," said Guffy. "Mebbe drop by Red Garrett's an' see if he's bin able to make a start yet. Then I'm goin' up to the house. You likely want me anymore?"

"No, you go on home. See you here first thing in the morning."

"You bet," said Guffy, and went.

Harry and Freddie and Morton played gin rummy. Freddie, who played a quiet, steady game, won eleven dollars from Morton and a dollar fifty from Harry. Morton was a bad loser. His mood didn't improve when they drew cards to see who was the one to go out for food and he got the chore.

They ate the barbecued ribs at the card table, drank a beer, got ready for the night. Morton was insistent they stand guard over the money, so they drew lots for shifts. He drew first shift. Freddie lay down, closed his eyes, and was asleep immediately. Harry had trouble getting to sleep, but finally drifted off. Morton sat in the big bamboo chair, pistol by his side, facing the door. Morton took his job very seriously.

Monday morning broke bright, calm, and clear. A pleasant high of eighty-two was predicted and the five-day forecast was excellent. The old hands agreed it was as good a fishing day as they'd seen and a damn fine way to kick off the tournament.

Harry, who'd drawn the dawn shift, had the coffee-pot going when Freddie and Morton awoke; Freddie, well rested from four hours' sleep, Morton, gritty eyed and peevish, not looking forward to another day and especially another night on Hog Cay. He needed his eight hours' sleep, he said, and last night he hadn't closed his eyes for worrying about the money.

"Relax, Morton," said Harry, "we'll be taking it to the bank at ten o'clock. After that, you can sleep all you like."

The fishing tournament competitors, officially registered and their fees paid, their boats stripped for action, equipment checked and rechecked, gaffs sharpened and bait boxes filled, set out for their particular locations, each chosen through a mystical mixture of experience and folklore. Blue marlin they were out to get, no other fish counted. Blue marlin, arguably the most spectacular fighter of the big-game fish. In these waters, a four-hundred-pound blue was reckoned to be a very good fish, but the local experts predicted that in this year's tournament a marlin of over two hundred and twenty pounds would stand a good chance of winning.

The judges' yacht sailed out with the competitors to fire the gun announcing the start of the fishing day, to see that the arcane rules of the tournament were followed, and to settle disputes. Spectators' boats followed to share vicariously in the excitement.

Harry watched as the boats headed out into deep water. Momentarily, he regretted that he and Guffy weren't going out with them, battling to a finish with some big, beautiful fish.

Bob Hammersley had dragged himself out of sleep around seven-thirty with his usual hangover and sour stomach. As usual, he woke up with a post-drinking erection. He pulled the sheet back from Sally and cupped a hand over the firm, pink cheeks of her bare bottom. She stirred, knocked his hand away, and drew the sheet over her head. Bob considered pushing her onto her back and reminding her of her principal function in life, but he had a lot to do today and didn't want to start things off with a big flaming argument, so he had a couple of cold beers instead.

Mike Cholski hadn't slept well. All night, variations of the scheme to break into the bank's safe had jumbled through his mind, and each variation had ended in disaster. If he had any possible option, he'd tell Bob he wasn't going through with it tonight. Tonight . . . ! He felt sick at the prospect.

The morning plane from Nassau touched down at seven minutes to nine. The two bank tellers, Peter Marriott and Charles Dawson, were on it. They were both young men in their twenties, looking forward to trouble-free banking careers and, ultimately, to promotions to comfortable positions as managers of major branches in civilized places like Bermuda or Kingston, Jamaica. To gain experience they currently were on the Out Island circuit, and they didn't like it very much. Peter Marriott, the senior by six months, had the courtesy title of manager while on Hog Cay. Customers liked to be able to talk to a manager.

The two young men wore English suits, carried plastic raincoats, and brought with them their ledgers and operating cash and so on in bulging, European-style leather briefcases. In a canvas duffel bag were four strong sailcloth sacks with heavy brass eyelets around the necks designed to be fastened with big old-fashioned padlocks. When Peter and Charles returned to Nassau the sacks would be filled with money and checks. No one had ever tried to steal these bank money sacks, not on Hog Cay, not on any other of the Out Islands.

Harry, who knew them through his occasional transactions at the bank, joined them and their police constable escort as they walked to the bank.

"Good morning, Mr. Marriott, Mr. Dawson."

"Good morning, Mr. Foster," said Peter Marriott, who made it a point of knowing every customer, even the most casual. "Beautiful day for the tournament, isn't it?"

"It is," Harry gravely agreed. "I'd like to leave a couple of boxes in your safekeeping until tomorrow. My boat's in for repairs and I don't want to leave these boxes lying around. The contents are quite valuable."

"I don't think that presents any problems, Mr. Foster."

"Thank you, Mr. Marriott."

"Our pleasure, Mr. Foster."

After he left Messrs. Marriott and Dawson, Harry hired Uncle Joe and his wheelbarrow. With no private cars and few taxis on Hog Cay, wheelbarrows were an accepted and practical way of moving luggage and personal belongings. Uncle Joe, a strong,

117

white-haired, ageless Bahamian had a large barrow and was much in demand. Harry nabbed him outside the Angler's Rest Hotel and walked with him back to the bungalow.

"In a wheelbarrow?" shrieked Morton. "In a god-dam wheelbarrow!"

"Cool off," said Harry. "We put the boxes in the barrow, throw in a few other bits and pieces, and Uncle Joe takes them the way he takes stuff a dozen times a day. Everyone knows Uncle Joe and his barrow, nobody will pay any attention. We go with him, acting natural, and once we get to the bank Freddie and I will take the boxes in and check them into the vault. Foolproof."

"I don't like it," said Morton. "I don't like the idea of wheeling a million bucks through the street in this place."

Freddie dragged the boxes from under the bed, carried them out, and dumped them in Uncle Joe's barrow. Harry added a canvas grip and a garment bag draped across the boxes. The load looked perfectly innocent. Headed by Uncle Joe and his barrow load of money, the small procession headed to the bank. As Harry had prophesied, they attracted not the slightest attention. No one gave them a second look . . . except for a slim, casually well-dressed young man carrying an aluminum fishing-rod case. The young man's name was Frank d'Angelo.

Frank d'Angelo and two other men had arrived on Hog Cay less than an hour ago. They'd come by boat, a green-and-white Glastron cruiser, to be specific. They left Miami before daybreak, made a fast run across and headed toward the end of the Island, down where no people lived and Hog Cay degenerated into a tangled mass of mangrove swamp. This unlikely landing place had several advantages, not the least of which being it allowed Frank d'Angelo to enter Hog Cay without being seen by anyone, particularly customs officers or policemen.

It had meant, of course, that Frank had a mile and a half walk carrying a canvas grip and his aluminum fishing-rod case. But Frank was young and kept himself in top physical condition; the morning was mild, so the walk presented no great hardship. When he'd gotten close to the lively part of the Island, Frank used the shelter of an abandoned shack to change from the old clothes he'd worn up to this point into white pants, a red and white striped polo shirt, Topsiders and a sailing jacket. Under the sailing jacket was his .22 pistol in a shoulder holster, and in the aluminum fishing-rod case a folding-stock Paratrooper semi-automatic .30-caliber carbine. Spare ammunition and the silencer for the pistol he carried in the pocket of his sailing jacket. He then hid the canvas grip under a pile of debris and set off to find Harry, Freddie, and Morton.

He'd expected this to take some time and was prepared to take that time. If it transpired that they had already left Hog Cay then Frank would simply follow them to the next stop on their itinerary, which he knew in detail. Frank d'Angelo was a man who worked slowly, carefully, and purposefully, as do all good professional killers. He was therefore agreeably surprised to see his quarry come out of the Fish and Game Club together with an old white-haired man pushing a wheelbarrow. Naturally, he followed them.

When Uncle Joe stopped outside the bank, Frank d'Angelo wrongly assumed the old man was simply taking a rest, but when Harry and Freddie lifted two large and obviously heavy cartons—two cartons that exactly matched the description he'd been given of the cartons that contained a million dollars—and

119

carried them into the bank, Frank quickly reassessed
the situation. His associates in the Glastron cruiser
had been sent over to retrieve the money, while his
own mandate was to kill the three men who'd
brought it from Miami to this island. Now, a new
element had been added. Why the money had been
taken into the bank, Frank d'Angelo couldn't understand; this didn't fit the expected procedure. It should
be on a boat named the *Rimshot*, en route for Haiti.
Presumably, at some point the money would be taken
out of the bank and would continue on its journey—
that is, unless it was being deposited, and it was hard
to comprehend why one million dollars would be
deposited in a tiny branch bank on an insignificant
island. There was no logic to it, and Frank d'Angelo
was a very logical young man.

But when Harry and Freddie came out of the bank
less than ten minutes after they'd gone in, Frank
d'Angelo's logical mind told him that quite obviously
the money had not been paid in as a deposit—no
bank teller could count a million dollars in ten
minutes, and no bank teller will accept money for
deposit without first counting it. Frank d'Angelo
added this factor into the equation and came up with
the simple and completely logical answer: the cartons of money had merely been entrusted to the
temporary care of the bank for safekeeping. Why? It
didn't really matter, although it did indicate that the
progress of the *Rimshot* had been delayed for some
reason such as a change of plans or modification or
repairs to the boat . . . each a perfectly reasonable
reason for a stopover. This delay, while inconvenient,
was of no great significance to Frank d'Angelo, because Frank, in addition to being a very logical young
man, was also a very patient young man.

The old man with the barrow went on his way and Frank followed the three back to the Club bungalow, so he now knew where he could find them when he needed to. By this time his two associates should have brought their boat down the Island from the point where they'd dropped him off, docked it, and cleared customs like any other visitors to Hog Cay. Frank d'Angelo would have breakfast and then join them on board.

Guffy was waiting outside the bungalow.

"Where were you?" Harry asked him. "Bright and early you were supposed to be here, remember?"

Morton and Freddie went into the bungalow, Guffy beckoned to Harry to follow him as he walked a few paces up the path.

"That boat, the green-and-white job we seen at Al Parsons' dock, you know, the one with the two guys on it that tried to jump us?"

"What about it?"

"I think I seen it."

"Where? Here, d'ya mean?"

"Here. I was walkin' up from home earlier on, an' I think I seen it comin' down from Mangrove Point an' headed for the docks."

"You sure? Did you get a real good look at it?"

Guffy held up his binoculars. "I watched it through my glasses, had it in good sight for mebbe a minute. If it wasn't the same boat, it was the double of it, an' you don' see too many of 'em around. Two guys on it. You recall what those two looked like?"

Harry thought. "I remember they were both fairly young . . . The one with the shotgun had slicked-back black hair and sunglasses with yellow lenses, like pilot's glasses. The other one . . . I might know him if

121

I saw him again, but I couldn't be sure, we were kind of busy at the time. Bit taller . . . light brown hair, I think.''

Guffy nodded. "The one drivin' the boat I seen had black hair, slick, like you say, like it had oil on it, an' he wore big yellow shades. The other one was sittin' down an' I didn't get much of a look at him, but he had brown hair, I'm pretty sure of that.''

"Looks like they followed us.''

"That's what it looks like.''

"How the bloody hell did they know we were here?''

Guffy shrugged. "How did they know we was goin' to be at Al Parson's dock?''

Harry shot a look back at the bungalow. "We'd better go and see if we can find this boat. I'll tell those two we're going over to Red Garrett's to check on the *Rimshot*. If I tell them there's a chance we've been followed, Morton will have a hemorrhage.''

Harry went into the bungalow, told Freddie and Morton he was going to check progress on the *Rimshot's* repairs.

Morton wasn't at all happy with the prospect of spending another day on Hog Cay. "A whole day to kill, a whole day in this place . . . jeeezus, I'll go outta my mind.''

"Go and lie on the beach," said Harry. "Get yourself a tan.''

"I ain't seen a beach," said Morton. "Is there a beach on this shitty island?''

Harry pointed. "The other side. Five minutes walk across the island, about a quarter mile up, there's a terrific beach. No one ever goes there. No docks, no bars, no stores, nothing, just sand. Good swimming there, but don't go beyond the reef.''

"Why not?"

"Sharks."

Morton paled. "Oh Christ, sharks! An' I'd kinda liked to go swimmin'!"

Freddie said, "I know what I'm gonna do. I'm gonna buy myself a cheap fishin' pole an' I'm gonna fish off the dock. Haven't done that in years. Catch up with you later." Contentedly, he wandered off.

"Looks like you're on your own, Morton," said Harry.

"Were you serious about there bein' sharks out there?"

"I was kidding," said Harry. "Every so often someone says he's seen one, but I never have. In any case, they can't get inside the reef. Stay inside the reef and you'll be safe, I promise, and that gives you a quarter of a mile. How far do you want to swim?"

"Oh, not that far," said Morton, "I'm not that good a swimmer, but it does seem dumb to be on an island in the Bahamas an' not go swimmin' don't it?"

"If we're here tomorrow, I'll take you diving, that's really something in these waters."

"No . . . no . . . not another day," Morton whined. "I mean, how long can it take to fix a propeller?"

"That's what I'm going to find out," said Harry. "Don't worry, Red'll have us out of here tomorrow."

"I hope so, I sure as hell hope so." Then as Harry went out through the door, Morton called, "They never come inside the reef, eh? The sharks, I mean."

"Like I said, I've never seen one yet," Harry called back. This wasn't strictly true. He had seen them on several occasions, but they'd been small, harmless nurse sharks that lazily gobbled up smaller fish, posing no threat to humans. He decided not to spoil Morton's planned dip in the ocean by telling him this.

It was most unlikely that Morton would see one, but if he did, while it might scare the living daylights out of him, he would be quite safe, and it would give him something to talk about for the rest of his dull life. Over the years, the sluggish and innocuous nurse shark would probably metamorphose into a predatory killer from whose great jaws Morton had barely escaped. "Enjoy your swim, Morton," said Harry.

Harry and Guffy checked each dock in turn along the main strip. With so many of the boats now out at sea, this didn't take too long. No sign of the green-and-white Glastron. They finally ran it to earth in the dock attached to Captain Scott's Out Island Freight Service, a dock little used by tourists or fishing competitors who chose to be closer to the main action. The Glastron was tucked between two ungainly old freighters.

Using Guffy's binoculars, Harry focussed on it from a distance.

"Sure looks like the same boat, Guffy. Even got the same brown curtains over the cabin windows. I'll bet money it's the same one."

"I think so," Guffy said. "See anybody movin' around inside?"

"No one in the cockpit, and I can't see into the cabin . . . wait . . . hold it."

As he watched, a man came out of the cabin, quickly grabbed something from the cockpit, and ducked back inside.

"That's him," said Harry. "That's the son of a bitch pulled the shotgun on us."

"Great," said Guffy. "Now what?"

Harry took Guffy's arm, led him away from the dock. Harry was smiling. "Now what? Now we do our duty and let Sergeant Welsh know that two dangerous criminals are on Hog Cay."

"We do, do we?" said Guffy. "Oh my."

Sergeant Welsh was at his desk in the whitewashed one-room, one-cell police station.

"Sergeant Welsh," said Harry, "as a law-abiding visitor to this island, I feel it is my duty to report that two armed and dangerous criminals are loose on Hog Cay, endangering the lives of visitors and residents alike."

Welsh laid down his pen. "Do you mean those two up at your bungalow?"

"No, I mean the two on the green-and-white Glastron cruiser now docked at Captain Scott's Out Island Freight Service."

The sergeant tipped his chair back against the wall, looked long and hard at Harry. "Who are they and what have they done?"

"I don't know who they are, but they're from Miami, and as I said, they're armed and they're trouble, believe me."

Sergeant Welsh stood. "I don't know what's behind this, but I'll find out, I'm sure." He stood, buckled on his Sam Browne, took his regulation Webley service pistol from the drawer of his desk, got his cap from a peg, squared it on his head, and led the way out to his Jeep.

At the dock, the sergeant parked the Jeep and strode firmly toward the green-and-white boat. Harry and Guffy followed. Without hurry, the sergeant stepped into the cockpit and rapped on the closed cabin door. It was cautiously opened. The black-haired man saw the sergeant. The brown-haired man joined his partner at the door. "What's the problem, Sergeant?"

asked the brown-haired man.

Harry stepped on board, Guffy stayed up on the dock. The black-haired man spotted Harry and, reflexively, brought up a shotgun.

The sergeant kicked the door wide open and piled into the cabin, pistol in hand. The black-haired man, knocked off balance, swung round, the shotgun leveled. The sergeant cracked him across the head with his .45, and Black Hair went down. His partner raised his hands in surrender. As he handcuffed the pair, Sergeant Welsh said to Harry, "I want to see you at the Station . . . follow me up, right now, understand?"

He led his prisoners to the Jeep, prodded them into the rear seat, and took off. Harry and Guffy walked to the police station. The prisoners were in the cell, and the sergeant was waiting for Harry. He pointed to the cell. "Those two . . . what's your connection with them? They're scum—they aren't wanted criminals, but they're on the undesirables list, mixed up with the mob that runs the casinos . . ." He slapped his hand on a pile of Wanted flyers and photocopied information sheets that lay on his desk. "They're down here as enforcers, debt collectors, leg-breakers, bully boys. Have they got a score to settle with you? Are you on the mob's shit list? Are they over here after you?" He didn't wait for Harry to reply, but hammered on. "If you're in trouble with them, that's your concern. My concern is keeping this island free of such garbage. You bring trouble here, I don't need you. I gave you fair warning, so now I'm coming down on you. Get those other two, your so-called charter party, off Hog Cay as soon as your boat's fixed and don't come back. You hear me?" He pointed a finger at Guffy. "What about you, Guffy? I've known you for years and you've never caused me grief. Are you involved in this in any way?"

Harry broke in. "He's not. He just signed on as my mate for the charter . . . you know I always have Guffy with me if he's available, he's done nothing wrong."

The sergeant looked from one to the other. "We'll see. I'm going to be on your tails until you're gone. When will your boat be ready?"

"Tomorrow, I hope," said Harry. "We're on our way over to Red Garrett's to find out."

"The sooner the better," said the sergeant. "Now get out of here."

As they made their way to Red Garrett's, Harry said to Guffy, "You can pull out if you want to, I'll understand. I didn't know what I was getting you into."

Guffy walked beside him, head down. "I think mebbe that'd be for the best," he said finally. "This is shapin' up into somethin' I hadn't reckoned on. I'll hang around till the boat's ready, then I think I'll stay here an' let you go on your way without me. I'll fix you up with another mate. Not here, not while the tournament's on, but I kin arrange for Wally Smight or Packy Isaacs over on Sabling Island to go with you, they're both good boys. You'll be okay with either of them."

"If you say so, Guffy," Harry said sadly. "I sure hate us to break up like this."

"Yeah, me too," said Guffy. "But I give it a lot a thought. Looked at it this way and that, an' the upshot is I reckon I'll take a raincheck this time."

Red Garrett, at least, had good news. The *Rimshot* was up on blocks and Red was working on it.

"Not as bad as it could have been," he said, wiping his oily hands on a rag. "The one prop's chewed up, we knew that, but I got a replacement comin' over on the afternoon plane. The shaft wasn't bent. Knocked outta line an' a bearin' shot, but otherwise okay. I'll have it back in the water sometime tomorrow."

ELEVEN

The beach on the north shore of the Island was, as Harry had said it would be, a gentle arc of clean white sand with no people, no houses. To get to it Morton had to follow a path through sea grass and tangled vines and then scramble down a steep sand slope. The reef that Harry had told him about was some hundred yards out at this point and ran almost the whole length of the beach. In two places, rocky promontories jutted out from the shore and joined up with the reef, creating a lagoon-like stretch of sheltered water. Beyond the reef the breakers rolled in across three thousand miles of Atlantic, unimpeded until they hit this reef of this small island in the Bahamas.

Morton took off his shirt and pants. Underneath he had on a pair of modest boxer swimming trunks. He folded his clothes, put them on a rock well back from the water's edge, and weighted them down with his shoes. His gold-rimmed bifocals he tucked inside one shoe. He tested the water, waded out a dozen paces, and found the clarity of the water played tricks with its depth.

Morton wasn't a bad swimmer. He did a pretty good crawl for fifty yards, floated on his back for a while, then swam underwater and saw some sergeant-major fish, a sand dollar, and a long, thin, eel-like fish that looked dangerous, but wasn't. He then swam to shore, waded out, toweled himself, put on his bifocals and sat on a rock while the sun warmed him through. After ten minutes of that, Morton remembered the warnings his wife always gave him about sunburn, so he put on his shirt and shoes.

He walked up the beach, picking up shells and pieces of driftwood that he hurled into the ocean. When he reached one of the rocky promontories, he climbed up it, careful of the sharp, coral-encrusted rocks, and found a place where he could look down at the breaking waves forty feet below him, pulling back as spray from the larger waves threatened him.

Back on shore, on the sea grass above the beach, Frank d'Angelo sat under a wind-bent Australian pine and watched Morton. Watched him swim, watched him dry off, watched him walk out onto the rocks. From his rod case, Frank took his carbine, unfolded the stock, released the safety, sighted, fired, and missed Morton by an inch. Morton spun round in the direction of the gunshot and Frank hit him in the neck with his second shot. The force slammed Morton back. Dying, he fell, bounced twice on the coral rocks, tearing his body, his face and his clutching hands, and was dead when he hit the water.

Frank d'Angelo casually looked around him. No one in sight. He'd reduced the odds. Chances were it would be a while before Morton's body was found, and then only after the waves and rocks and fish had worked on it.

He cleaned his gun, put it back in the rod case and strolled to the Ocean View for lunch. Later he might try to improve his hand by killing another of them. Not the one called Harry Foster, he needed him to get the money from the bank. One of the other two. The Bahamian, maybe. Frank didn't like blacks.

Freddie bought a Japanese fiberglass baitcasting rod and a reel at the Island's only bait and tackle shop. Back home he'd seen the same outfit for $8.95 at Richway. Here, it cost him twenty dollars. He also bought a tin pail and some conch to cut up for bait. For nearly two hours he fished and caught a bucket full of grunts and small jacks and a couple that looked like perch. He ate two Hershey bars while he fished, and was at peace. When he was through, he gave the bucket of fish to a Bahamian kid who was sitting near him. Earlier, Freddie had given him a chocolate bar, so they were now firm friends. As an afterthought, Freddie gave him the rod and reel.

It wasn't until late afternoon that Freddie met up with Harry at the bungalow and they realized neither of them had seen Morton for several hours. They waited awhile, then went to look for him, but he wasn't in any of the stores, or on the docks, or at Red Garrett's. As he wasn't a drinking man they didn't bother with the bars, but did check the places that served food. No sign of Morton.

Then Harry remembered he'd told Morton about

the north-shore beach. He told Freddie and they agreed it was unlikely Morton would still be there at this time of day. But they decided to go over and take a look.

Morton's pants and towel were still on the rock where he'd left them.

"How good a swimmer was he?"

Freddie shrugged. "I dunno, but he couldn't come to much harm in that water, could he?" He pointed to the lagoon.

"It's deeper than it looks," said Harry. He went through the pockets of Morton's pants. "He's got his glasses with him, at least, he didn't leave them here. I doubt he went swimming with his glasses on."

"Nor with his shirt and shoes on," said Freddie. "No trace of them. Maybe he went for a walk along the beach." He slowly scanned the beach, shielding his eyes from the late sun. "Can't see him anywhere."

Harry was looking out to the line of rocks that extended to the reef. "He might have walked out there, to watch the waves. People do that."

"He might." said Freddie.

They walked to the rocks, climbed up, went to the end and looked down at the waves as they crashed against the base.

"He might have come out here and then slipped," said Harry.

"Could be, he had lousy eyesight even with his glasses."

"If he did fall, he'd have been hurt. These rocks can cut you to pieces."

"I guess," said Freddie.

They started to walk back. Harry bent down, looked at a flat rock, wetted his finger then rubbed it on the rock. Freddie knelt on one knee beside him.

"That's blood," said Harry. "There's more over here," said Freddie.

Harry lay face down, inched himself forward and looked over the edge of the rocks. Caught in a crevice, halfway down, glinting in the sun, were Morton's gold-rimmed spectacles. Harry beckoned over his shoulder to Freddie. "Take a look here." Freddie carefully lay down beside Harry. "That looks like Morton's glasses."

They got up. "Reckon he fell? Reckon he slipped and fell over the edge?" Freddie asked.

Harry shook his head. "If he'd fallen accidentally there wouldn't be blood up here. On the way down, yes, but not up here. No reason for it."

Freddie again lay down and looked over the edge, squinting his eyes. "There's blood down there, I can see it."

As Freddie got to his feet, Harry said thoughtfully. "So the way I read it, he fell, but not accidentally. And he wasn't pushed, the blood up here proves that."

"He coulda had a knife stuck in him," said Freddie.

"Or been shot," said Harry, turning to look back at the beach.

"Yeah, but who coulda done it?" asked Freddie, thinking out loud. "We know why somebody mighta wanted to do it, don't we? Gotta be the money, an' that takes us back to Miami and them two characters on Al Parson's dock, don't it?"

"Freddie," said Harry, "I've got something to tell you." He told Freddie about the green-and-white boat and the two men who were now in the Island jail. "But we didn't see anybody else there, and when I got rid of those two I thought that was it. Looks like there's at least one more, though."

"Yeah, looks that way."

"Of course, we may be jumping to conclusions," said Harry. "Maybe nothing's happened to Morton."

"An' then again, maybe somethin' has," said Freddie.

Harry looked around him. "In which case we're standing out here like ducks in a shooting gallery."

They scrambled back along the rock ridge to the beach, collected Morton's pants and the towel, and made their way to the bungalow. Guffy was there. Harry stayed by the screened window when he came in and looked back down the path.

"Who you lookin' for?" asked Guffy. "Morton? I was wonderin' where he was, meself."

"We think he may be dead," said Harry. "We think someone killed him out on the rocks at North Beach."

"Oh my Lord," said Guffy. "Who?"

"We think somebody else came across from Miami with those two we gave to the sergeant. So be careful. Watch yourself."

"I'll surely do that," Guffy said fervently. "This thing's taken a real nasty turn, ain't it?"

Freddie threw Morton's pants into a corner, got his gun, and sat in the bamboo chair, looking out of the window. "One thing," he said, "If there is someone lookin' for us, he's got a big advantage. He knows who we are but we don' know who he is."

"That don't make me feel no better," said Guffy.

"Nor me," said Harry.

Frank d'Angelo sat at a table in the Fish and Game Club dining room. The table afforded a good view of the Club's grounds. It was too far for him to see into Harry's bungalow, but he knew the three of them were there. If the right opportunity came along, he might change his mind about killing the Bahamian next. He might get rid of the older guy, the one called Freddie, the one with the big ugly face and big ears. He'd seen him around. Mr. Chambers used him a lot, him and that Jew with the gold-rimmed spectacles. *Had* used him, that is, the Jew wasn't much use to anybody anymore.

The first day of the Blue Marlin Tournament had ended. Three boats came in flying pennants proclaiming they'd each gotten a fish. Ninety-one pounds was the biggest, so no one was considered seriously as being in the running for the trophy, but you never knew.

The booze flowed. Parties on boats, parties in bars, parties in the Fish and Game Club. Everybody bought drinks for everybody. Battles with fish were refought, failures were justified, advice given, information exchanged, and petty rivalries blossomed. One or two arguments developed into minor fights that a handshake and a round of drinks put into history. The short stretch of the Queen's Highway that arthritically wound through Hog Cay's temporary Action Center channeled an erratic tide of free-spending, glad-handling revelers.

The sensible ones would call it a day before midnight and blearily crawl into their bunks and beds. Those made of sterner stuff would get down to some serious drinking. Hell, they didn't need sleep to fish the next day . . . well, a couple of hours at the most, then they'd be fine.

Bob Hammersley and Mike Cholski watched the madness from the after-deck of the *Moonglow.*

"Look at 'em," said Bob, "look at all that luv'ly money out there. I was up at the bank earlier, nosin' around, doin' a bit of research as you might say, an' you shouldda seen the deposits was bein' shoveled in, all the weekend takins. I seen that effer Cap'n Scott pay in a bloody great bag a money, musta bin four or five grand, I wouldn't doubt. An' he was only one of 'em stashing it away for us."

He stuffed half a ham sandwich into his mouth, chewed, swallowed, washed it down with gin. The other half of the sandwich he offered to Mike, who shook his head. Mike hadn't eaten all day, the constant awareness of what they planned to do in a few hours' time left him without appetite.

"Jus' think," said Bob, "we're soon gonna have our hands on that loot. Only thing we got left to do is work out where our first layover's gonna be. We wait there a bit, throw the fuckers off our track, then we can waltz over to Mexico, like I said. 'Course, if it comes to that, we don't need to go all the way to bleedin' Mexico. There's a coupla boys up in Jacksonville do a neat job on hot boats."

"Let's stay away from the mainland," Mike said. "Too many people know me, anywhere there's boats, I mean."

"I'm easy, I don't care where we go so long as we get off this shitheap of an island. But first things first, where do we make for soon's we've done the bank? That's your department, you're the bloody skipper."

"I know fifty places they'd never find us," said Mike. "Don't forget I been sailing these islands for over fifteen years."

"We don't need fifty, we need just one good one."

"Lemme think," said Mike. He thought, then heaved himself out of his canvas chair. "Come below with me."

From a cupboard in the main cabin Mike hauled out a thick stack of charts and maps. "I got the best set of charts on the Island," he said, remnants of past pride surfacing. He dumped the charts on a table, pulled up a chair. Bob stood looking over his shoulder. Mike sorted through the charts, happy to be doing something purposeful, happy to feel the thick, familiar charts again between his fingers. He went through a dozen, unfolding each, briefly scanning it, then refolding it. Bob watched, impatient.

"All those bloody islands," he said, prodding a chart, "an' you can't find one where we can hide out for a day or two? Christ, don't seem like askin' very much of you. Thought you knew fifty."

"It's gotta be right," said Mike, still unfolding and refolding charts. He unfolded yet another, slapped his hand down on it. "Stupid I am, stupid. Of course I know one . . ." He smiled reminiscently "That's one island I should remember." He pointed. A small island had been inked in by hand and then circled in black marker. "See? Right there."

Bob waved his hand imperiously. "Could be a map a the bleedin' moon for all I know. You say it's what we want, I'll take your word. Looks in the middle a nowhere to me. You draw that in?"

"Yes, I marked it in."

"You got in the right place? Can you find it again?"

Mike still smiled. "I don't even need the chart to find this one again."

"Okay, I was just askin'," Bob said. "And what's that smile on yer face all about?"

"A girl," said Mike, memories washing over him. "A girl that chartered the boat for two weeks to go island hopping, go to all the places people never go. Two weeks, an' apart from a couple of crew, there was just me an' her. Jeeeezus, what a ball we had ourselves, an' most a the time we spent on that island." He put his finger on the inked-in spot on the chart.

"Why is it marked in?"

"Because it doesn't show up on the regular charts. Lotsa places like that in the Bahamas. Little islands that never bin charted, specially when it's one of a bunch of small islands, like this is. Got missed in the first maps, an' lotsa the new charts are just copies of the old ones, mistakes an' all." Again the smile of sheer remembered bliss came over his face. "Oh my God, what a two weeks that was."

"Don't let's start draggin' up your romantic past, and don't let's pick a place jus' because you got your ashes hauled there Christ knows how many years ago."

Mike came down to earth. "It's a perfect spot, honest, just what we need."

"An' you sure you can find it again?"

"With my eyes closed," said Mike, the dream returning.

"Maybe," said Bob, "but don't fuckin' try it with me on board."

"I'm dead serious," said Mike. "This island is exactly right. It's uninhabited, no one sets foot on it from one year to the next. We could hide there till Doomsday and nobody would spot us—not that they'd think of comin' there to look for us in the first place. It's a good run, 106 nautical miles straight across the Bahama Bank. North of Stirrup Cay and the Berry Islands, I s'pose you might consider it part of the Berrys."

"Don't bother givin' me all that nautical crap," said Bob, "just get us there."

Guffy went home to Lucy for the night. Harry and Freddie walked across to the Club for dinner. Frank d'Angelo was leaving as they entered. He brushed against Freddie and regretted that it wasn't the right time or place to stick a knife in him, since he'd never have a better opportunity. Frank was now staying at the Club, a bribe had got him a room. Not a luxury bungalow, not one of the suites reserved for wealthy members of long standing, just a slip of a room with a cot and a dresser, a room that was pressed into service only at tournament time.

Harry and Freddie ate Island lobster and steak. They talked. Freddie said he knew most of the boys in the Lauderdale-Miami area who hired out for jobs like hijacking a million dollars or killing somebody to order. Harry didn't ask him how or why he knew them.

"But," said Freddie, "I don't know those two turkeys that came after us. From the way they screwed up I don't figger them as big league. Pullin' a shotgun on a cop? Not cool, they panicked, an' that ain't the mark of a pro. They're either strickly amateurs or small-time toughs."

"The sergeant seems to think they're bully-boys, to quote his own words. Enforcers, leg-breakers, he called them."

"That fits," said Freddie, "all muscle an' no brain."

"What really bugs me," Harry said, "is the way we almost walked into that setup back on the dock. Somebody knew the whole routine and they were waiting for us. That means someone set us up. Who? And they also knew we were coming across to Hog Cay."

"The sixty-four-thousand-dollar question," said Freddie. "I don't know the answer. Has to be an inside job, but I didn't think anybody knew Mr. Chambers' plans except me an' Mr. Chambers. Even poor old Morton didn't know until the last minute. Shouldn't we oughta call Mr. Chambers an' fill him in?"

"No. Tomorrow we'll be out of here. We just hang in, make the delivery, then we tell Mr. Chambers. Why worry him?" Harry cut into his steak, speared a piece of the meat on his fork, lifted it to his mouth, put the fork back down on his plate. "A thought's just occurred to me. What about Mrs. Cellini? She knew. When I gave Chambers a map I'd made showing how to get to Al Parson's dock, I told him to be careful not to lose it, and he said he'd get Mrs. Cellini to make some copies."

"Rose Cellini . . . ?" said Freddie. "Christ, Rose Cellini's bin with Mr. Chambers for more'n twenty years. Funny old bird, I know, bad tempered and everything, but she looks after Mr. Chambers like a nursemaid looks after a baby."

"And she's loyal to him? No resentments she's been carrying? No fights?"

"Oh, they fight an' argue all the time, always have, but it don't mean a thing. But let anybody say one word against Mr. Chambers an' Rose would rip his eyes out."

"So we can rule out Mrs. Cellini?"

"We can't rule out nobody," Freddie said flatly.

"If you had to take a guess," said Harry, "how many others are we up against? On the Island, I mean, how many more came over with those two on the Glastron?"

Freddie considered the matter critically, professionally. "Now you're askin' me somethin'. How many we still got gunnin' for us? Well . . . I'll tell you. I'd say that at the most, two, but quite likely, jus' one. One guy on his own can jus' melt into the background, shift an' move around as he pleases, no havin' to rely on a partner who might let him down. That's the way the real pro works."

"But he had two partners," said Harry, "he didn't come here alone."

"An' a good thing for him he didn't rely on the jerks, ain't it? The way I see it . . . the way I'd have set it up, would go like this. Three guys come across, they drop the hit man off at some quiet spot. That way, nobody even knows he's here. The hit man's job is to shorten the odds . . . get rid of one, two of us, me an' Morton, most likely. Then all the muscle boys gotta worry about when they boost the money from your boat is takin' care of you, an' they won't see you as much of a problem. You're a motel-keeper, an ordinary joe, you ain't a professional hardcase, like me an' Morton."

"Morton . . . ?" said Harry, "Morton was an accountant."

"Among other things," said Freddie, ambiguously. "Morton wasn't no pantywaist, believe you me, despite the way he looked. Sharp kid, Morton, I'm surprised he let himself get suckered into that situation, I honest to God am."

"So I was wrong about Morton being an accountant. What about you, Freddie, what are you?"

Freddie's homely face cracked with a grin. "Me . . . ? Oh, I'm just an old guy works for Mr. Chambers. A security guard, sort of."

"Sure you are, Freddie," Harry said, and let it go at that.

"I wonder if our hit man knows about his two friends," said Freddie. "I wonder if he knows they bin' scratched?"

"The Island's been buzzing with the news that the sergeant arrested them. Five minutes after it happened there wouldn't be a soul in the place didn't know about it. It isn't every day something exciting like that happens on Hog Cay. They'll be talking about it for years."

"Guess so," said Freddie. "You know, speakin' of those two, we should do something about their boat."

"How d'ya mean."

"Like fixin' it so the hit man can't use it to make a getaway."

"Right on," said Harry. "Let's go fix it." He called for the bill.

Cap'n Scott's Out Island Freight Service dock was deserted. While Freddie stood guard, Harry slipped aboard with a pair of side-cutters. He was back on the dock in five minutes. In one hand he had the side-cutters and in the other, a bunch of lengths of electric wiring. He showed them to Freddie, then pitched them into the water. "That'll slow him down," he said.

The night slowly wore down. Hog Cay was in full drunken swing. On the terrace of the Ocean View, King Jumbo and his Island Trio pounded out "Yellow Bird," "Land of the Sea and Sun," and "Kingston Market" in turn. Newfound friends put their arms around each other and sang along, pitching money into Jumbo's straw hat on the floor in front of the group.

A conga line started from the steps of the Red Lion, led by a fat lady in tight lime-green pants, a T-shirt bearing the words "I'm Hot To Trot," and a borrowed captain's cap.

Sergeant Welsh drove slowly past in his Jeep.

Midnight came. One o'clock approached. Sergeant Welsh drove back to the police station. Constable Mathews heard him coming and got busy with paper work kept in reserve for this time.

"Any problems?" Welsh asked as he came in.

"No trouble, Sergeant, they bin as quiet as two mice."

The sergeant looked through the cell bars at the two men now asleep on their thin mattresses. He'd called Nassau to report their arrest and Nassau said they would be over to collect them. That made the sergeant happy. Usually he had to escort handcuffed prisoners to Nassau on a regular Pollack's flight, and that was a nuisance. It made the passengers uneasy and it wasted two days of his time, more if he had to stay for the arraignment and even more if he had to return later for the trial.

And the prisoners he did escort were invariably guilty of simple crimes like assault or petty robbery, uncomplicated crimes of no great importance. But this situation was different. Harry Foster had opened this can of worms and the sergeant wanted to know why, wanted to know what lay under the surface. He'd questioned the two men individually and together and got nowhere. One thing was clear, they'd been a threat to Foster and he'd neatly taken them out of the action. Why? What threat? To his own satisfaction the sergeant had connected them with the other two, the two Foster said had chartered his boat for a fishing trip. He didn't buy that story, not one iota of it. He'd stake his stripes that those two in the Club bungalow were villains.

The whole bunch were on Hog Cay for some reason. Something was going on that he couldn't get to grips with, and the Sergeant didn't like that. He always knew what was going on . . . except for this time. So far no crime had been committed. Oh, carrying guns, resisting arrest, he could make that stick, but that wasn't the end of it. Why were they here?

Sergeant Welsh wasn't a patient man.

"Give me the keys," he said to Constable Mathews. Mathews got them from the hook and took them to Welsh. The sergeant unlocked the cell door, strode in, and kicked the metal frames of the bunks.

"Up," said the sergeant, "get up, both of you."

Protesting, the two climbed out of their bunks.

"Stand together," the sergeant said. "That's better. Keep your arms down at your sides. Good. Now I'm going to ask you some questions, the same questions I've been asking you from the start. This time, I want the answers."

The black-haired man laughed. "We bin through this ten times already. You're not gonna get any answers, can't you get that through your dumb cop head?"

Sergeant Welsh hit him in the stomach, and as he straightened up, arms wrapped around his belly, Welsh slapped him across the head with his open right hand, a roundhouse swing that knocked him back against the metal bunk. The brown-haired man said, "I'm a witness to that. It was an unprovoked attack, you're gonna get nailed for that."

Welsh moved in on him. "Am I?" he said conversationally, "Am I, now?" Unhurriedly, he took his massive service pistol from its holster and stuck the muzzle under the brown-haired man's chin, jamming it into his throat. "I'm going home now to get a few hours' sleep. I'll be back, and I'm going to take you up the Island where it's quiet and no one can see us and you're going to answer all the questions I feel like asking you. I'll take you first, and if you don't tell me what I want to know, I'm going to shoot you. Then I'll come back for the other one, and I'll take him up the Island, and if I have to, I'll shoot him. But you're first, so think about that while I'm gone."

He holstered his gun, marched out of the cell, out

of the police station. Mathews waited until he heard
the Jeep take off, then put on his uniform jacket and
cap, buckled on his gun belt, checked the cell door,
and waited for Constable Ivers, who was five minutes
late already, to report for duty.

Constable Ivers rushed in. "Sorry I'm late, man,
there's a big party at the Ocean View an' it could be
trouble, man. Cherry Taylor's on a bad drunk, an' you
know how Cherry likes pitchin' bottles through windows when he's drunk. You might look in at the
Ocean View, will you, man?"

"I'll look in," said Mathews and left to start on his
rounds.

From the deck of the *Moonglow*, Bob and Mike
watched Sergeant Welsh drive past toward the police
station. Bob checked the time. "He's goin' back to the
station to sign off," he said wisely. "Ten, fifteen
minutes from now you'll see that black fucker
Mathews come past an' head up the hill for his nightly
go at Maudie."

They waited. Mathews was a few minutes behind
schedule. He'd checked the Ocean View, the party
was winding down and losing its steam. Cherry
Taylor had passed out on the street in front of the
Ocean View's big front window, an empty beer bottle
in his hand. Constable Mathews had taken the bottle
from him and left Cherry to sleep it off.

"He's late," said Bob, "Usually the bastard's as
regular as clockwork."

Mathews appeared, turned sharp right up a path
that gently climbed to a group of cinder-block one-
story houses.

"There he goes," said Bob, smugly, "Just like I
fuckin' told you he would." He stood. "Ready mate,
'ere we go."

Mike stood beside him. He didn't feel at all well.

Bob looked at him. "What's the matter with you?"

"Nothing," said Mike.

Bob finished his gin, pitched the empty glass over the side of the boat, belched, hitched up his pants. "Then let's get movin', for crissakes."

TWELVE

Mike followed Bob down the *Moonglow*'s gangplank onto the dock and along the road. The moonlight was unnervingly bright and hard-edged. They stayed on the shadowed side as they passed the Ocean View, where lights still burned and a handful of drinkers were still hard at it.

Some hundred yards ahead on the ocean side sprawled a sagging-roofed wooden shack, the equipment shed for Scott's Marine Salvage Company. In it were stored old helmet-type deep-sea-diving gear, compressors, winches, oxyacetylene torches, rope and cables, and boxes of rusted tools. Bob smashed the padlock from the door with a rock, and while Mike kept nervous watch he went into the shed and came out pushing a two-wheeled metal dolly that had cylinders of gas and a cutting torch strapped to it. In his pocket he'd stuffed welder's goggles and a pair of work gloves.

With Mike ahead of him, acting as a scout, Bob trundled the dolly from the shed to the edge of the Queen's Highway. It was only about two hundred yards to the bank, but to get there meant wheeling the dolly down the road in full view of anyone who passed them or looked out and saw them. The ocean side of the road was completely open at this point, no buildings, no cover. On the opposite side, a scattering of single-story stores separated by patches of sand and bushes stretched as far as the bank. None of the stores had lights on in their windows or in the living quarters behind them. This side of the road offered the only protection, so Bob pushed the dolly across the road, the wheels shrieking on unoiled bearings.

Three Bahamian men appeared, hooting and yelling and chasing after each other as they kicked an empty beer can ahead of them. Bob moved back into the shadows between a gift shop and a dejected grocery store and waited for them to go by. Mike beckoned to him when the coast was clear and Bob came out from the shadows, checked in both directions, then set out for the bank at a brisk trot. Mike tried to ignore the high-pitched shriek from the wheels.

When they reached the bank, Bob hauled the dolly up the side path and round to the back of the building. Mike stayed with him and they stood, breathing heavily, listening carefully. From the road, they couldn't be seen. The Island was quiet—a dog barked, another dog bayed mournfully in reply, and then there was nothing. The moonlight sliced past them, leaving them in deep shadow.

"So far, so good," said Bob. He unfolded a clasp knife and tried to open the bank's back door.

148

"They've got it bolted from inside, the bastards," he said angrily. To the right of the door was a small casement window set high off the ground. "I'll have a go at this," he said. Balancing on the dolly, with Mike steadying him, Bob efficiently slipped the latch with his knife then pushed the window open. He jumped to the ground. "In you go," he said to Mike, and boosted him through the window. From inside, Mike unbolted the back door and Bob wheeled the dolly into the bank.

The bank's vault was a safe in the manager's office. It looked impregnable. Almost five feet tall and four feet square, it dominated the tiny room. On the door of the safe was cast a fearsome lion's head and in a scroll under the lion were the words "Jos. Crump & Sons, London. Est. 1867." A big brass handle, worn and polished with use, was set by an old-fashioned keyhole of enormous size.

"Bloody antique," said Bob, "all fuckin' show." He prepared the oxyacetylene torch. "You go round the side and watch the road. Anything wrong, bang on the back door."

Mike went out, Bob put on the gloves and goggles and lit the torch. Mike watched the road, furtively peering around the side of the building and ducking back at imagined sounds or shifting shadows. Bolder, he made a crouching run to the front of the bank and hid in the shadowed cover of an hibiscus bush by the front steps. From here he had a much better view. From time to time he looked at his watch, once shaking it to make sure it was still running. When fifteen minutes had crawled past, he thought he'd better go back and see how Bob was making out. He opened the back door a crack and could see the reflected hot blue flame from Bob's torch, and in a panic ran to the front of the bank to check if the intense light could be seen through the plate-glass window, but all was well. If you went right up to the window and looked over the frosted-glass lower part with the gilt lettering on it, then you could see a glow from the office, but from the road you couldn't see a thing. Again he made his crouching run around to the back. As he got there, Bob pushed the door open, the welder's goggles hanging around his neck.

"Done," said Bob. He led the way back into the manager's office and pointed to the safe. Where the lock had been was now a ragged-edged hole. "Like I said, all bloody show. Looks very grand, but it's a piece of junk, cut like butter, it did."

Mike put out a hand, Bob pulled him back. "Don't touch it, you nit, it's still hot."

They waited. Then using the leg of a metal chair as a lever, Bob pried open the safe door, Mike close behind him, straining to see over Bob's shoulder. On the top shelf in the safe were bundles of U.S. and Canadian currency. Bob took out a packet. On the paper wrapper was written in black marker, "$1,000 US." He riffled through the bills as if to confirm the money was real, then passed it back to Mike. "Find somethin' to put this lot in. Jus' look at all that luv'ly loot, will ya? Who said there ain't no Santa Claus."

Mike found two canvas money sacks and Bob relayed bundles of notes. They filled one of the sacks. "That's it," said Bob, that's the lot. How much do you reckon we got?"

"Some of them last stacks was small bills," said Mike, "ones and fives."

"It's all bleedin' money," said Bob. "How much we got?"

"I been keeping count," Mike said proudly. "I know to the penny. There's 11,500 in U.S. money, 1200 Canadian, and 475 Bahamian."

"A good start," said Bob, "but not enough. Not enough by a long bloody chalk. What else they got in here?" He bent down to look deeper into the safe. At the back of a lower shelf were ten flat, gray-metal safety deposit boxes. "Stick these in a bag," he said to Mike. "Who knows what might be in the bastards."

Almost filling the lower half of the safe were two cardboard cartons, one had held Tide detergent, the other, Dewars Scotch Whiskey. They were fastened and sealed with metal industrial strapping and rope. Bob pulled out one carton, hefted it, looked critically at it.

"Now what d'ya s'ppose is in these that warrants them being kept in the safe?"

Mike was getting anxious, he had the two canvas sacks in his hands and wanted to get away. "Can't be much," he said, "not packed in cardboard boxes. Leave 'em. Let's get outta here, we've got enough."

"Not so fuckin' fast," said Bob. He got out his clasp knife and cut an opening like a mail slot in the side of one carton. He angled the box in a shaft on moonlight to better see what was inside. "Christ! It can't be."

"What can't be?"

"I think this bloody box is full a money . . ."

"Lemme see . . . lemme see . . ." said Mike. He peered through the slot, looked at Bob in disbelief, then forced his hand through the slot, tugged, and came out with the torn half of a bank note. "Foreign money . . ." he said scornfully, "It's fulla foreign money."

Bob snatched it back, examined it. "This is a thousand-franc note, Swiss, nearly as good as dollars, these are." He looked down at the two cartons. "I dunno what else is in these sods, but if it's more of the same, we're laughin' chum, we're laughin'." He unstrapped the gas cylinders from the dolly, laid them on the floor, then stacked the two cartons on the platform of the dolly and pushed it toward the back door. "Let's move our arses, I think we hit the fuckin' jackpot."

Outside the bank they looked up and down the Queen's Highway. The Island had finally turned in for the night. "All clear," said Bob. "Christopher's dock. On the bleedin' double." He wheeled the dolly with Mike following, swinging a money sack from each hand. At the dock, Bob took the cartons off the dolly and carried them by the ropes. "Fourth slip to the left," he said. "The red-and-white boat."

The slip below the Uniflite cruiser Bob had picked out was empty, the one above it held an outboard runabout. Bob climbed onto the red-and-white Uniflite and peered through the cabin window.

"Nobody home," he said. "Like I told you, they sleep on shore." He tried the door of the cabin, it was unlocked. Mike passed down the cartons then stepped into the boat with his money sacks. They carried the cartons into the cabin and closed the door.

"This is a bit of all right," said Bob, looking around the broadloomed, white-leather-upholstered interior.

"Pretty dumb, leaving it unlocked," said Mike. "Askin' for trouble."

"Half the idiots do," Bob said. "Trustin' lot of bleeders. Let's get this thing started up. You drive it, that's your department. Just gimme a minute." He went to the control console. From his various pockets he took a small pair of pliers, a plastic case that held a screwdriver and assorted bits, a pair of wire cutters, and a roll of electrician's tape. With practiced ease he hot-wired the boat's starter. "Benefits of a misspent youth," he said.

Mike slid behind the wheel, familiarizing himself

with the layout. "Very nice. For a powerboat, very nice indeed."

"All set?" said Bob.

Mike nodded. "Any time."

"Right," said Bob, "let's get goin'."

They untied the lines. Bob started the engines and Mike expertly reversed the boat out of the slip. With the engines ticking over, Mike took the boat out and through the reef. Only then did he turn on the running lights. "Hang on," he called to Bob. The rev counter rapidly climbed and Mike leveled off at around 2200. The twin 310 hp Johnson & Towers diesels were now driving them at roughly twenty-two knots, close to their top end. "That should do us," said Mike. "Not the fastest boat in the water, but it'll get us there."

Bob went into the cabin, turned on the lights, opened the built-in bar, made two stiff gin and tonics and carried them back into the cockpit. "Here, have a drink while I get those boxes open so we can see what we really got." He dragged one carton over to a deeply padded leather chair, took a slug of his drink. Then with his cutters, he snipped the ropes around the carton and cut through the metal strapping. Upon opening the folded flaps of the carton he saw revealed stack upon stack of U.S. dollars, Swiss francs, and British pounds. Wordlessly, he dragged over the second carton and repeated the operation. The contents of the second carton duplicated the first.

"Holy shit," he said, lifting out layer upon layer of bundles of currency.

"Well, what's the score?" Mike called over the noise of the engines.

"I dunno," Bob shouted back. "I dunno what this foreign money's worth, but apart from that, there's a fuck of a great load of good old U.S. greenbacks. If there's less than a couppla hundred grand here, I'm gonna be awful bloody disappointed."

"You kiddin'?"

"No bleedin' way."

Mike let out a rebel yell. "Show me, for crissakes, lemme see it for meself."

Steadying himself against the motion of the boat, Bob carried up one of the cartons and held it for Mike to see into it.

"Holy shit," said Mike as, with his free hand, he scrabbled through the bundles of money.

"My sentiments exactly," said Bob.

Peter Marriott and Charles Dawson, the bank tellers, were eating their breakfast of bacon and eggs, toast, marmalade, and tea, when Sergeant Welsh strode briskly up to their table in the dining room of the Angler's Rest Hotel and told them their bank had been robbed.

"Good heavens," said Peter.

"Good heavens," echoed Charles.

They put down their knives and forks, dabbed their mouths with their napkins, neatly folded the napkins, and followed the sergeant to the bank.

Harry and Freddie pottered around killing time—Red Garrett had promised the *Rimshot* would be ready for them at noon—and packed their bags.

"What are we going to do about Morton's stuff?" Freddie asked.

"Is there anything there of any value?" said Harry.

"He left his wallet here."

"You better take that with you. Does he have a wife and family?"

"Yes. He's got two kids. One's just a baby."

"Will she be all right for money?" said Harry.

"Mr. Chambers will look after her."

"Good. Let's take a walk, we've still got a while to wait."

"Okay," said Freddie. "I'm gonna take my gun. Stick close to me, keep your eyes open."

In silence they walked along the path and up to the Queen's Highway. "What's the excitement?" Freddie said. "Must be a fire or something." Ahead of them, people were running toward the docks. They followed the runners. A crowd of at least fifty was gathered around the front of the bank, pointing and chattering excitedly. Constable Mathews, tired from two hours with Maudie and less than an hour's sleep, tried to handle the mob.

"What happened?" Harry asked Mathews.

"The bank's bin' robbed."

Harry and Freddie looked at each other. "Where's the sergeant?" Harry asked Mathews.

"Sergeant's round the back," said Mathews.

A smaller crowd had collected at the back door and was trying to see inside the bank. Harry and Freddie elbowed a way through them. Sergeant Welsh, Peter, and Charles were all in Peter's office. Charles was on his knees, picking up scattered papers while Peter tallied up what had been taken. Harry and Freddie came in on the run.

"Did they get my boxes?" Harry asked Peter Marriott.

Sergeant Welsh answered. "They got everything in the safe except some papers and ledgers. If your boxes were there, they got them too."

Harry sat on the edge of the desk and rubbed his hand over his face. Freddie suddenly looked a lot older.

"What was in those boxes of yours?" Peter Marriott asked.

"Papers," said Harry. "Valuable papers."

The sergeant smiled wolfishly. He knew precisely what was in the two cartons. His prisoners had answered his questions late last night, and he hadn't had to shoot either of them.

"Do you know who did it?" said Harry to the sergeant.

"Yes. Bob Hammersley and Mike Cholski."

"Bob Hammersley and Mike Cholski . . . ? How do you know? Where did they go?"

Patiently Sergeant Welsh explained. "They stole a boat, a thirty-six-foot cruiser belonging to a Mr. Martell. He went down to his dock just before six, and the boat was gone. Bob Hammersley and Mike Cholski have serious financial problems, and they're nowhere on Hog Cay. Circumstantial evidence, I admit, but to me it adds up. As for where they went, I have no idea. If I knew, I'd be on my way there."

Harry had to agree there was logic to the sergeant's reasoning, but he persisted. "Do you have any idea of when they took off?"

"They were seen leaving Cholski's boat around one-thirty this morning. How long it took them to open the safe, I can only guess. An oxyacetylene torch was used—they left the gas cylinders behind, as you can see. So, allowing them an hour to do the job, steal the boat, and take off, all we can assume is they left the Island some time between 2:30 and 6 A.M."

Without emotion, Freddie said, "We've got to find them."

The sergeant glared at Freddie with open dislike. "And what is your interest in this, Mr . . . ?"

"Makepeace. Freddie Makepeace."

This was the first time Harry had heard Freddie's last name. He didn't think it was very appropriate.

"And the other one, your companion, the one who

isn't here. What's his name, and where is he?"

"Morton Sumway," said Freddie. "Morton's around someplace."

"You still haven't told me why you're so concerned with finding Hammersley and Cholski. Were those 'valuable papers' yours?"

"No, but I'm responsible for seeing they get where they're supposed to be goin'."

"And where's that . . . ?" asked the Sergeant.

"None of your business," Freddie said amiably.

The sergeant's eyes went cold and blank. He took a pace toward Freddie, then stopped, the icy flash of rage now under control. "You're making me very angry," he said. "Everything that happens on Hog Cay is my business."

Harry stepped in. "Are you going to make a search for them, sergeant?"

Sergeant Welsh slowly turned from Freddie to face Harry. "What do you expect me to do? Swim out and see if I can find them? In which direction should I swim? This has been reported to Nassau and a helicopter will be sent here. The only chance of finding them is with a helicopter."

"My boat will be ready in an hour; I'm going to look for them," Harry said.

"No you won't," said the sergeant. "I know I told you I wanted you off Hog Cay, but circumstances have changed. This is an order. You stay here on Hog Cay until I say otherwise, I'm not through with you yet. Do you understand?"

"Sure, Sarge," said Harry, "I understand."

Harry and Freddie left the bank and set off for Red Garrett's boatyard. Standing apart from the crowd around the bank was Frank d'Angelo. He'd followed the two from the Club to the bank, had learned of the robbery, had watched Harry and Freddie run into the bank, had watched them come out empty-handed and obviously perturbed. From the way they were walking and talking it was clear that something was very wrong. His analytical mind rationalized that it was entirely possible the million dollars had been stolen along with the bank's money.

Frank picked up his rod case. He considered following Harry and Freddie, shooting them at the first opportune moment, then fading from the scene. He also fed into his personal mental computer a most interesting set of data.

1). Harry Foster had to recover the million dollars or be accountable to Mr. John Chambers.

2). If Harry Foster did not recover the money, then Mr. John Chambers would come down hard on Harry Foster, and Mr. Chambers was a most unforgiving and vindictive old man.

3). Frank's two moronic associates were now in jail and could not, therefore, carry out their assignment, namely, to hijack the million dollars and return it to certain parties in Miami. Not to John Chambers, but to certain other parties who were very angry with John Chambers.

4). Frank d'Angelo was the only one left who could assume the responsibility for carrying out the hijacking and returning the money to those certain parties.

5). But Frank's contract only required him to kill Harry Foster, the ugly Freddie Makepeace, and his Jew-partner Morton Sumway. His fee for this was a modest $25,000.

6). The shifting winds of chance had dealt new cards in this game, with Frank d'Angelo holding the best hand.

7). Playing that hand carefully, Frank d'Angelo could scoop the million-dollar pot. For himself.

All this data Frank examined coolly and objectively. He factored in the risks and consequences, the variables and the unknown quantities. The important unknown quantity was Harry Foster. What would his next move be? When Frank d'Angelo knew that, he'd then have to decide what his own next move would be. Until then, keep calm, think logically, act decisively.

Frank went through the exercises his psychiatrist had taught him: mind control, emotion control, relaxation. The pressure behind his eyes abated. It really was going to be a pleasure to eventually kill those two.

Harry stopped and looked out at the infinity of the tranquil ocean. "In an hour the *Rimshot* will be ready," he said to Freddie, "then we go after them. What we've got to work out is where we go."

Freddie stood by his side and looked where Harry looked. "We'll never find 'em until we've got some idea where they've gone. That's a mighty big ocean out there. Say they push the boat twenny, twenny five-knots, with a start like they've got they can be better'n a hundred miles in any direction before we even get started after 'em. Be like lookin' for a needle in a haystack."

I know," said Harry, "put it like that and you're right, we'd never find them. What we've got to do is outthink them . . . or at least, think their way." He sat on the edge of the road, his feet in the sand, Freddie sat beside him. "With those two," Harry went on, "Bob Hammersley's the one who would have planned this, but Mike Cholski is the one who knows boats and knows these waters."

"So?"

"So, I'm betting that Mike would be the one to pick

where they were going. If you were in their shoes, what sort of place would you pick?"

Freddie scanned the horizon as if looking for the answer. "Two kinds of places, depends on what sort of chance I wanted to take. One, big risk, but fast, I'd make for the mainland, down in the Keys, say, or up the west coast toward Naples, lose meself in the Everglades . . ."

Harry broke in. "Not the mainland. Nassau will have the police, the Coast Guard, and probably the Marines out by now."

"Right," said Freddie, "that's why I said it would be fast but a big risk. Most likely what I'd do is hole up on some island where there was no chance of being found, wait till the heat was off, then make my move."

"I'll buy that," Harry said. "I'll just add one thing. I wouldn't head for anywhere too far away, I'd want to get under cover as fast as I could."

"Check," said Freddie. "Let's think about that. A thirty-six footer, the sergeant said they took. Okay, assuming it's a stock boat, standard engines— probably diesels—and assuming they got out of here in a hurry, then eased off a bit to save fuel, they'd have a range of about 400, 450 miles, if the tanks were full, of course."

"Even if they were only half full, they'd still have a range of a couple of hundred miles."

"They gotta make two runs, remember," said Freddie. "First run to their hideout and second, they gotta go on to wherever it is they're plannin' to go, so they'll have to save some gas for that. I don't reckon they'd dare put in for gas anywhere in this area."

"Okay, let's say half and half on the gas. In that case we're after some safe spot within a hundred-odd miles from here, somewhere you can hide a boat and not be found."

"So how many places are there like that?" Freddie asked.

Harry threw up his hands. "One hell of a lot."

"So where do we look?"

Harry sighed. "I don't know, I have no damn idea."

On the way to Red Garrett's, Harry and Freddie passed the dock where the *Moonglow* was tied up. "That's Mike Cholski's boat," said Harry, pointing.

"I can see why they didn't try and get away in that," said Freddie.

"Got quite a history, that boat. Mike Cholski bought it about ten years ago from an old guy named Bergmann. A Swede. Over eighty when he quit, his eyes went on him, couldn't read his charts any more, and he had the finest set of charts you ever saw, or that's what everybody says. Should have been in a museum, they say, but apparently he gave them to Mike when Mike bought the boat . . ." Harry stopped and thoughtfully tapped one finger on his chin.

"What?" said Freddie.

"I had a flash. You go on over to Red Garrett's and see how he's doing. I'm going on Mike's boat, maybe I can dig up some clue that might point us in the right direction."

"From his charts?"

"From his charts . . . and his logs."

Freddie looked doubtful. "Maybe . . . maybe . . . if he didn't take them with him. Still, worth a shot. I'll see you back here."

Freddie continued on toward Red Garrett's boat-yard, Harry went aboard the *Moonglow*.

From the doorway of Scott's Wines & Spirits, Frank d'Angelo watched him.

THIRTEEN

Thirty minutes out from Hog Cay, on an empty ocean with no land in sight, Mike reduced speed until they were making a steady fifteen knots, the diesels of the Uniflite running silk-smooth, the deep V hull effortlessly slicing through the light seas. Mike Cholski was not a powerboat fan, but he was enjoying himself.

Bob wandered round the boat, looking into cupboards and closets, checking the liquor and food supplies. On the floor of one closet was a stack of newspapers, the top one a week-old copy of the *Wall Street Journal*.

"Swiss Franc Shows Strong Gains," he read out. "Glad we got a lot of 'em."

"Any idea what a Swiss franc's worth?" Mike asked.

Bob waved the paper. "They give all the exchange

quotations in this bleedin' capitalist rag, don't they? I'll take a look and see." He carried the newspaper back to his chair by the money cartons. "Got a pen or pencil up there?"

Mike picked up a ballpoint from the console, threw it to him.

"Now we can find out just how much we did cop," Bob said.

For half an hour Bob sat and counted bank notes and converted the Swiss francs and British pounds into U.S. dollars. Finally he said, "I got it figgered out."

"How much?" said Mike.

"Without splittin' hairs and ignorin' the odd cents here and there, I make it one million, one hundred and thirty-eight thousand, seven hundred and eighty-eight dollars."

"How much . . . ?" Mike said faintly.

"One million, one hundred and thirty-eight thousand, seven hundred and eighty-eight dollars."

"You gotta be wrong," said Mike. "You must have a decimal point in the wrong place or something."

"Believe it or not, mate, I used to be good at math at school. Used to be able to do square roots in me head when I was ten. I ain't got it wrong."

"A million bucks . . ." Mike took a deep breath. "A million goddam dollars."

"Got a nice comfortin' ring to it, ain't it?" Bob said. He stuffed the bundles of money back into the cartons then poured himself a large Chivas Regal from Mr. Martell's excellent stock of liquor. For Mike, he uncapped a beer. "No 'ard liquor for you, mate, drinkin' and drivin' don't mix."

Some hours later, Mike beckoned to Bob to join him at the wheel. "That's where we're goin'." Ahead,

Alan Cullimore

barely visible above the horizon, lay a chain of low-lying islands. The miles clocked off, Mike changed course a few degrees. A single island, smaller than the others, now lay directly ahead. As they drew closer, Bob could see it was about half a mile long and sloped up from the rocky northern tip to a central plateau of sand and sea grass some twenty feet above sea level. The south end of the island hid in a jungle of mangroves, and it was to this south end Mike headed.

Bob put down the binoculars. "Friendly lookin' fuckin' place, I must say."

Mike watched the depthsounder, it showed forty feet of water but spun rapidly back as the water got shallower. He again reduced speed. "There's a channel we gotta find. Reef is no problem this end, but there's sandbars we gotta look out for an' they shift all the time." The island was now less than two hundred yards away. Mike throttled back until the boat barely made headway.

"There it is, that's what I'm looking for." He pointed to a wind-eroded rock formation that rose from the ocean like some piece of avant-garde sculpture. Just past this, Mike swung the boat in a gentle arc and followed a deep, narrow channel that led into the interior of the island. In places, the channel was almost overgrown by the tangle of mangroves and only just wide enough for the boat to inch its way through. But quite suddenly, the channel widened into a lagoon about the size of a regulation basketball court. The border of the lagoon was heavily wooded and covered with a dense profusion of flowering vines and bushes. Huge turtles watched the boat from the sloping, sandy bank; herons and spoonbills and wood ibis flapped off in alarm at its approach, but

164

quickly settled again further up the lagoon and went back to wading and fish catching.

Mike cut the engines and they anchored in about eight feet of water. The stillness wrapped around them. Even the sounds of the waves breaking on the shore less than a hundred yards away were blanketed by the curtain of trees and vines.

"Christ, it's hot," said Bob. He slapped his arm. "Fuckin' mosquitoes . . ." He slapped again. "I'm bloody well being eaten alive."

Mike found a can of insect repellent and they sprayed each other. "How long you reckon on stayin' here?" he asked Bob.

"No hurry. The longer we leave it, the better. There's plenty of canned food and booze on board, so let's have a drink and relax an' enjoy it . . ." He swiped at a mosquito ". . . as much as these sodding things will let us."

He made two mammoth drinks and they took them and the insect repellent up to the flying bridge and sat on the padded bench. Bob looked around him at the impenetrable mass of mangroves and vines and ropes of violently colored blossoms, at the shrieking flocks of exotic birds, the lumbering turtles. "I take back what I said about bein' in no hurry," he said. "Drive you bonkers if you had to spend much time in this tropical bleedin' paradise, wouldn't it?" He took a drink. But I gotta admit you were right, not much chance of the fuckers findin' us here. Where d'ya reckon we should make for next? How we doin' for gas?"

Mike took a thoughtful drink of Chivas Regal. "I been giving that a lot of thought. What I think we should do is make a run for Grand Bahama."

Bob looked at him as if Mike had lost his senses.

"Grand Bahama . . . ! Christ, go there and we might as well wave a flag an' yell 'Here we are, come and get us.' "

"No," said Mike, shaking his head wisely, "think about it. Take Freeport. Place is always full of tourists, trippers, the gamblin' nuts, hundreds of boats, cruises arrivin' every ten minutes, everybody comin' an' goin' all the time. We just dress up like tourists—" He looked at Bob's filthy pants and stained linen jacket. "—there's bound to be something on board we can wear . . . an' we slip in with everybody else, tie up anywhere we can find, drift ashore with the money, an' disappear into the goddam crowd. Find ourselves a place to stay where they ain't likely to ask questions. An' we got an advantage on that score. With all the mob boys an' crooks an' shysters in that place, nobody does ask too many questions, not if they know what's good for them."

Bob tilted his glass, drained it. "You know . . . it's not such a bad bloody idea at that, an' at least it's part of effin' civilization."

"It would work," said Mike, "trust me." A thought hit him. "Changin' the subject, did you open them safety-deposit boxes? What was in them?"

"I dunno," said Bob. "I never bothered. With a million bloody dollars lyin' on the floor, I couldn't care less what's in them."

"All the same," Mike said, "we don't want to miss anything. People stick all kinds of valuable stuff in safety-deposit boxes."

"You're right, let's take a look see. Give us somethin' to do."

They carried their glasses down to the cabin. Mike made fresh drinks while Bob stacked the flat tin boxes on a table, then got a heavy screwdriver and hammer. One by one he forced open the lids of the trays and passed them to Mike. In the first tray was nothing of worth: an insurance policy, a will, and various papers and documents. In the second box there was little of interest to them except an old pocket watch with an enameled, flower-decorated face. Mike gave the winding stem a few turns and the watch ticked, probably for the first time in years. The third tray yielded nothing. Bob became impatient. The fourth tray was an improvement: six gold Spanish pieces and ten U.S. twenty-dollar gold coins. In the fifth tray, under a bundle of handwritten letters tied with a blue ribbon, was a red leather wallet and, folded inside it, a piece of black velvet. Between the layers of velvet were six rings. One was a Victorian wedding band, wide and heavy. There were two dress rings with small rubies and diamonds set in gold filigree. An eternity ring of alternating tiny emeralds and diamonds, a child's ring with a pearl set in a gold heart, and a diamond solitaire, the square-cut, blue-white stone a good half inch across. While Bob's attention was on prying open the next box, Mike slipped the solitaire ring into his shirt pocket. The remaining safety-deposit boxes held nothing of any importance.

Bob examined the various items. The gold coins he stacked up like casino chips, clinked them from hand to hand. "It all helps, it all bleedin' well helps."

Sally was one of the last to find out about Bob and Mike and the bank robbery. Sergeant Welsh drove to the pool hall and found the place closed. It had been half-past three when Sally closed the bar and almost four by the time she got into bed, so it took a while for the sergeant's pounding on the door to rouse her from her nineteen-year-old's deep sleep. She called out that she was coming, pulled on jeans and a shirt and opened the pool-hall door to him.

"What's he done now?" she asked routinely.

The sergeant came in, cleared his throat. "Your husband and Mike Cholski robbed the bank during the night and have taken off in a stolen boat."

"Oh, the silly buggers," Sally said. "Do you know where they've gone?"

"I hoped you might have some idea of that. Something your husband said to you at some time. The name of an island, a town, a city, in the Islands, the United States . . . anywhere. Some place he's said he'd go if he had money. We all play games like what we'd do and where we'd go if we won a sweepstake or someone left us a lot of money—did your husband ever do that?"

"He daydreams all the time," said Sally. "Can't keep his feet on the ground for a minute. Always dreaming up some scheme that's going to make him a fortune, but nothing ever comes of any of it, of course. But I don't remember him ever saying anything about any special place he'd like to go. One day it's back to New Zealand, the next day England or South America. He's always vague, always up in the clouds. I've begged him to stay away from that Mike Cholski. He's no good, that one. Bob isn't too bad on his own, but when he gets with Mike, anything's likely to happen."

The sergeant sighed. Like all women, Sally would defend her own man, even if that man was Bob Hammersley. "If you think of anything, you'll let me know, won't you?"

"Oh, yes," said Sally. "You'll be going after him, I suppose?"

"As soon as the helicopter arrives from Nassau."

A pause. "You won't shoot him, will you?"

"Not unless I have to. I don't shoot people who give

168

themselves up or who don't shoot at me."

"Oh well," Sally said, "that's something."

From the pool hall, the sergeant drove back to the police station and got on the radio to Nassau to see if there was any news of the helicopter. Nassau told him he would have it some time today, that was the best they could do. They were tied up with a freighter full of dope they'd stopped at sea, and a robbery involving a few thousand dollars on one of the Out Islands had to take its place on their priority list. A general alert had been issued, they said, so why didn't the sergeant write up his report and wait till they got there. And would the sergeant not use that kind of language on the air.

Sergeant Welsh switched off the radio in a fury. The hell with Nassau, he'd managed without them in the past, and he'd manage without them now.

Harry sat at a table in the *Moonglow*'s main cabin amid a shambles of dirty glasses, empty bottles, cigarette butts, unwashed plates, crumpled candy wrappers, and empty potato-chip bags and wondered how a man could lose enough pride to treat a boat that way.

He'd swept the tabletop clear of litter, then gone over the entire boat, collecting every map, chart, and log he could find. These he'd arranged in neat stacks on the table and was slowly and methodically going through them, looking for some clue, some notation, some log entry that might provide a tip-off as to where Bob and Mike had fled.

Until fairly recently, Mike had kept good logs, precise and detailed. For the most part they were records of one or two-day diving charters, and for these he'd given the bare facts: dates, times, position, weather, and a few brief comments.

Dating back three, four, five or more years were the logs of longer charters, some of several weeks, and here Mike had written up much longer and more graphic accounts. Harry read these carefully, for many of the *Moonglow*'s charters had been to remote locations and to little and seldom-visited islands.

Freddie came down through the hatch and into the cabin.

"Red's almost through," he said. "We'll have the boat on schedule. Any luck here?"

"It would help if I knew what I was looking for," said Harry. Freddie pulled up a chair and sat quietly while Harry continued to read through the log. He stopped at one page, turned back to the previous page, read through both pages again. "I don't know if this means anything," Harry said, tapping a page with his finger, "but he's written up two pages on this charter and made a rough drawing of an island, complete with map references. Listen to this . . .

Natural harbor cannot be seen from off shore. We would not have found it if we had not explored the island on foot. Entrance and channel, six to eight feet of water, sand bottom. Heavily overgrown with mangroves and vines. Approx. one hundred yards up channel, lagoon approx three hundred and fifty feet long by twenty to twenty-five feet wide. Eight to ten feet of water . . .

Harry's finger moved further down the page.

. . . On west bank of lagoon found remains of wooden bucket and old pistol Professor Warton said date back to pirate days and that lagoon might have been used by pirates hiding from British Navy as almost no chance of being found here. Possible as channel could have been wider back then . . .

He glanced up at Freddie. "Apparently Professor Warton was the one who chartered the boat. Don't you find it interesting that the Prof said this lagoon would make a good place to hide a boat if you were on the run from the authorities?"

Dubiously, Freddie said, "I s'pose. You thinking Mike Cholski might have remembered this island and this lagoon and gone there now? Kind of a long shot, ain't it?"

"We've got nothing else to go on," said Harry. "Not so far, anyway."

A further twenty minutes of reading the log and checking charts added nothing. Guffy put his head over the edge of the hatch. "Fifteen minutes, an' we're set to go," he shouted down.

"We . . . ?" said Harry. "You including yourself in this wild-goose chase?"

"Thought I would," said Guffy. "You'd prolly get lost without me."

Frank d'Angelo watched Harry and Guffy and Freddie leave the *Moonglow*. Tucking the rod case under one arm, he let them get some distance ahead, and then followed them.

Sergeant Welsh saw Harry, Freddie, and Guffy leave the *Moonglow* as he was on his way to the bank, and tried to guess what Harry might have been doing on Mike Cholski's boat. For a moment he considered the possibility of Harry being involved in the bank robbery, but good sense told him no, it didn't add up.

In twenty minutes the *Rimshot* had taken on its full load of gas—main tanks and reserve. The fresh water Harry kept down to seventy-five gallons, no one would be bothering with showers. Canned and dried food they had in plenty. Firearms were checked, air tanks filled, all systems—mechanical, manual, and electronic—tested. They were all set to go.

Frank d'Angelo mingled with a small group of bored tourists on the dock who had nothing better to do than watch the *Rimshot* being made ready. In his white pants, baggy blue sweatshirt, and Topsiders, Frank fit right in.

Guffy untied the last of the lines. Harry and Freddie were in the cockpit, Harry at the wheel. Frank d'Angelo went to the very edge of the dock. Guffy walked forward to the bow rail, boathook in hand. Harry eased the *Rimshot* away from the dock. Frank d'Angelo stepped from the dock to the *Rimshot*'s transom and from there down into the cockpit. From under his sweatshirt he slipped his silenced .22 pistol; in his left hand he carried the rod case. He walked forward—Frank was very light on his feet. Neither Harry nor Freddie saw or heard him. Frank stuck the muzzle of the .22 into the back of Harry's neck. Freddie turned, froze.

"Just keep going," Frank said to Harry. "No fuss, no tricks. Try anything, I'll blow your brains out, and if the ugly old guy tries anything, I'll blow your brains out. Either way, you're dead."

Guffy came back along the side deck from the bow of the boat and jumped down into the cockpit. "Drop the boathook," said Frank. Guffy dropped it. "Now come here. Stand next to the old guy where I can see you. That's good," he said, as Guffy lined up beside Freddie. Frank turned his attention back to Harry. "Nice and easy now. Think of me as a passenger. Nice and easy 'til we're clear, then let's go get the money."

"What money?" asked Harry, looking rigidly ahead.

"Don't get smart, you know what money. One million dollars of Chambers' money, the money you let those two bums get away with. The money you're going after right now."

"I don't know where the money is. We're checking out the boat, that's all. It's been repaired and now we're checking it out."

Frank viciously jammed the gun into Harry's neck, pushing his head forward. "I've followed every move you've made, so don't try and con me."

The *Rimshot* was now through the reef. Strung out ahead were a line of tournament fishing boats, on their way back in for lunch. Harry turned the wheel a fraction; maybe he could get close enough to cause some kind of disturbance, draw attention.

"Keep well clear of those boats," said Frank. "Obey all the rules."

They passed the boats. The closest one blew its horn in greeting, Harry courteously replied with the *Rimshot*'s horn.

"That's it," said Frank, "that's the idea."

Gradually they left the tournament boats behind. Harry held the *Rimshot* to about ten knots, which seemed to satisfy d'Angelo. With Hog Cay over the horizon and open sea all around them, Frank jerked his head at Freddie. "You . . . go to the back of the boat." Freddie took a step. "Don't come any closer to me," Frank warned, "don't get cute." Freddie slowly walked toward the stern. As Freddie passed him, Frank transferred the muzzle of the gun from Harry's neck to the middle of Freddie's back, right on his spine, and prodded Freddie ahead of him. Freddie stopped a few feet before he reached the transom. "All the way," said Frank. Freddie took another step and was now hard up against the transom. Frank moved the gun up to Freddie's head. "Lean over, old man."

Freddie took a deep breath, stood straight-backed.

"Lean over, I said," Frank yelled.

"No," said Freddie, "I'm not going to make it easy for you."

Harry slammed the throttles wide open and spun the wheel hard over. Freddie grabbed the fighting chair and managed to save himself from going overboard as the *Rimshot* tried to stand on its side in a crazy tight turn.

Frank d'Angelo dropped his rod case as he lost his footing and was flung across the boat. As Frank scrambled to his feet, Harry immediately spun the wheel in the reverse direction. Caught completely by surprise, Frank stumbled against the low transom, pitched forward over it and into the ocean. Harry cut power, turned the *Rimshot*, and went back. Frank d'Angelo wildly treaded water, one hand raised as he frantically called for help.

"We can't let him drown," said Harry, as he brought the *Rimshot* alongside the terrified man.

"No," said Freddie, "we can't let him drown." He leaned far out over the side, extending his left hand. Frank grabbed it. Freddie pulled him close to the side of the boat, shot him through the forehead, then let his body slide back beneath the waves.

FOURTEEN

Through his binoculars, Sergeant Welsh followed the *Rimshot* until he finally lost it against the horizon in a haze of sea and sun. The boat was heading due east—not that this helped much, but unless Harry was playing some elaborate evasive game, it meant he wasn't making for the Florida mainland, which lay to the west, or Grand Bahama to the north. That left five thousand square miles of hundreds of island and cays spread over a length of six hundred miles where he could be going. In his forty and some years, the Sergeant hadn't covered one quarter of this scattered Bahamian territory.

He put the glasses back in their case and, shielding his eyes from the glare, scanned the cloudless sky for his promised helicopter. One-thirty was the most recent word from Nassau—he should definitely have his copter by one-thirty, they said.

The sergeant had taken a gamble when he'd deliberately let Harry go. He was convinced Harry knew where Bob Hammersley and Mike Cholski were bound for, and it was this pair of bastards the sergeant ached to get his hands on, the pair who'd violated his virgin parish, the pair who'd pulled off the one and only major robbery on Hog Cay since it had come under the sergeant's stewardship. And the sergeant had also gambled the helicopter would arrive in time. In time for him to let Harry get a fair start, then fly a pattern in the copter that would keep tabs on the *Rimshot*, and the *Rimshot* would lead him to Hammersley and Cholski. Unless the chopper arrived soon he would have gambled and lost. And the chopper was late. Someone in Nassau had screwed up, but someone in Nassau always screwed up; they couldn't organize a two-car funeral.

Where in Christ's sacred name was that helicopter?

If Harry got more than an hour's lead, the Sergeant would never track him. An hour was twenty miles or more, and in the immensity of the empty ocean, a thirty-eight-foot boat was easy to lose, especially when a stiffening breeze broke up the surface of the water as it now did.

There was still the puzzle of why Harry had been on the *Moonglow*. The sergeant had gone down into the filthy cabin and seen the piles of maps and charts and logs on the table where Harry had left them, but they told him nothing. He did note that a page of a log had recently been torn out. If Harry had been the one to tear it out, it could only mean it was because that page contained information Harry wanted or needed. The sergeant was building a case on the flimsiest of circumstantial evidence, and he knew it, but it was all he had to go on.

He'd better get back to the station. There might be a signal from Nassau.

Constable Ivers flagged down the jeep half way to the station. Ivers was running, and it took something of unusual significance to cause Ivers to run.

"Constable Mathews, he want you down at Sanders' Point," panted Ivers.

"What for? What's he doing down at Sanders' Point?"

"They found a body, sergeant. They want you there afore they move it."

"Whose body?"

"They didn't say, sergeant. Jes' told me to come and get you."

"All right, constable. You go back to the station. Call Nassau and see if the 'copter's on the way."

"Don't know how to work the radio, sergeant."

"Turn it on and listen, you can do that, can't you?"

"Yes, sergeant. I knows how to turn it on."

"Just switch on, and listen. If they say anything to us, write it down." The sergeant gunned the Jeep in the direction of Sanders' Point.

The Point was on the north shore, a long finger of enormous coral-covered slabs of rock haphazardly tumbled in some giant upheaval. Constable Mathews, two teenage boys in swimming trunks—flippers and snorkels on the rocks beside them—and a group of the people who automatically are drawn to accident and death, stood in a half circle around a body trapped at water level between two coral spurs. The sergeant shoved them aside and bent down to look at the body. It was in bad shape, bloated by its time in the water, battered by rocks and torn by coral. Fish had eaten away parts of the face and flesh from the fingers. The remnants of running shoes were still on its feet and the boxer swimming trunks had stayed intact, the elastic waistband buried deep in the grotesquely swollen stomach. The sergeant didn't know the man, or if he did know him, he couldn't identify him from these obscene remains.

"They found him," said Mathews, pointing to the two teenagers.

Sergeant Welsh went over to the boys. "Tell me about it. What are your names?"

"My name's Darryl Mason," said the older of the two boys, "and that's my brother Jack. We're from Coral Gables, our dad's fishing in the tournament."

"How come you found the body?"

The boys looked down at it, then quickly back up to the sergeant. "We came here because they told us it was a good place to snorkel," said Darryl. "They said the coral and the fish here were neat." He pointed to a protected deep pool, some short distance out. "We fooled around there for a while and I followed a big fish, grouper I think it was, and I came up here . . . and . . . it was staring right at me . . ." He shuddered. "It didn't have any eyes . . . but it was sort of looking right at me, and . . . excuse me . . ." He ran to a rock, leaned on it, and vomited.

"Is that what happened?" the sergeant asked the younger boy.

White-faced, the boy silently nodded.

"Where are you staying?"

"At the Ocean View. Me and Darryl are in room seventeen."

"I'll give you a ride back," said the sergeant. He faced the morbidly fascinated voyeurs who clustered around them. "The rest of you, go home. Nothing more to see." He waved his hand in dismissal. To Mathews, he said, "there's a tarp in the back of the Jeep. Get it, will you."

Mathews got the tarpaulin and unrolled it on the rocks, and the ghouls who had started to drift away flocked back to watch Mathews and the sergeant lift the sad, misshapen body out of the crevice in the rocks and onto the rubberized sheet. Only when the body was wrapped and stowed in the back of the Jeep did they leave. The sergeant and Mathews were in the front of the Jeep. "Get in," the sergeant called to the two boys. "Bit of a tight squeeze, but we'll manage."

The boys looked at the tarpaulin-covered bundle in the back of the Jeep, looked at each other, and shook their heads. "We'll walk," said Darryl. "It's not that far."

Bob Hammersley and Mike Cholski sat in canvas captain's chairs in the stern of the boat, drinking Mr. Martell's Remy Martin and smoking Mr. Martell's smuggled Havana perfecto cigars. Mr. Martell had good taste and the money to indulge it. They'd made their dinner on Mr. Martell's canned lobster, canned artichoke hearts, and a bottle of decent Burgundy. The brandy and cigars topped it off nicely. A black and white striped canopy protected them from the sun and the breeze now blowing up the channel kept down the mosquitoes. For the moment, life was very pleasant.

Mike waved his cigar at the lagoon. "I was right about this place, wasn't I? Nobody could find us here."

"I grant you that," Bob conceded, "but it sure as bloody hell ain't my idea of a place to live permanent."

They smoked for a while, then Bob said, "What you goin' to do with your share?"

Mike considered. "I'm going to get another boat, a steel ketch. Work out of the Caymans or the

Windwards. Martinique's a good place, but there's money in the Caymans. What about you?"

"I seen enough of the bleedin' Islands to last me," said Bob. "Thought maybe I'd go back to England, I was there for a time, you know. Buy a pub an' take things easy. Seaside town on the south coast . . . Brighton, somewhere like that." He tasted his Remy Martin. "Quite honestly, mate, I'm gettin' sick of movin' around, an' I ain't gettin' any younger, neither."

"Know what you mean," said Mike. "That makes two of us. But I gotta have a boat, I'm not happy unless I got a boat."

"Wouldn't worry me if I never saw another bloody boat as long as I lived," said Bob. "No, a nice pub would do me fine."

"What I should do," Mike said, "is forget big boats and buy a motel on the coast somewhere. That way I'd have somewhere to live, have an income, an' I could have a sailboat, even a small one, even a sailin' dinghy . . . no. I'd want somethin' bigger than that."

"Let's not start countin' our chickens too soon," said Bob, suddenly down. "We gotta long way to go before we're in the clear."

"Still want to try for Grand Bahama?"

"Unless we come up with something better. It was your idea. You backin' off?"

"No."

"Then Grand Bahama it is." Bob passed his empty glass to Mike. "Pour us another shot a that brandy."

At twenty minutes past two, the helicopter arrived from Nassau and put down on Pollack's Air Service's concrete square. Sergeant Welsh was waiting, and he let out his breath in a long, disgusted sigh when he saw who it was climbed out of the passenger's seat in the bubble. Chief Inspector Lowe. Fifty-five years old, nearly thirty years on the force and, in the sergeant's opinion, a bureaucratic, politicking, alibiing twit.

"Inspector Lowe," the sergeant snapped, saluting smartly.

Lowe's eyebrows went up. "A bit formal, aren't you, Welsh? No need for that carry-on. What's going on here? Any developments?"

"Sir," said the sergeant. "Suggest we take the Jeep back to the station and you read my report."

"Good idea," said Lowe, "but go easy on the 'sir' stuff."

At the station, Lowe read Sergeant Welsh's report and asked some fairly intelligent questions. The sergeant kept to the facts and offered no opinions, he wasn't going to give Lowe a chance to nail him later.

"Not a lot of money involved for all this commotion, is there?" said Lowe. "The helicopter, my time, your time, all the calls backward and forward to Nassau, getting the American Coast Guard excited, alerting all the other Family Islands, and so on. A lot of it's the bank's doing, of course. They were very upset when they heard about your balls-up. What's all this about two cartons of valuable papers, property of a Mr. Harry Foster? I should have a talk with this Harry Foster, where is he now?"

The sergeant cleared his throat. "He's on his boat, sir."

"Send for him, there's a good fellow."

"Well, sir, when I said Mr. Foster was on his boat, I meant he was at sea. Left about two and a half hours ago. I had no reason to detain him."

"You're probably right," said Lowe, losing interest. "What have you planned to do about this affair? How d'ya propose to make use of the copter. Costs a damn arm and a leg to keep that thing in the air, and we can't spare it for long, you know."

Keeping all expression from his face, sergeant Welsh said, "Had the helicopter arrived on time, sir . . . as promised, sir, I proposed to carry out a search for the stolen boat in which the two bank robbers escaped. I assume, sir, that police detachments on Grand Bahama, Abaco, Andros, Eleuthera, and the smaller islands have already been warned to be on the lookout for them."

"Of course they have," Lowe said testily. "I told you we had been in touch with the other Family Islands, didn't I? What the devil d'ya think we've been doing? And as for the hold up with the copter, we were busy with twenty million dollars' worth of cocaine. Got 'em cold. Made us look damn good, I can tell you. Sort of publicity we need these days. Got myself interviewed for television. What d'ya think about that, eh?"

"Congratulations, sir," said Sergeant Welsh. He shifted in his seat. "If there's nothing else. sir, I'd like to take off in the 'copter as soon as possible."

"Not much hope of finding them, is there?"

"Always a chance, sir."

The inspector shrugged. "Good luck, anyway. You take off, nothing much I can do to help by coming. I hate those bloody machines, in any case. I'll take a walk around, haven't been on Hog Cay in five years. Marlin tournament's on, isn't it?"

"It is, sir," said the sergeant, on his way to the door. "I'll report back, sir."

"Don't leave it too long," said the inspector, "I want to get home before dark."

The pilot had refueled the helicopter and now sat chatting with the pretty Bahamian girl in Pollack's office. He had found out she wasn't married, that her regular boyfriend was over on Cat Cay for the week, and that if the pilot didn't have to return to Nassau that night, she would go to bed with him if he gave her a ride in the helicopter. At this point, Sergeant Welsh hauled him out of the office.

"Where to, Sarge," the pilot asked, after they'd buckled in and lifted off.

"East. East for fifty miles, then we'll start sweeping. Ten degrees each side at first."

"Whatever you say, Sarge. What are we looking for?"

"Thirty-eight-foot cruiser, white hull."

"Good luck," said the pilot, and settled down to some dull flying and erotic thoughts about the Bahamian girl with the big tits in Pollack's office.

Harry sighted the island, dead on course. He steered for the rocky north end, cut speed way back, and cruised parallel to the shore while Guffy scrutinized the island through binoculars. Freddie sat in a canvas chair, legs braced, a telescopic-sighted .303 rifle resting on the side rail of the boat.

About an eighth of a mile from where Mike's log showed the hidden channel to be, Harry killed the engines and they anchored offshore in twenty feet of water. He got into a pair of swimming trunks and around his waist buckled a webbing belt that had a metal ring sewn to it at the back. In an aluminum cylinder the size of a scuba air tank he stuffed rolled-up jeans, a long sleeved black sweater, a pair of high-topped sneakers, and a can of bug-repellent. On top of these he put the machine pistol and two thirty-round magazines, then fitted a watertight rubber cap over the cylinder's open end. Guffy fastened the cylinder to the ring on Harry's belt with a length of thin nylon rope.

Holding the cylinder under one arm, Harry slipped over the side of the boat and swam to the rock-strewn beach, the aluminum cylinder bobbing behind him on the surface of the water. In the shallows he stood, hauled in the cylinder, and carried it up the steeply shelving beach to where the sea grass and bushes grew thick. There, he dressed in his jeans, sweater and sneakers, sprayed himself with repellent, snapped one magazine into the machine pistol, put the second magazine in his hip pocket, and hid the cylinder behind a rock.

He waved to Guffy and pointed along the beach. Guffy waved back in understanding. Keeping close to the protective rocks, shrubs, and stunted trees, Harry moved quickly along the shoreline until he came to the mouth of the channel. Through the binoculars, Guffy kept track of him.

Bob and Mike still sat in the stern of Mr. Martell's boat. They'd finished Mr. Martell's bottle of Remy Martin VSOP Reserve and were a third of the way through a bottle of his Benedictine. With the approach of evening, the breeze had stilled and mosquitoes were out in force. Insect repellent kept some away and the liquor largely compensated for the rest, but neither repellent nor the Benedictine deterred the clouds of vicious, almost invisible sand flies that swarmed in to reinforce the mosquitoes.

"Jesus," said Mike, "we're gonna have to go inside."

"Be hotter'n buggery in the cabin," said Bob.

"At least the screens will keep these damn things out." Mike scratched at his wrist, puffy from sand-fly bites.

"Before we go in," Bob said, "an' changin' the subject completely, you got me a bit confused. Just how did you discover this earthly Garden of bleedin' Eden?" He swirled Benedictine around in his brandy snifter. "Accordin' to the yarn you pitched me back on Hog Cay, you spent two weeks here rogerin' some broad. Then awhile ago, you was on about you and a professor findin' a bucket an' pistol here . . . the guy who said this was likely a pirate's hang out. You oughtta get your stories straight, mate. Don' know what to believe where you're concerned."

Mike swatted a mosquito on his forehead, examined the blood-engorged remains, and wiped his hand on the underside of his canvas chair. "Best charter I ever had," he said grinning like a fool. "This professor was from one of them Ivy League colleges, got a grant to research a book on Anne Bonney—you know, the lady pirate—an' the prof had a theory she used the Berry Islands as a sort of base of operations and probably hid some of her loot on one of the islands and holed up to wait it out when things got hot. That's why we were here; this particular island matched up with what Anne Bonney had written in her journal . . ." He swept a hand in an arc. "Not right in this spot, I don't mean, but on this island. We anchored off the north end, didn't have any of this to contend with . . ." He raked his ankle with his nails.

"What about the bleedin' girl?" said Bob. "Where does she come in or was you jus' makin' that part up?"

Mike winked, theatrically. "I'm gettin' to the juicy part. This prof was a woman, not more'n twenny-six, twenny-seven, an' looked like she shouldda been a Penthouse centerfold. Built like there's no tomorrow. Stacked, she was, 'nuff to drive you outta your mind . . . knockers on her like . . ."

"Get on with the fuckin' story," Bob said impatiently.

"Gotta be told right," said Mike, stringing out the suspense. "Now, when I told you we was here alone, apart from the couppla boys I had crewin' for me, that's not strickly true. The prof had an assistant, 'nother girl, a student, she was. Well, every mornin' the prof an' the girl would set off with their cameras and surveyin' gear an' their charts, an' the prof would mark off a section of the island an' then leave her assistant to do the work. The prof would come back to the boat an' I'd bang the ass off her for the rest of the day. Christ, I musta laid her fifty times. What a randy bitch she was, couldn't get enough of it, an' she had some pretty kinky habits considerin' how well educated she was . . . an' on top of that, I had the assistant a few times, too. Man oh man oh man, what a charter that was."

Bob nodded wisely. "Mus' be somethin' about higher education that turns women on. Best fuck I ever had in all me born days was in England. Headmistress of a posh girl's school. I was workin' there as a handyman an' I was fixin' the furnace one day an' this old gal came down to the furnace room, grabbed me, slung me down on the floor an' bloody near killed me. Strong as an ox, she was. Screamin' and yellin' an thrashin' around . . . she was something else, that one. You never can tell, mate, you never can tell."

Mike flailed at the unseen sand flies attacking his neck. "That's enough, that does it. You stay here if you like, but I'm going in." He filled his glass with Benedictine, pushed back his canvas chair, and ran for the hatchway to the cabin.

With infinite caution Harry followed the channel as it widened then opened up into the lagoon. Through the trees he saw Mike stand and run back to the hatchway and the cabin. Bob stayed in his chair at the stern of the boat, the bottle of Benedictine at his side.

Harry waited, eased off the safety of the machine pistol and, testing every step, taking advantage of every piece of cover, approached the boat. The stern faced him almost square on. Forty feet from the boat rose an outcropping of rock. Harry carefully kept this between him and Bob as he cautiously covered the last stretch.

Bob finished his drink, stood, belched, went to the transom, unzipped his fly and luxuriously peed into the lagoon. When he'd finished, he shook off the last drops, zippered up his fly, and looked up at Harry standing on the bank twenty feet from him, the machine pistol pointed at his head.

"Oh shit," said Bob. "Wouldn't you fuckin' know it would be you."

Mike came up from the cabin. "Did I leave my—" He saw Harry, didn't believe what he saw. "How—how the hell did you know we was here? How did you find us . . . ?"

Harry raised the muzzle of the machine pistol and fired a short burst into the air. A wave of gulls and wading birds took off, shrieking in panic.

On the *Rimshot*, Guffy heard the signal shots and started the engines. Freddie hauled in the light anchor and Guffy took the *Rimshot* along to the mouth of the channel, cautiously up the channel, and into the lagoon. Freddie cradled his rifle, relaxed and ready. Harry still stood on the bank, covering Bob and Mike. Guffy brought the *Rimshot* alongside the other boat. Freddie stepped across to it from the *Rimshot*.

"Where's the money?" he said to Bob.

"What money you talking about?"

Freddie slowly raised the rifle. The front sight stopped a foot in front of a spot directly between Bob's eyes.

"It's all here," said Bob, "so don't do nothin' fuckin' silly."

FIFTEEN

Sergeant Welsh made the copter pilot fly the search pattern until failing light and the falling levels in the gas tanks dictated they return to Hog Cay. The pilot was delighted. He and Inspector Lowe would now have to stay overnight on the Island, and that meant he'd be climbing between those lovely brown thighs of the girl in Pollack's office. He had to shift in his seat at the thought of it.

Sitting beside the pilot and tiredly looking down at the seemingly endless ocean that threw back at them the reflected glare of the dying sun, the sergeant told himself the search had been a long shot from the outset. The late arrival of the copter from Nassau had turned it into a million-to-one shot that hadn't paid off. Blame Inspector Lowe, blame Nassau, blame the system, but don't blame him—it wasn't his fault he'd failed to find Harry Foster's boat.

He closed his eyes. The whole chain of recent events flashed by in perfect sequence. Harry Foster and his so-called charter. The fuss on the green-and-white boat that Harry had initiated, and that ended in the arrest of those two hoodlums. The bank robbery. The two cardboard cartons of "valuable papers" that were indeed valuable—a million dollars valuable. Harry Foster on Mike Cholski's boat. Harry Foster taking off after Hammersley and Cholski. The drowned man whose body nobody has claimed and no one on the Island had reported missing. The drowned man had to be the second of the two men in Harry Foster's charter. He'd seen the older man, Freddie Makepeace, get on the boat with Harry Foster and Guffy when they gassed up and left in such a hurry, but now he really thought about it, he hadn't seen the second man, the younger one with gold-rimmed spectacles, for a full day before that, even though he'd kept tabs on them. What was the man's name . . . ? They'd told him in the bank, following the robbery. The older man had told him . . . Milton . . . ? No. Morton . . . Morton Sumway. Dear oh dear . . . his memory wasn't what it used to be. Not so long ago he could recall information like this automatically, without effort. Tiredness, maybe. Age, more likely. Anyway, everything pointed to the drowned man being this Morton Sumway. If this was so, Morton Sumway's death hadn't seemed to bother the other two, and there had to be good reason for that.

The sergeant slumped deeper into his seat. God, what a tangled mess it was, but he'd sort it out, he wouldn't stop until he did. It had all happened on his island, in his backyard, and he'd get to the bottom of it and someone would pay. How much of this should he tell Inspector Lowe when he got back? So far he'd simply reported the facts, no speculation, no suspicions of there being anything beyond the bank robbery to cause concern.

Sergeant Welsh debated the issue with himself and decided to tell Inspector Lowe nothing.

Reconciled to, but not pleased by the thought of having to stay the night on Hog Cay, the inspector had taken off his uniform jacket, loosened his tie, removed his red-banded and gold-braided cap, and now leaned on the bar of the Ocean View, democratically allowing the big, bearded Canadian behind the bar to buy him Canadian Clubs with a twist on the rocks. From the way the man talked and behaved he appeared to be the owner of the establishment, and Inspector Lowe made a mental note to check on the immigration status of this Marcus Marchand, the man everyone called the Professor.

Although Marcus Marchand had a built-in aversion to authority in any form, with puffed-up, patronizing bastards like this one across the bar occupying a special place in his loathing, he kept the inspector's glass filled and chatted with him whenever he could spare the time, because the Professor had the distinct feeling the inspector could make trouble for him, and enjoy doing it.

Chief Inspector Percival Lowe relished his rank and the authority it carried. All through his early years he'd resented and envied the insufferable British who governed the Islands and relegated native Bahamians, such as himself, to low-paid, menial subservience. When the Bahamas became self-governing, and native Bahamians—such as Inspector Lowe—took over the responsibility of running the show, they filled their newly acquired roles and functions as figures of authority in heavy-handed and arbitrary fashion. They had learned well from the examples set by their deposed British masters, with the result that it was impossible to imagine a more arrogant, ill-humored, vindictive collection of minor bureaucrats and civil servants. And, like their ex-masters they were, for the most part, lazy and profoundly inefficient.

There were exceptions, Sergeant Welsh being a classic example of a native Bahamian proud of his lineage and passionate in his desire for peace and dignity in his Islands. Tom Welsh bitterly knew that the Out Islands—or Family Islands as they had been redesignated by some public relations man—were shamefully neglected by the Bahamian government and its swollen ranks of functionaries. For Government was centered in prosperous, wheeling-dealing Nassau, and Government was concerned only with matters of self-interest—important issues such as patronage and payoffs and protection of its duly elected or appointed rights to the perks and privileges and numbered bank accounts that automatically went with being Representatives of the People.

To Government, the Out Islands that extended like a string of beads from just off the Florida coast down to the West Indies, were a worrisome nuisance; their requests for money for schools, housing, medical services, roads, and employment opportunities never seemed to stop. So the Government did its best to ignore them. Which explained without justifying the insidious growth of drug-related activity that was rapidly replacing tourism as the Bahamas' principal source of revenue.

This was something which, as Chief Inspector Lowe liked to tell the press, was firmly under control and would be ruthlessly stamped out in the forseeable future. He knew better.

Chief Inspector Lowe pushed his empty glass across the bar to the Professor. "I imagine," said the inspector, "you know these two, this . . . er . . . Hammersley and the other one, quite well?"

"I know them. Terrible pair, awful people."

"And why do you say that?"

"Owed money to everyone on Hog Cay. Hammersley used to beat up his young wife. Disgusting creature, Bob Hammersley. Drunk all the time, mouth like a sewer, and Cholski wasn't much better." He poured the inspector his third shot of Canadian Club.

"Thank you," said the inspector. "And this Harry Foster, you know him?"

The Professor was immediately on guard. "Yes, I know him." He stroked his bushy beard and waited to see where this Lowe character was leading the conversation.

The inspector added a twist of lemon to his Canadian Club. "And what sort of man is he?"

"Oh, basically a good type. Pays his way, minds his own business, well-liked. A quiet man."

"Is that so? A quiet man?" The inspector sounded moderately surprised. "I understood that Foster and this Hammersley person were always fighting. Didn't they have one set-to right here in this bar?"

The Professor tugged at his beard. The inspector had been digging. He'd sensed the wretched man was trouble right from the time he'd come through the door with his uniform jacket off and his shirt unbuttoned, just like one of the regular guys. "Oh . . . that was nothing."

"Hammersley had to go to hospital, didn't he?"

"Bloody nose, that was all. Wouldn't stop bleeding. Nurse Jones up the clinic patched him up in five minutes."

"I see. And what about the fight they had in Hammersley's pool hall? I understand a shotgun was fired and Hammersley was beaten into unconsciousness with a bottle."

"I know nothing about that," said the Professor. He caught a signal from a customer with an empty glass. "Excuse me, inspector, I'll be right back."

The inspector had indeed been digging, and there were questions he wanted to ask Sergeant Welsh when he returned. He'd read the sergeant's reports covering the past few days, and while Welsh couldn't be faulted for what the reports said and the way they were worded, the inspector was an old hand at report writing and recognized a snow job when he saw one. It was what the sergeant had left out of his reports that interested him. That's why he'd been digging and prying and gossiping all afternoon.

From across the water he heard the chop of the helicopter's rotor blades. He already knew from Sergeant Welsh's radio contact that the search had been unsuccessful.

The inspector had left his uniform jacket and cap in the Jeep parked outside the Ocean View. Constable Mathews waited for him, because the inspector refused to drive the vehicle himself. Lowe put on his jacket, pulled up the knot of his tie, settled his cap forward over his eyes, checked the overall effect in the rearview mirror, popped a mint in his mouth, and told Mathews to drive him to meet Sergeant Welsh.

Tired, angry, and frustrated, Sergeant Welsh was not looking forward to a session with the inspector, and felt a lot worse when he saw Lowe sitting in the Jeep, waiting at Pollack's, with Mathews driving like some damned chauffeur. Easy to see the inspector was a Nassau desk man; do him a power of good to be posted to one of the more remote Out Islands for a spell.

"Too bad that was all for nothing," said the inspector. "Lost him, eh?"

Sergeant Welsh counted to ten. "Yes, sir." He climbed into the back of the Jeep and Mathews drove them to the station. The sergeant would have given his eyeteeth to stop for a cold beer or two but he didn't think this was a good time to suggest it. At the station he settled for a quick wash and a mug of instant coffee.

The inspector waited for him by his desk, standing with his back to the room, looking out of the window at late-returning tournament boats as the sergeant walked in with his mug of coffee and sat behind his desk.

"So," the inspector said, "as I predicted, you didn't find them."

"No, we didn't find them," the sergeant wearily repeated.

The inspector turned from the window. "I'm sure you're anxious to call it a day—we all are—but there are some questions raised by this bank robbery and other goings-on that bother me."

"I'll do my best to answer them . . . sir," said the sergeant.

"I'm sure you have an answer for everything. We'll start with those two men in the cell. I've read and reread your reports, and this fellow Foster you've been chasing seems to have got himself involved at every twist and turn. Take that affair on the boat where you arrested the two men you've detained.

Apparently you took action on Foster's information they were carrying weapons, is that not so?"

Impassively, the sergeant said, "That's what happened, sir."

"Hmmm . . . Leaving that for a moment and moving on to the bank robbery," said the inspector, "again we meet Mr. Foster, and it's common knowledge he's had several fights with the Hammersley character who was one of the robbers."

"Everybody fights with Bob Hammersley," said the sergeant.

"Possibly, but not everybody sleeps with his wife," the Inspector murmured.

"I can't say about that, sir."

"Welsh, I do wish you'd stop calling me sir all the time. I told you about it before. I would hate to think you were being subtly offensive . . . you aren't are you, Welsh?"

"No, sir . . . no, Inspector."

"Good. Let's press on. It is also a strange coincidence that Foster should leave two mysterious cardboard cartons in the bank's safe the day before the bank was robbed by Hammersley and that other one with the Russian name . . .

"Cholski . . . I believe it's a Polish name . . . sir."

"Cholski, that's it. And as soon as his boat was repaired, Foster took after them and you made no effort to prevent him leaving, and some long time after that you did search for him, but to no avail."

Sergeant Welsh felt a terrible sense of doom. The inspector was playing back to him all his own troubling thoughts. "Let me repeat my reasoning, sir . . . I mean inspector. Knowing it was impossible to track down the escaped perpetrators of the robbery, who had some five or six hours' start on us, I took a chance in allowing Foster to leave, believing I

196

would be able to follow him and that he would lead me to Hammersley and Cholski."

The inspector walked round the sergeant's desk and sat in the visitor's chair opposite him. He leaned his elbows on the desk. "For an island of this small size, sergeant, and recognizing your past record for keeping things very much under control here, there seem to have been an extraordinary number of unresolved and most peculiar things taking place on Hog Cay in the last few days. The body found by those two boys . . . incredible that on such a small island nobody would miss the man, isn't it?"

The sergeant pressed his thumb and forefinger against his closed eyes. "The conclusion I reached, sir, was that the drowned man was a visitor, here on his own and therefore no one reported him missing."

"Possible," said the inspector. He leaned further across the desk. "And what about the second body? Was that man another visitor, here on his own, with no one to report him missing?"

Sergeant Welsh's feeling of doom grew blacker. "The second body . . . sir?"

Inspector Lowe was enjoying this. "While you were flying around in the helicopter, one of the tournament boats fished it out of the water and brought it in. Young man, been shot through the forehead. Probably a pistol at point-blank range."

The sergeant let this sink in. "Any identification, sir?"

"No. White, late twenties, most likely. Typical tourist from the way he was dressed. But no wallet, no identification. However, he did have over three thousand dollars in his pocket."

"Then he certainly wasn't a typical tourist," the sergeant said resignedly.

"Hardly," said the inspector. "I wonder if we can

consider him another piece of the puzzle you've got yourself saddled with?" He sat back in his chair, smiled. "Anyway, sergeant, I'm off first thing in the morning; got to get back, work's piling up. I'll expect to hear from you very shortly that you've sorted all this out. But between you and me, as long as you just get the bank its money back, I don't think anybody in Nassau is going to get too upset about the rest of it. Of course, I'll be interested to see how you resolve it, but that's between the two of us, isn't it?"

He stood. "Now, sergeant, let me buy you dinner and a couple of rounds of drinks. All goes on my expense account. Then, a good night's sleep. Oh . . . you can put me up for the night, can't you?"

"Be a pleasure, sir," said the sergeant.

They were all squeezed into the cabin of the *Rimshot*. Harry, Freddie, and Guffy in canvas chairs lined up facing Bob and Mike who were sitting on one of the bunks. Freddie had exchanged his rifle for Harry's machine pistol, which he held in his lap, finger resting on the trigger. Two battery-powered lanterns mixed their yellow light with the last red rays of the evening sun that filtered through the trees. A battery-powered fan did little to stir the dead air.

The million dollars and the money and safety-deposit boxes from the bank had been checked and locked away. Mike was uncomfortably aware of the big solitaire diamond ring buttoned in his shirt pocket under a wad of Kleenex.

"So, crack of dawn," said Harry, "you two are going in the other boat. Guffy will drive and Freddie will see you behave yourselves."

Freddie raised the machine pistol and winked at them.

". . . if we have any trouble with you between now

198

and then, we'll leave you here and come back for you . . . if we remember."

"I like that better," said Guffy. "Why don't we do that an' save a lot of messin' around?"

"Hey . . . you can't do that," Mike said in a panic.

"We can do anything we want to," Harry said, "so don't you forget it. I'll follow you in this boat, then back in Hog Cay we'll hand you over and be heroes for catching you and getting the bank's money back."

"Then we can get on with our fishin' trip," said Freddie. "we've lost three days already thanks to you creeps."

"Some fuckin' fishin trip," said Bob. "Who d'ya think you're foolin'? Who takes a million bucks with them on a fishin' trip? I wasn't born yesterday, ya know."

"Maybe not," said Freddie, fondling the machine pistol, "but you can be dead today if you don't watch it."

"Look, I gotta proposition," Bob said. "Make life a lot simpler for everybody. You three fuck off with your money, let me an' Mike have our bit from the bank, they'll never miss it, an' you tell 'em you couldn't find us. Now, that's reasonable, isn't it?"

"I've got a better proposition," said Harry. "We keep everything, take you out a couple of miles in the boat you stole, and sink it, with you two on it. How's that?"

"I like that even better'n jus' leavin' 'em here," said Guffy.

"Me too," Freddie said thoughtfully. "I don't know why we're botherin' to go all the way back with them. We'll be kept hangin' around answerin' a lot of fool questions, and that one," he pointed to Mike, "that yellow-bellied son of a bitch is goin' to shoot his mouth off about us and the money. He'd do anythin' he thought would make them go easier on him."

"No . . . no . . . not me," Mike whined. "I wouldn't do nothin' like that, honest."

Harry stood and stretched. "The only reason we're going to take you back is to keep my record and Guffy's record clean. If you start yapping about a million dollars in cardboard cartons, people are going to think you're out of your skull. Valuable papers I told the bank and the sergeant, valuable papers I said was in them. If anybody wants to check, that's what they'll find in them: valuable papers."

"What kinda valuable papers?" Freddie asked, frowning.

Harry shrugged, grinned, "Whatever I feel like putting in the cartons. Could be old newspapers, who's to say they aren't valuable to me?"

"I tell you one thing," said Bob. "This heat's bleedin' diabolical. At least you could open some cold beers."

They left the lagoon in the pink false light of predawn, with Guffy at the wheel of the *Glastron* as the lead boat. Bob and Mike sat with their backs to the transom, each with his thumbs tied behind his back with hundred-pound-test braided nylon fishing line. Freddie contentedly watched them from the fighting chair, the machine pistol across his knees. He'd fallen in love with the deadly little gun, so Harry had made him a present of it. During the night Bob and Mike had given them no trouble: Mike had sat quietly, reflecting that life had been very unfair to a man who had never done any real harm to anybody and who only wanted to sail big, beautiful boats. Bob, philosophically chalking up the whole thing as yet another load of the crap that always got dumped on him, wondered how long a stretch they'd get and how he could shift the blame onto Mike.

Harry tailed Guffy in the *Rimshot*, off to one side and clear of his wake. Hundreds of gulls escorted the two boats for a while, flying low, swooping down on them, raucous and bad-tempered, but in twos and threes they peeled off and flew back to the familiar sanctuary of their island. Harry liked having the *Rimshot* to himself and relaxed at the wheel. It was a faultless morning, the boat's engines sounding good as they effortlessly sliced off the miles.

He felt at peace, he felt satisfied, complete. Then his unconscious conjured up images of Sally. Sally lying naked on the beach, her arms upstretched to him. Sally with her battered and bruised unlined little-girl face. Sally defending Bob because her young pride demanded she stick with the man she had married. Harry caught sight of his own face reflected in the mirror above the console, and he looked curiously at his reflection as if he hadn't seen himself for a long time. He saw the tanned, forty-year-old skin that had thickened and coarsened and the deep lines that ran from his nose to join the corners of a mouth that seldom seemed to smile any more. And his eyes . . . he blinked rapidly . . . he didn't know the eyes at all. Women used to fall in love with his eyes, tell him they were fascinating . . . cold, but fascinating. The pale blue eyes he saw reflected in the mirror were fatigued. The lids drooped, the right one more than the left. The once clear bright whites now shot with tiny burst blood vessels or whatever it was caused those red lines. And the deep crowsfeet. . . . He opened his eyes as wide as he could, and the crows feet went, leaving in their place white tracks of skin that hadn't seen the sun.

Harry looked over his shoulder, as if to see if anyone was watching, then shook his head in embarrassment. He'd read that forty-year-old men can go through menopause, like women. In fact, he'd seen it happen to other men and had been impatient, intolerant, full of good advice. Had told them to snap out of it, buy a new boat, find a good two-hundred-dollar hooker, have an affair, get a new job, move to a new town. Was it happening to him? Was he into a change of life? What to do? Try the geographic cure he preached to others? Sell the motel? Sell the *Rimshot*, get himself a bigger boat and take off to somewhere far, far away? Take off for the Pacific, for the Marquesas, or Papeete, or Bora Bora or Pago Pago, names from boyhood books of South Sea island adventure, islands with dusky maidens in grass skirts. He automatically positioned the places in the charts of his mind, working out routes and distances and fuel consumption in programmed reflexes.

Harry the loner. Why was it his daydreams spirited him away to remote places where no one knew him? To be a free agent, answerable to none? Even when he'd asked Sally to leave Hog Cay and come away with him he'd instinctively rejected marriage, home, and permanence. It hadn't always been this way, but it sure as hell was that way now. Why?

"I don't know," he said aloud. "I don't know."

When they were half an hour out of Hog Cay, Harry radioed ahead and, after a lot of hassle, made contact with Sergeant Welsh. The sergeant told him to make for Avery Wilke's old dock halfway up the Island. Nobody had used it in years, but it was still serviceable, and if they pulled in there their arrival could be kept quiet. The sergeant got off the air fast; no questions, no hows, whys, whens, and wheres. Those would come later.

* * *

A Bad Day in the Bahamas

So, when the two boats pulled in at Avery Wilkes' rotting dock, only Sergeant Welsh was there to meet them. He handcuffed Bob and Mike together in the back of the Jeep and took from Harry the bank's money and the contents of the safety-deposit boxes, but didn't mention the two cardboard cartons of valuable papers. The sergeant told Harry and Guffy to report to the station immediately after they had taken care of the boats, and drove off with his prisoners.

Harry and Guffy took the two boats to Christopher's dock. Mr. Martell was glad to get his boat back although he complained about the missing Remy Martin and Chivas Regal.

Sergeant Welsh escorted the handcuffed prisoners into the single cell, which was now empty, Nassau having collected the two previous occupants. "Take the cuffs off them," he said to Constable Mathews, and then to Bob and Mike, "Empty your pockets, on the bunk." They did, and the sergeant looked at the pile of crumpled small bills, loose change, a dirty handkerchief, half a pack of the Dunhill Special cigarettes that Mr. Martell always smoked, a sweat-stained and worn leather wallet of Mike's that held a tattered address book, a few business cards, and two condoms. He pushed the things around with the tip of a pencil. "Is that all?"

The two nodded. The sergeant patted them down, prodded Mike's shirt pocket. "What's in there?"

"Just Kleenex," said Mike.

"Take it out."

Mike dropped the wadded Kleenex on top of the other stuff. The sergeant hooked his finger into Mike's pocket and came up with the diamond ring.

"You lousy fuckin' chiseler," said Bob.

The sergeant held the ring up to the light, then dangled it on his pencil in front of Mike's nose.

203

"Where did you get this?"

"I've had it for years," said Mike. "My grandmother left it to me in her will."

"Bleedin' liar," said Bob. "I know where you got it. It was in one of them safety deposit boxes we took from the bank. What a bloody lousy thing to do to a mate." He took a roundhouse swing at Mike. The sergeant blocked the punch.

"That's enough," said the sergeant. "I'll put the cuffs back on you if I have any more of that. Lock 'em up," he said to Mathews, who swung shut the heavy old iron-barred door and locked it with the giant iron key that hung from an iron ring the size of a saucer. Bob watched the ritual. Get his hands on a fork or a teaspoon he could have that open before you could say Jack Robinson. "You goin' to ask that sod Harry Foster about his boxes of bleedin' valuable papers?" he called through the bars. Sergeant Welsh walked away without answering or looking at him.

"A million bloody dollars, that's what in them boxes." Bob shouted after him. "Ask him where he got that."

The sergeant stopped, turned, walked slowly and deliberately back to the cell. "You, Cholski, did you see what was in those cartons?"

Mike shot a glance at Bob. "Yes, we opened them, I saw what was in them."

"And what was in them . . . ?" asked the sergeant.

Mike smiled vindictively at Bob. "Oh . . . just a bunch of papers. Didn't look like they was worth anything to me."

"You silly fucker," said Bob. "What a shit you are, mate."

The sergeant pointed at Bob. "Do you still say there was a million dollars in them? Seems a pretty far-fetched story. Well, do you?"

Bob weighed the chance of being believed. "No," he said surlily, "I just made it up."

The sergeant left them. At his desk he put through a call to Nassau and reported to Inspector Lowe the capture of Hammersley and Cholski.

"Good work," said the inspector. "Did you recover the money?"

"Yes, every penny the bank reported as stolen."

"The bank will be pleased to hear that. I'll let them know immediately. This will look good on your sheet, Sergeant. Write up your report and let me have it, soonest."

"I can't take the credit, sir, it was Foster who brought them in."

"Was it, now? Well, that's not important in the scheme of things. You've got them and the money, and that's all that really matters. Don't complicate things more than you have to. Far as Nassau's concerned, you're the one who planned the search and capture. Letting Foster help you was a clever move. Well-thought-out operation, glad I could be there to help you pull it off. I'll pop up and see the superintendent, make sure he hears the story from the horse's mouth. The super's a director of the bank, this'll make him happy. Wheels within wheels, Sergeant. Make sure you send your report for my eyes only. Want to add my comments to it. Polish it up a bit, if you know what I mean. Got to go now, Sergeant. Once again, congratulations." He signed off, broke the radio connection.

Sergeant Welsh switched off at his end. Crafty old bugger, by the time he was through with the report it wouldn't have much resemblance to the original. Add his comments, polish it up . . . sure. By the time Chief Inspector Lowe had worked over the report, it was unlikely that Sergeant Welsh, Hog Cay Detachment, would get more than a passing mention.

Harry and Guffy came into the station. Harry looked at Welsh's tired, resigned face. He looks old, Harry thought. He looks the way I feel. The starch has gone out of him. Something's happened to make him look like that. Wonder what?

The Sergeant lifted a hand in greeting.

"You wanted to see us," said Harry.

"Yes . . . I do." Welsh wearily opened his report pad, hunted through his desk drawer for a pen. "Sit down," he said. "Tell me what happened."

Harry started at the point where he'd found Mike Cholski's old log on the *Moonglow*. The Sergeant nodded absently, made a few notes. Harry bypassed the part about the young man with the gun who'd jumped them on the *Rimshot* and whom Freddie had shot, and moved on to locating the lagoon on the island that was part of the Berrys. The Sergeant laid down his pen, looked out through his window at the expensive sport fishing boats and luxury yachts.

"So I swam ashore . . ." said Harry.

The Sergeant stood, closed his report pad. "Let's go and have a drink," he said. "Let's go to the Ocean View and have a drink or two and maybe a piece of their fish. What d'ya say to that idea, eh? I've seen enough of this bloody place for one day."

"I like the idea," said Harry.

They went to the Ocean View, sat at a table at the back, and the Professor brought them drinks. The sergeant slowly tipped soda water into his whiskey, absently stirred the ice cubes with a swizzle stick, took a small sip of the drink, put the glass down on the table.

"You know," said the sergeant. "I'd like to make inspector before I retire. Not chief inspector or anything grand like that, just an ordinary run of the mill inspector. I need the pension that goes with being an inspector, I don't particularly want the job." He took another small sip of his drink, put the glass down. After a long pause, he said, "I need the pension so that when I retire I can go back to the island where I was born, build a cottage by the ocean, be with my people, live a decent life, and never once think about what goes on more than a mile from my backyard. I won't read a newspaper, listen to the radio, and I never want to hear a word about drug smuggling, people shooting each other, people robbing each other, or about crime in any shape or form . . ."

Another tiny sip of his drink, barely tasting it.

". . . and to make Inspector means I've got to get the promotion, and all promotions come from Nassau. And I know that to get the promotion I've got to be a good boy, not upset anybody, mind my *p*'s and *q*'s, play the game, go by the rules, do as I'm told . . ."

Another long pause.

"So I've got to make a decision, haven't I?" The sergeant spoke out loud, neither wanting nor expecting a reply from the other two at the table, but weighing the consequences of the two courses of action he could follow. "Do I write up a report that's a lie but makes me, the department, and above all, the top brass come out smelling like roses, or do I tell it the way it really happened, officially record the fuckup it actually was? My decision. No one can make it for me, can they?"

He again picked up his glass, held it in front of him, looked long and hard at it, concentrating his attention on it. Abruptly, he tilted the glass to his lips and emptied it in one long swallow. He banged the empty glass down hard on the table, grinned at Harry and Guffy as if a great weight had been lifted from him and he hadn't a care in the world.

"I've just made that decision," he said, and the old strength was back in his voice, the old fire in his eyes. "Screw 'em. Screw the whole damn politicking bunch of 'em. They're going to get the truth, the plain, unvarnished truth. Screw the mealymouthed bastards. Now let's have another round of drinks. My treat."

The drinks came. The three men clinked their glasses together in a mutual toast.

"Long life," said Guffy.

"And everything we want from it," said Harry.

"Damnation to the enemy," said Sergeant Welsh. They drank. The sergeant raised his glass to Harry and Guffy. "That was a smart bit of work you did. Those two would have got away, otherwise. However much it pains me, I've got to hand it to you."

Harry and Guffy modestly accepted the sergeant's qualified praise.

"Was nothin'," said Guffy.

"Luck, really," said Harry, "but we got them, that's the main thing. Pity Freddie isn't here with us right now. I propose a toast to Freddie Makepeace."

Again they clinked glasses.

"Freddie Makepeace," they chorused. They drank. The sergeant set his glass down with slow deliberation. "Which brings me to my next point," he said, eyes on Harry. "Brings us full circle, as it were. What I said to you that night we had our heart-to-heart chat still stands. I want you and Mr. Freddie Makepeace off my island within twenty-four hours. Before sundown tomorrow. Understand?"

Harry digested this. "You're a hard man, Sergeant."

The sergeant smiled. "Keep that thought at all times, Mr. Foster."

SIXTEEN

Sally heard that Bob was back on Hog Cay from one of her regular customers. The news caught her at a time when she was feeling pleasantly untroubled. The lunch trade had been brisk. In fact, business was getting better every day. She'd had the plywood taken down and the shattered window repaired, had experimented with making a kettle of conch chowder which proved popular with her customers, and Captain Scott had filtered down word to her that as long as Bob wasn't around she could stay on in the pool hall with only a small increase in rent.

And now, Bob was back. In jail, to be sure, but he was back. She'd prayed that he would never be back. She had also prayed that he wouldn't get caught and be sent to prison, but in most of her prayers she'd asked that she'd never see Bob Hammersley again. But he was back, and again he was a problem. He was her husband and she'd have to stand at his side, help him if she could, let him know that he could depend on her for support. She was his wife, and that's the way things were supposed to be between man and wife.

She told her customers she was closing the bar for the day, went into the horrible bedroom, brushed her hair, put on fresh lipstick and a touch of eyeshadow. Back in the bar she emptied the cash register and put the money in her jeans pocket. There were still a number of people at the bar; she knew them all.

"I've got to go out for a while," she told them. "That's why I'm putting up the Closed sign. Keep tabs on what you drink and you can settle up with me later."

Sally walked into the police station stiff-backed and determined. She practiced smiling.

Sergeant Welsh pointed in the direction of the cell. "He's in there."

In the cell, Bob and Mike sat elaborately ignoring each other. Sally stood close to the bars. Bob looked up.

"Bob, I know what you did was wrong," Sally said, almost as a recitation, "but from what I hear, they've got all the money back so things shouldn't go too bad for you. And don't worry. I'm going to get a lawyer from Nassau to help you. I'm your wife, Bob, and I'll do everything I can to help you."

Bob looked down at the floor, then up at Sally.

"If you really want to help," he said, "why don't you fuck off and leave me alone."

On the street, Harry waited for Sally to come out of the police station. He'd seen her go in and assumed she'd gone there to see Bob. The girl just never gave up. Why he waited, he wasn't sure, but he waited just the same. She came out, crying. Harry went to her. Teary eyed, she shook her head and walked away. He fell in beside her, saying nothing, stayed with her all the way to the pool hall. She didn't once look at him, as head down, dejected, she trudged along, thinking only she knew what. At the pool-hall door, she stopped, faced him.

"They'll send Bob to prison, won't they?"

"Yes."

"How long for?"

"Depends on the bank and the judge. Could be anywhere from six months to ten years. My guess is three."

"Three years?" She thought on this, then said, "I'd be twenty-three when he got out—if I hung around and waited for him, that is. What should I do, Harry?"

"Come with me. Don't even go through that door. Come with me. There's nothing here for you any more."

"Three years isn't long to wait," Sally said. She brushed her hand across her eyes. She had stopped crying. "I've got a business, it can make me the money I need, and I can save up. I can put something aside every week. I've made nearly a hundred-and-fifty-dollars profit these last two days. That's the best we've ever done."

"That's very good," Harry said, "but the tournament doesn't go on all year round, don't forget that. Don't knock yourself out trying to make something of this ratty place. Don't waste your time, don't waste your life. You want a business to run? I told you I'd set you up in something, didn't I? The offer still holds."

That did it. Sally folded her arms, stood with her back against the pool-hall door, outraged. "Ratty place, is it? Wasting my time, am I? Well thank you, Harry Foster. The hell with you, Harry Foster. I don't need you to tell me what I should do. I don't need anybody to tell me what to do. I'll run my own life, thank you very much indeed!" She spun round, pushed open the poolroom door, and ran inside.

Harry didn't follow her. He'd meant well, he told himself. He'd been trying to help her, he told himself. Yes, and you really blew it, didn't you, he told himself.

Cursing himself for an idiot, for once again laying himself wide open for Sally to once again make it clear that her life, now and in the future, did not include him, he walked back to the bungalow at the Fish and Game Club. Freddie was there, lying on the bed, shoes off, reading the *Miami Herald*.

"Hey, I found a store here gets the *Herald*," he said happily. "Jus' readin' up on all the local gossip, seein' what everybody's bin up to while I was away."

"I want to get going," said Harry. "If we get organized, we can get out of here in an hour and make Chub Cay before dark. We've got to get that money to Haiti, remember? And we're three days behind schedule, so let's roll."

Reluctantly, Freddie folded up his newspaper, swung his feet to the floor. "Okay, but I got to have a shower an' change my clothes. I stink." He stood, unbuttoned his shirt, and peeled it off. He had the hard-muscled body of an old-time miner. "Be five minutes," he said, making for the bathroom.

There was a knock on the bungalow's screen door. Through the mesh of the screen Harry could see Chester, the Club's handyman. Chester had a piece of notepaper in his hand. Harry opened the door, Chester gave him the piece of paper.

"Message for you, Mr. Foster. Gentleman from Miami called, said it was important."

"Thanks, Chester." Harry gave him a dollar. The message was short and to the point. "Important you phone me at home. Immediately. I will wait. Most urgent. John Chambers." A Miami telephone number was given.

Harry carried the piece of paper back into the bungalow, reading the terse message again. "Freddie . . ." he called. "Message from John Chambers."

Freddie came out of the bathroom, a towel wrapped around his waist. "What's it say?"

"He wants me to call him at home. Urgent, he says."

Freddie took the piece of paper from Harry and read the message for himself, as if to confirm what it actually said.

"I'll go up to the Club and call him right now," said Harry.

"Wait for me," said Freddie, "I'd like a word with him."

From the Club's office, Harry placed the call. He waited out the crackles, empty silences, whirrings, and clickings, and eventually, Chambers' phone rang.

Thin and faint, a man's voice said, "Hullo?"

"Is Mr. John Chambers there?" Harry shouted.

"Who wants to talk to him?"

"Harry Foster. I'm returning his call."

"Just a minute."

A long wait, then Chambers came on the 'phone. "Is that you, Harry?" said Chambers.

"Yes," said Harry, registering that Chambers had never called him Harry before . . . always Mr. Foster.

"This is important, Harry. I've been trying to reach you. I called Andros, but they told me you hadn't arrived yet. They said you'd contacted them to say you'd been delayed, so I tried Hog Cay again. Glad I got you. Listen carefully, Harry. I want you to cancel our arrangements. Do not deliver the merchandise, is that clear, Harry? Do not deliver it, I've had to revise my plans."

Harry covered up the mouthpiece, turned to Freddie. "Something funny going on here." He took his hand away, and said, "I understand, Mr. Chambers. What am I to do with the merchandise, return it to you?"

"No, Harry. Do nothing. I want you to hand it over to two of my representatives. They will arrive on Hog Cay around 10 A.M. tomorrow. They will sign for it, and you will no longer be responsible for it. Is that understood, Harry?"

"Understood, Mr. Chambers, but we've got a problem this end. I'd like to suggest a change in that arrangement."

"A change, Harry? Hold on a moment."

Silence at Chambers' end for some ten seconds. He came back on the line. "A change, Harry? What sort of change?"

"We shouldn't transfer the merchandise on Hog Cay," Harry said. "There's a lot going on here. A bank robbery, some big fuss over a shipload of drugs that went aground. There's cops crawling all over the place. Everybody who comes in and out is being searched and checked. Boats, too. All boats are being stopped and searched. You can't move here for cops and customs men. That's why I've stored the merchandise at another location."

Freddie was looking at Harry as if he'd gone out of his mind. Harry pantomimed that he'd explain later. After another and longer silence, Chambers said, "That sounds like a sensible move, Harry. Exactly where is this new location?"

"Er . . . is it safe to tell you over the phone, Mr. Chambers?" Harry was playing for time.

"Yes, it's safe. Tell me the location. I must know the new location." There was now a thread of tension in Chambers' voice.

"Very well. It's Bright's Cay. Three miles due south of here. A very small island, very safe, no one lives on it. No one ever visits it."

"How do you spell that?" Chambers asked.

Harry spelled it out, then added, "Three miles due south, did you get that, Mr. Chambers?"

Another pause, then Chambers said. "Yes, I got that, Harry. Ten A.M. tomorrow, my representatives will meet you at Bright's Cay. Thank you, Harry. Would you pass on a message to Freddie for me? I don't need to speak to him, just tell him Pat Shields sends his regards and hopes to see him soon. Will you do that, Harry?"

"I'll tell him. Is that everything, Mr. Chambers?"

"That's everything. Good-bye, Harry."

In Miami, John Chambers hung up his phone.

"You did that nicely," said the man who was standing close by Chambers, a silenced pistol pressed against Chambers' head. "Didn't he do that nicely, Sol?"

"Very nicely," Sol said.

"Yes, very nicely indeed," said the first man, and shot John Chambers.

"What the hell was that all about?" Freddie asked as Harry hung up.

"Something's screwed up, Freddie. Something's gone very wrong."

"With Mr. Chambers . . . ?"

"I think so. In fact, I'm sure it has."

"What did he say?"

"He said he wants us to turn the money over to two of his representatives. Tomorrow." Harry looked around the club office. "Let's go back to the bungalow."

They talked as they walked. "I don't get it," said Freddie. "What representatives? Did he tell you their names?"

"No. Just said they be here at ten tomorrow."

Freddie shook his head in bewilderment. "Mr. Chambers doesn't have any representatives, he doesn't work that way."

"Another thing," said Harry. "He called me Harry at least ten times. He's never called me Harry, always Mr. Foster."

"Did he?" said Freddie. "That's not like him. Mr. Chambers ain't big on usin' first names. And what was all that malarkey you was giving him about the place crawlin' with cops an' shiploads of dope goin' aground?"

"I'll tell you in a minute," said Harry. "The big thing that made me think something strange is going on is that he told me he'd called Andros and they told him I'd been in contact with them because we'd been delayed. Now that's crazy, I haven't been in contact with the Andros operator about anything."

"I don't like this," Freddie said. "I don't like the sound of this at all."

"Oh . . . and he gave me a message to pass on to you. He said Pat Shields sends his regards and hopes to see you soon. Who's Pat Shields?"

"Pat Shields," Freddie said, "has bin' dead ten years . . . God rest his soul. Pat Shields was my best buddy, an' Mr. Chambers knows that. That's a tip-off. That's Mr. Chambers' way of lettin' me know everything ain't kosher. I smell a setup. I hear Mr. Chambers loud 'n clear tellin' us to watch our asses."

"Me too," said Harry. "That's why I pulled that Bright's Cay switch. On Bright's Cay we've got a chance to get a good look at these two representatives before they see us. We've got the chance to watch our asses."

They reached the bungalow, went in.

"You couldn't tell if there was anyone else there with Mr. Chambers, could you?" Freddie asked.

"If he'd been on his own, why would he go through that routine?"

"That was dumb," said Freddie. "Forget I asked."

Harry filled the coffeepot, put it on to perk. "Somebody's very anxious we don't deliver this money to Haiti."

"Yeah," said Freddie, "that's for damn sure."

"First on Al Parson's dock, then here on Hog Cay, and now this call telling us to forget it. I guess we don't go to Haiti."

"I guess," Freddie said absently. He sat on the bed, head down, arms dangling between his knees, lost in his worrying thoughts.

"On the phone," Harry said, "someone was putting the screws to John Chambers, telling him what to say."

"Right," said Freddie.

"Who?"

Freddie shrugged, didn't answer.

"You know more about this whole business than you let on, don't you, Freddie?"

"Maybe."

"Then answer me some questions. One, who is it we were supposed to deliver the money to in Haiti? Chambers wouldn't tell me. Said someone would let me know when I needed to know. Was that someone you?"

"Yeah," said Freddie. "It was me."

Harry turned down the flame under the coffeepot which had just started to perk. "So tell me."

Freddie stayed, sitting on the bed, head down, arms between his knees for a full minute, then said, "It was Mr. Chambers."

"Mr. Chambers . . . ? said Harry. "He was going to be in Haiti? We were taking the money to John Chambers . . . ?"

"There's a lot you don't know," said Freddie.

"That's the understatement of the year. Are you going to tell me all the things I don't know, like what's going on? Just what it is I've got myself into? Like when this stopped being a fishing charter for covering up a little harmless money smuggling, and that was all? Do I really know who and what John Chambers is? Do I?"

"No, you don't," said Freddie. "If you hadda known, you'd never have taken on the job. That's why you was picked, because you didn't know nothin' about nothin'. That's why Mr. Chambers could trust you."

"The innocent babe," said Harry. "The innocent sucker is more like it."

"No, we figgered you for a straight-up guy who wouldn't try an' pull any stunts on us. We liked the look of you, so we hired you."

"We . . . we . . ." said Harry. "Suddenly it's 'we.' We is you and John Chambers, is it?"

Freddie stood, went over to the stove, poured himself a cup of coffee. "You gotta remember I've been with Mr. Chambers over twenny years. I was closer'n family to him. I looked after him—for over twenny years I looked after him. Never let him down, not once in over twenny years."

Harry was losing patience. "Look, let's start at square one. Who and what is John Chambers?"

"That's not his real name," said Freddie. "Don't make no difference to you what his real name was, but it wasn't John Chambers."

"Was . . . ?"

Freddie came back with his coffee. "Yeah . . . was. I figger Mr. Chambers is dead by now. That's why I'm tellin' you all this."

Harry accepted this pronouncement of Freddie's without comment. So many bizarre and improbable events, people and revelations had been thrown at him in the last few days, he was rapidly becoming shockproof.

"An' export import wasn't Mr. Chambers' real business, it was gamblin'," Freddie said.

"John Chambers was a gambler?" Harry said incredulously. "A professional gambler . . . like Nick the Greek?"

Freddie looked pityingly at him. "No . . . Mr. Chambers wasn't a gambler, he ran gamblin', he controlled most a the gamblin' in South Florida. You know . . . jai alai, football, horses, dogs, slots, wheels, lotteries—you name it. If it was gamblin', Mr. Chambers got his cut off the top. He was Big Man in gamblin', too big for some people's tastes. They wanted to cut him down to size. Some of the new trash that's movin' in to Florida, was tryin' to get rid of him and take over, get the picture . . . ?"

Harry nodded. He got the picture.

"But Mr. Chambers wasn't the sort of man you push around," Freddie went on. He didn't stay Big Man all those years by runnin' scared . . ." Freddie chuckled. "Perfec' gentleman he was till you crossed him, an' if you did, God help you."

The chuckle faded. Freddie's big, ugly face drooped. "He wasn't getting no younger, though. Day came when he made up his mind he'd had enough, time to pull out an' take things easy. But he couldn't jus' retire like your average businessman, he had too many enemies, too many people who figured they had a score to settle with him. Mr. Chambers was a marked man, an' he knew it."

Harry took up the story. "So he decided to disappear from Florida, reappear in Haiti, and have me deliver him a million dollars to take care of his old age, right?"

"That's about the size of it," said Freddie. "'Course, he wasn't plannin' on stayin' in Haiti, but where he was goin' after that, he didn't even tell me."

Harry got a can of beer from the refrigerator. "It all makes sense in a weird kind of way. Get Chambers out of the way and grab his million dollars. Everything wrapped up nice and neat. No loose ends."

"That's about it," said Freddie.

"With me the patsy in the middle," said Harry.

"That's the way it's turned out," Freddie agreed. "But not just you. Me an' poor little Morton got the short end of the stick, too, if you think about it."

"And someone's known every move we made, ever since we started out."

"Rose Cellini," said Freddie. "You first put that thought in my mind, an' you called it right. It's gotta be Rose Cellini. I'll take care of Mrs. Rose Cellini if it's the last thing I ever do."

"Well, Freddie," Harry said. "Now I know the full story and where I fit into it, let me tell you what I'm going to do. I'm quitting. I want out. I'm through. I'm going back to running a motel. A dull life, but a safe one. First thing in the morning. You can worry about these two representatives who're coming for the money at ten. I'll be long gone by then."

"Can't say I'd blame you," Freddie said sadly. "You take off an' leave me here by m'self, me an' the

million bucks. You go on home, an' don' give me
another thought. You go back to your motel an' sleep
easy. Don' you worry you head about them two
tomorrow going to Bright's Cay, realizin' they been
given a bum steer, then comin' back here lookin' for
us, findin' me here all on my lonesome, a sittin' duck,
a lamb ready for the slaughter. Don' you give it a
second thought."

Harry pitched his empty beer can into the waste-
basket. "Good try, Freddie, but it won't work. You
don't have to wait around. You can come with me. Let
them have the money. If John Chambers is dead, he
sure doesn't need it, and if he doesn't need it, your
responsibilities are over. What's it to you any more?
Pull out with me, that way you'll live to sleep easy,
like me."

"Can't do that," said Freddie. "I don't know for
absolute sure Mr. Chambers is dead, an' if there's one
chance he ain't dead, then he's still relyin' on me.
Over twenny years he's relied on me an' I never let
him down, an' I ain't goin' to now. Till I know for
sure, me an' that money don' get separated as long as
I got a breath left in my body. You go. I stay."

"You play dirty, Freddie," said Harry. "You play a
real lowdown, dirty game. You're banking on me
having some kind of conscience, aren't you?"

Freddie smiled innocently. "It's up to you, Harry.
It's your decision."

Guffy came through the bungalow door carrying a
platter covered with a white cloth. "Hi, you guys.
Lucy cooked up a whole lotta barbecued ribs, so I
thought I'd bring some down for you."

"Great," said Freddie. "Nothin' I like better'n a
barbecued rib." He lifted the cloth, took a rib,
stripped the meat from the bone with his square,
strong, yellowed teeth.

"What time you shovin' off tomorrow?" Guffy asked. "Goin' early on the first tide?" He shook his head sadly. "The sergeant really laid it on the line, dinn't he? Funny man to understand, the sergeant. There he was, buyin' us drinks, everybody toastin' everybody else's good health an' so on, an practickly in the same breath he tells you to get off the Island. Don' follow the man's reasonin' some times."

"I do," said Harry. "It's pride. Afraid to show weakness, got to keep proving he's a hard man."

"He sure is a prideful man," Guffy said. Again the sorrowful shake of his head. "I guess tomorrow we say good-bye, for a while, anyways. Gonna be quiet on Hog Cay without you."

"Before we say good-bye," Harry said, "we've got one more thing left to do before we go back. In the morning, how'd you like to take a run over to Bright's Cay with us?"

"Bright's Cay . . . ?" Suspicion flickered across Guffy's broad, black face. "What you goin' to Bright's Cay for? Ain't nothin' on Bright's Cay . . . is there?"

Casually Harry said, "Oh, we've got a date to meet a couple of people there. Freddie wants to see them, don't you, Freddie?"

"That I do," Freddie said. "That I certainly do." He destroyed another rib.

"And I'm going with Freddie to keep him company. We need you to drive the boat for us." Harry took a rib. "Last time we'll be together. How's about it, old friend?"

Eyes narrowed, Guffy looked from one to the other. "I got the distinc' feelin' there's more to this than a nice little boat ride to Bright's Cay. What say you tell ole Guffy the rest a the story?"

So Harry told him.

Guffy listened, then said, "An' you is proposin' to

get there ahead a them an' set up a kinda reception committee for these two gents, would that be it?"

"That would be it," said Freddie.

"An all you want me to do is drive the boat? Not get mixed up in nothin'? Jus' stand 'n watch?"

"Right," said Harry. "Nothing more than that."

"I dunno," Guffy said. "I tole meself a while back I dinn't want no more part a this, said you'd have to find yourself a new mate. An' what happens . . . ? I ends up on that junket clear across to the Berry's chasin' after them two loonies."

"Sure, sure," said Harry. "And as a result, you're a local celebrity. One of the brave capturers of two notorious bank robbers, two escaped criminals."

"Bullshit," said Guffy. "Mosta the folks I know was hopin' they'd get away with it."

"Won't be like that this trip," said Harry. "Bright's Cay's only three miles from here. Quick trip over and back, and that's the end of it all."

"I dunno . . ." Guffy again said. "The sergeant saw me comin' over here with these ribs an' pulled up in that Jeep a his an' gave me another lecture on keepin' my nose clean."

"The sergeant won't know," said Harry. "Quick trip over and back, like I said. Will you do it?"

"Lemme think about it," said Guffy. "If I was to come, all I'd do is drive the boat . . . nothin' more. Not that I'm sayin' I will, mind."

Full of bristling pride and independence, certain she didn't need Harry's or anyone else's help or advice, Sally marched through the pool hall, efficiently tallied the tabs for the drinks the boys had poured themselves while she was down at the police station, collected the money from them, parried questions about Bob and his probable fate, served drinks, welcomed the steady trickle of customers arriving for an early kickoff to the evening's drinking, then went into her bedroom, sat on the edge of the bed, and burst into tears.

Awash in self-pity, she ran through the litany of her miseries.

"I hate this place," she bawled. "I hate Hog Cay. I hate Bob. I hate Harry Foster . . . and I hate myself." She fell back on the bed and curled herself into a sobbing question mark, pounded her fists into the mattress. "Why should I try? Why should I work my fingers to the bone? Who cares?" No answers came. "I'm twenty years old, I'm attractive, I've got my whole life in front of me. Why am I doing this? Why am I here?" Still no answers came. She stopped crying, sat up, swung her legs to the floor. "Screw everybody," she yelled. "Screw the whole rotten bunch of you. Screw Hog Cay."

That got things back on track. Sally sniffed a few times, wiped her nose, dried her eyes, and felt a lot better. As she brushed her hair she looked at herself in the mildewed mirror. "All right, that's enough of this nonsense. Let's do this thing in style."

With a determined smile fixed firmly in place, she marched back into the pool room, picked up a tin beer tray and a metal bar spoon and went around to the front of the bar.

"Excuse me," she said to Boxer Waring, who was sitting on one of the barstools peaceably enjoying his vodka and milk, "Can I borrow your stool?"

Boxer, who wasn't very quick on the uptake—he'd once been middleweight champion of the Bahamas but had been hit a lot since those days—blinked at Sally, then got off his stool. "Oh, sure you can, Sally. Here, have my stool."

Using Boxer's shoulder to boost herself up, Sally

stood on the stool and banged the metal spoon against the tin tray. "Listen to me," she shouted, "all of you listen to me," and banged the tray harder, holding it above her head for greater effect. The talk and laughter trickled to a stop. Someone pulled the plug on the jukebox and now Sally had quiet. The two-dozen drinkers at the bar end of the hall crowded round her, the pool players made their shots, then stood with their cues at attention by their sides.

"Thank you," said Sally. "I want to make an announcement. What I want to tell you is that we're going to have a party . . ."

"Right on," called out a few of the drinkers. Others waited for the catch.

". . . and the party's on me . . ." Sally yelled. "It starts right now and it goes on until it's finished, and we're going to have the best party Hog Cay's ever had."

All doubts removed, the pool hall exploded. Whoops, hollers, whistles, and cheers accompanied Sally as Boxer Waring lifted her onto his shoulders and carried her around the room.

And the party started.

Sally lined up her entire stock of liquor from one end of the bar to the other. Willing hands helped her drag out every case of beer she'd stockpiled. She emptied the cash register, added her fifty-dollar reserve to the pile of bills, and gave the money to Boxer Waring.

"Go down to the liquor store and get more booze, Boxer. I've got a feeling we're going to need it." She folded his massive, broken-knuckled hand over the money and kissed his gentle, battered face. "Come straight back, Boxer, won't you?" Sally stuck an open bottle of beer into his free hand. "Here, you might get thirsty on the way." The liquor store was three hundred yards down the road.

Kevin Scott, who operated the liquor store for his father, the Captain, listened to Boxer's story, made sense of it, and loaded a porter's dolly with liquor. He added, at no extra charge, a case of sweet, pink, champagne-type wine he couldn't sell at any price.

Word spread. Friends told friends. Tourists and visitors heard about the party and had the best time they'd had in the Bahamas. From the competition boats the captains and owners arrived—most of them had never before set foot in the pool hall. Big Daddy Brannigan, in good spirits because he'd got himself a two-hundred-and-thirty-pound marlin that day and led the field, was celebrating and ready for a party. Big Daddy sent his mate down to the liquor store with a fistful of money in case the party ran short at some time in the future.

Jumbo and his Island Trio, on their way to play at the Ocean View, heard the commotion, looked in through the pool-hall door, came in for one free drink, and stayed. The six-stool bar couldn't cope with the traffic so a second bar was set up on one of the pool tables.

And the party got into its stride.

Harry heard about it and wondered what was on Sally's mind. But he didn't go, and Freddie and Guffy didn't go, although Guffy was sorely tempted.

Just about everyone else on the Island showed up. The pink champagne-type wine donated by Scott's Wines and Spirits proved undrinkable, but Sally emptied the bottles into a zinc washtub, added vodka, rum, and creme-de-menthe and made a punch that some of the ladies declared delicious . . . for the ladies from the boats came to the party. Normally, the pool hall was not the sort of place they'd be caught dead in, nor was it the sort of place where they would have been welcome, but for the party, all barriers were down.

Princess Maya, the firedancer, showed up with Alice, her formidable bull-dyke friend and protector. Roger and Ralph, who lived in the elegantly converted stone cottage that dated back to settler's days, and who made hand-loomed caftans, put on their gayest clothes and an extra touch of makeup, and joined in the fun. Roger warned Ralph that if he got drunk and tried to pick up one of the Bahamian boys he would be sent packing, so Ralph confined himself to a few quick gropes in the crush.

Some of the ladies were at first uneasy in the heady broth of booze, music, and big Bahamian men who grabbed their hands and danced with them in a detached but most sexual way. But, as the evening wore on, the same ladies let their inhibitions and prejudices go hang and seriously wondered what they would do if they were actually propositioned.

Jill and Judy, the sixteen- and seventeen-year-old sibling nymphomaniacs, came to the party with no inhibitions and most certainly with no prejudices. They each had two double-vodkas-and-Coke, picked the biggest and best-hung men in the room, took them outside behind the pool hall, had a quick stand-up bang against a tree, and were back cruising the pool hall, all in the first fifteen minutes.

Sergeant Welsh drove up in his Jeep, slowed down, and kept going.

The party overflowed into the street and a second band was added; three local Bahamian teenage rockers brought their guitars, drums, amplifiers, and strobe lights. Extension power cords were strung round the side of the pool hall and in through the window of the men's washroom—which was also the women's washroom.

Around two o'clock in the morning, Big Daddy Brannigan—a natural bully—went around with a hat and collected $115.00. He added a hundred of his own, and Kevin Scott, who'd closed his liquor store to come to the party, was sent back to Scott's Wines and Spirits for more booze. This time Kevin contributed a case of suspicious Algerian red. It went into the punch; a bottle of apricot brandy took the bite out of it.

Sally eventually became one of the crowd at a party where no one knew or remembered who the host was. So, she left the guests, made herself a cup of tea, took it into the miserable living room, and reread an old *Cosmopolitan*. When she'd finished the tea she went into the bedroom, propped a chair under the doorknob, got into bed in her shirt and panties, and fell immediately asleep.

The party blasted on until the washed-out pink light of the dawn before the real dawn put everything back into unkind focus.

The rock band pulled the plugs on its amps and strobe lights. Jumbo had sunk into a coma, but the Island Trio still played: Doobie plucking unheard notes from his washtub bass; Maurice, fingers slack on his conga drum between his legs, gently massaging the skin of the drum in soft support, as Wes, bent low over his guitar, spun out simple chords and lovely melodies of centuries-old Island folk songs.

Most of the partyers had gone home, to their boats, houses, or hotel rooms. Big Daddy Brannigan still sat at the bar with two other last-ditch drinkers, each unwilling to be the one to call it quits. Two couples, eyes closed, arms around partners' necks, shuffled and swayed in no perceptible pattern. Boxer Waring danced by himself up in one corner of the room, from time to time snorting and throwing a short right cross or a left jab.

Under one pool table, Jill and Judy lay with their arms around each other, satisfied and asleep. Under the other pool table, a small, separate party was winding down. The four had long ago retreated from the main event and set up house with their own supply of liquor. The green baize of the tables, shiny and patched to begin with, was now scarred with cigarette burns and sodden with spilled drinks. Empty bottles, broken glasses, cigarette packages and butts, paper plates, and the remains of fried chicken and barbecued ribs covered the poolroom floor.

Maurice slowly folded over onto his conga drum. Wes came to the end of his lullaby, signaled to Doobie who woke Jumbo, and the Island Trio picked up its instruments and silently stumbled out into the sharp, clear morning. No one ever questioned why the Island Trio had four members.

As the light brightened and filtered in through the pool-hall window, cutting paths through the stale tobacco haze, the party to end all parties was finally over. In ones and twos the last survivors left, red-eyed, sour-mouthed, but with the bleary satisfaction of having seen it through to the end.

Sally awoke to complete silence. She got out of bed and tentatively put her head round the door into the bar, unsure of what she'd find. "Oh Gawd," she said. After a strong cup of tea and two slices of bread and jam, she put on her oldest jeans, tied a scarf around her head, and started to clean up.

SEVENTEEN

Harry and Freddie awoke with the dawn. Harry put on a pot of coffee, Freddie fried up bacon sandwiches. They took their breakfast onto the verandah of the bungalow and ate in silence. Guffy came down the path, joined them.

"As long as all I do is drive the boat, I might as well come with you," he said. "Nice morning for a ride to Bright's Cay. Snakes don't bother you, do they Freddie?"

Freddie looked up from his bacon sandwich. "Snakes? Waddya mean, snakes?"

Harry licked his fingers. "Don't listen to him, that's just an old wives tale."

"What is?"

"According to local legend—and you know how these crazy stories get handed down—there's poison-

230

ous snakes on Bright's Cay . . . s'posed to hide under the rocks and in the trees. It's a load of nonsense, there's no snakes on Bright's Cay, but these snakes which don't exist are the reason why none of the locals will go near the place, let alone set foot on it. Which is also one of the reasons why I picked it for our meeting."

"You sure about the snakes?" asked Freddie. "Snakes give me the creeps."

"No snakes, take it from me."

"Not so sure about that," Guffy muttered. "Anyways, don't make no never mind to me, I'm stayin' on the boat."

They went back into the bungalow, washed their breakfast dishes, got ready to leave. The two cardboard cartons that held the million dollars they left under the bed. At the beginning of the mission, these had been guarded and watched with unblinking care. Now, battered, salt-water stained, flaps torn, stolen, recovered, and killed for, the cartons had become abstract pieces in a Monopoly game in which the players made up the rules as they went along.

At eight-thirty Harry eased the *Rimshot* away from the dock, and under clear skies they leisurely cruised down to Bright's Cay, Guffy at the wheel, Harry and Freddie sitting in the stern, watching the boat's wake lazily curl away into the distance.

Bright's Cay was a pretty island, roughly kidney-shaped and scarcely a quarter of a mile long, a place of wind-ridged sand dunes, patches of lush sea grass and solitary travel-poster palms. The wide, gently sloping, white sand beaches and shallow waters made for safe swimming for children, but the snake myth kept locals away and tourists and visitors never found Bright's Cay.

In the sheltered curve of the island, Harry anchored the *Rimshot* in the shallow water, and he and Freddie waded ashore with their gear. They had first circled the Cay to determine if any other boats were there: not a single boat was anchored or approached.

Harry and Freddie now searched the island, checking possible hiding places.

"Clean," said Harry as they met up again.

"Not even a snake," said Freddie.

Harry looked at his watch. "Thirty-five minutes to go. No saying they'll stick to the time, so easy does it."

They stood in the shade of a palm tree and waited . . . watched and waited.

"Boat coming," said Harry, and passed the glasses to Freddie. "Keep looking," Harry said. He took off his shirt and pants; under his pants he wore swim trunks. From the gear piled at the base of the tree he picked up flippers, mask, snorkel, and spear gun. Guffy signaled from the boat that he saw the approaching cruiser. Freddie lay flat, legs spread army-style, behind a low sand dune, and he lined up a telescopic-sighted .303 carbine on the approaching boat.

"Must be them," Freddie called to Harry. Even without binoculars it was now plain the boat was headed for the cove where the *Rimshot* was anchored.

"We'll soon find out," said Harry.

From a canvas bag, Freddie took the towel-wrapped machine pistol, slammed in a magazine. Unhurriedly, Harry sauntered a hundred yards down the beach, put on his flippers, mask, and snorkel, and carrying his speargun, waded into the ocean, then ducked under the surface and swam out into deeper water. He came up, again swam under water, resurfaced, and generally carried on like a not very expert diver.

The boat came closer. It was a trim, thirty-five-foot Trojan with lots of speed. The driver stayed parallel with the shore and made a fast run past the *Rimshot*, then turned the boat in a tight arc and cut power. The Trojan settled in the water; the driver brought it by for a second look and pulled alongside the *Rimshot*. Guffy was in the cabin, the door closed; the *Rimshot* apparently had no one on board. A black-haired man with a drooping moustache and blue-lensed sunglasses was at the wheel of the Trojan. No second man was to be seen.

Along the beach, Harry waded out of the water, took off his flippers and, carrying his speargun and mask, started back. The Trojan pulled away from the *Rimshot* and, with engines ticking over, came closer to shore. The driver killed the engines and the Trojan came to rest with its bow on the sandy bottom of the cove.

Harry waved cheerfully to the droopy-mustached man and the man flipped one hand in token reply. When Harry was closer, the man pointed to the *Rimshot* and called out, "This your boat?" Harry waded through the shallow water toward him. "Not mine," he said. "Belongs to some people up the beach." He gestured vaguely and waded closer to the Trojan. "I've got my sailboat over the other side. Never been here before. Diving's lousy, isn't it?" Harry was now a bare five yards from the Trojan.

"Hold it there," said the man. "Don't come any closer."

"Why not?" asked Harry, wading another step.

The droopy mustached man reached behind his back, going to the waistband of his pants. Harry swung the loaded speargun so that it pointed at the man's stomach. "Leave it," said Harry, "Bring your hand slowly back where I can see it."

The man looked down at the serrated-edged spear sticking from the gun two feet from his belly. Slowly he brought his hand back.

"There were supposed to be two of you," said Harry. "Where's the other one, in the cabin?"

In answer, the second man came out fast from the cabin, holding an automatic pistol. He raised the gun in a two-hand grip, but took a fraction of a second too long getting set. Freddie shot him, his rifle bullet hitting the man in the shoulder, spinning him around. Lining him up in his telescopic sights, Freddie shot him a second time, this time through the chest. The man pitched backward, fell to the deck, very dead. Freddie got up from behind the sand dune, carrying the machine pistol, and walked to the water's edge.

"Okay," Harry said to the droopy-mustached man, who hadn't moved, "out you get." Droopy Mustache sat on the edge of the Trojan and slid into the water. Harry took the .38 revolver from the man's waistband, then pressed the point of the spear into his back. "Onto the beach," said Harry.

They waded to shore. "Bernie Ritter," said Freddie, "fancy meeting you here."

"Who is he?" Harry asked.

"He's nothing," said Freddie. "A punk who used to be a messenger boy for Mr. Chambers, a punk with big ideas, ain't you, Bernie?"

"Things has changed," Bernie said. "New deal. New people. Chambers is out, so back off."

"How do you mean, out?" Freddie said.

"Bang . . . like that out," said Bernie, aiming his pointing finger at his temple. "Out, like dead. Your old man is dead."

"I don't believe you," Freddie said. "I don't believe Mr. Chambers is dead."

Bernie laughed. "Oh, he's dead. I should know."

"I see," said Freddie. Then, to Harry, "Let the son of a bitch go."

"Let him go?"

"Yeah, let him go back to his new bosses. They ain't gonna be too pleased with him when he gets back without the money."

Harry lowered the speargun. Freddie walked down the beach, away from them. Bernie looked from one to the other to see if there was a trap, saw none, ran through the water to the boat, grabbed a rail and heaved himself over the side. As he stood, Freddie stitched Bernie through with a dozen rounds from the machine pistol. Bernie flailed in a spastic dance as the bullets hit him, then collapsed into the boat's cockpit, across the body of his dead partner. Freddie slowly walked back to join Harry. He dragged his feet like an old, tired man, an old man who knows he's no longer needed.

Guffy cautiously came out of the *Rimshot*'s cabin.

"We'll have to get rid of them," Harry said. "Let's do it now. Tell Guffy to bring the *Rimshot* out after me." He pushed the Trojan into deeper water and hauled himself over the transom. The cockpit was a bloody shambles. He picked his way past the bodies to the controls, started the engines, and headed the boat out to sea. Behind him he heard the *Rimshot*'s Chryslers turn over, catch, and fire.

Harry took the Trojan a mile out beyond the edge of the Bahama bank, where it could be ten thousand feet down to the ocean floor. He killed the engines and the Trojan drifted in the choppy seas. Blood-tinged water sloshed with the pitch and roll of the boat. Guffy brought up the *Rimshot* and slowly circled the Trojan. Harry left the wheel and from the galley took some rags and towels and a box of red-tipped kitchen matches from a rack over the single gas burner. Then he opened the hatch cover of the gas tanks, unscrewed the caps of the tanks, and soaked rolled-up towels in the gasoline. One towel he hung from a tank like a giant fuse. Working back, he laid a trail of the towels and rags, spaced a couple of feet apart, the last towel across the two bodies. He emptied the box of matches, except for seven or eight of the redtips, took one of these, scratched it alight, dropped it into the box, and as the cardboard box flared, pitched it onto the last of the gasoline-soaked rags and dived over the side of the boat.

Guffy swung the *Rimshot* toward him, but stayed well back from the Trojan. Harry swam toward the *Rimshot*, putting every ounce of muscle into the crawl. He counted to ten as he swam, then filled his lungs, dived, and switched to the breaststroke under water, conserving his air. Five seconds later the flames from the burning towels and rags, igniting in a chain reaction, reached the gas tanks, and the Trojan blew apart.

Harry felt the shock of the explosion under water, knew it was now safe to go up. Bits and pieces of the Trojan littered the surface of the water and close by him was something that could have been one of Bernie Ritter's arms. He swam to the *Rimshot*, Freddie pulled him on board. Guffy picked off charred chunks of wood and smoldering plastic that had reached the boat. Harry looked back to where the Trojan had been. Already, the flotsam was dispersing. In a few hours, the wind and waves and the fish would effectively take care of the remains.

"Let's go home," said Harry.

On the run back to Hog Cay, Freddie sat quietly, cradling the machine pistol. Guffy let the *Rimshot* cruise along at ten or twelve knots. From time to time, Harry looked at Freddie; the heavy, tired old man didn't want to talk. That was fine. Harry understood. Freddie felt Harry's eyes on him.

"I think it's about time I got into a different line of work," Freddie said. Slowly, painfully, he got out of his canvas chair. It seemed to take great effort for him to walk from the cockpit to the side of the boat. He dropped the machine pistol into the ocean. "I'll buy you another one," he said to Harry as he came back and again sat slumped in his chair.

As they approached Hog Cay, one of the competition boats came into sight, bait trailing behind it from antennae-like outriggers. Guffy gave the boat plenty of room. Up on the platform of the spindly tuna tower, the boat's mate recognized the *Rimshot* and waved, but he was too far away for Harry or Guffy to identify. More competition boats were thinly dotted along the mile-wide, unmarked ocean path that by common, unspoken agreement had been chosen as the most likely area to hit a good marlin. Through his glasses, Harry watched as one fisherman got a solid strike, saw him fasten the harness of his fighting chair, grab the rod from its holder, wait, set the hook, then begin his pumping, arm-wrenching fight. The fish broke water. The angler, whoever he was, had tied into a big broadbill. The beautiful fish again leaped in seeming slow motion, huge sail extended, head snapping in an effort to get free of the hook, then smashed back down into the ocean and headed for the bottom. The fight had only started.

Soon, Harry promised himself, sneaking a look at the empty fighting chair of the *Rimshot*, soon I'm going to take some time off and go fishing.

They tied up at the Club dock. "We've got to have a meeting," said Harry. "There's certain things have got to be decided. Let's have that meeting now."

"I got to make a coupla phone calls first," said Freddie. "Let's meet in the bungalow in fifteen minutes, okay?"

"Fifteen minutes," said Harry.

Freddie made his calls, and in the bungalow they sat in rattan chairs, a solemn-faced trio with decisions to make.

"The main issue," said Harry, "is what we do with the money. Just what do we do with one million dollars we can't deliver because the man we were supposed to deliver it to is dead." He looked at Freddie. "There is no doubt in your mind that Mr. Chambers is dead, is there, Freddie?"

"No, there's no doubt. One a the calls I just made was to Linc Butler, he was Mr. Chambers' driver. Been with Mr. Chambers nearly as long as me. Linc told me he was dead, shot through the head. Funeral's tomorrow."

"So, what do we do with the money?" said Harry.

All three turned to look at the two cartons wedged under the bed.

"Yeah, what do we do with the money?" Freddie echoed.

"Funny kinda situation, ain't it?" said Guffy, "A million bucks with no rightful owner."

"We've got to look at this logically," said Harry. "The money belonged to Mr. Chambers . . . how he got it, where it came from is none of our concern. Now he's dead, the money is part of his estate. "Does he have any family, Freddie?"

"His wife died a long time ago," said Freddie, "must be twelve, fifteen years or more. Hit by a car, crossing the street. I went to her funeral, too."

"Any children?"

"He's got a son," said Freddie. "A dentist in Wisconsin or Oregon or some such place. Got religion. Wouldn't have nothin' to do with his daddy. He'll give the money to his church if he gets his hands on it, one a them phony revivalist setups you see on TV. Mr. Chambers told me his son's given 'em millions. He can afford it, he's made a fortune outta real estate. He don't need no more money jus' to give to them religious hustlers."

"Nobody else? No other family?"

"Nobody else."

"Who knows we got the money . . . ?" asked Guffy. "Anybody else likely to come lookin' for it?"

"No, there won't be anybody else comin' over to try an' get their hands on it. Take my word," said Freddie.

"How can you be sure?" said Harry. "D'ya mean they're going to give up trying . . . ?"

"I made another phone call," said Freddie. "I took care a that."

"How?"

"I dropped the story in the right ear. I dropped the story that Bernie Ritter an' his friend grabbed the money on schedule an' took off with it, an was las' seen headin' south in a hurry—in the opposite direction from Miami, so Miami could wave good-bye to it."

"Will they buy that story?"

"They'll buy it. Look, nobody in that mob trusts nobody else," said Freddie. "They'll swallow the story cause it'll make sense to their crooked ways a thinkin'. By now the word's out that Bernie an' his pal made the heist an' copped the money for themselves, an' by now Bernie an' his pal will be on the mob's wanted list. Good luck."

With elaborate casualness, as if tossing out a whimsical idea, Harry said, "Of course, we could always split it three ways and let each of us worry about what to do with his third, couldn't we?"

Freddie and Guffy considered this.

"Have to be a four-way split," said Freddie. "I reckon poor old Morton oughta be figured in for a share. I know his wife an' kids could use the money, and I feel responsible for gettin' Morton into this an' gettin' him killed as a result. So we gotta count Morton in."

"All right," said Harry, "four ways, a quarter of a million each."

"It's more than that," said Freddie. "There's more'n a million there. Say three hundred thousand each, that would be closer."

"Three hundred thousand each," said Harry. "There's no way to trace this money, is there, Freddie?"

"No way in the world."

Each thought about the sudden windfall of three hundred thousand dollars in cash.

"Count me out," Freddie suddenly said. "I don't need it. I made money over the years. Mr. Chambers put me on to some good things, legitimate, mosta them. I got a twenty-two-unit apartment house in Lauderdale. I got a piece of a golf club up in Myrtle Beach. I set my son up in the contractin' business an' the kid's makin' more money'n he can spend. My daughter Laurel married a guy owns the Mother Nature's Delight hamburger chain. They just went public an' his end a it was seventeen million bucks, so they ain't hurtin'."

Harry said, "Well, I could use the money, but I don't need it. I've got my motel, free and clear, no mortgage. Got the *Rimshot*, all paid for. Got some money in the bank, and the motel makes me a fair living. There's nothing I need, so I'm going to pass, too."

Guffy rested his solemn black face in his hands. "Made up my mind long time ago I was gonna live an' die on Hog Cay. Got a house a sorts. Built it meself, don't owe nobody nothing on it. Got a few dollars savings, but not enough to last me. You two gentlemen so well off you don't need your share, but I'd like to put my name down for my piece a that money."

"There's one honest man," said Freddie.

"Dunno about honest," said Guffy. "Legally speakin' that money ain't ours to parcel out."

Freddie laughed, choked on his laugh. Harry slapped him on the back. "That money ain't exackly legal to begin with," Freddie said, after he'd caught his breath, "so I wouldn't worry yourself none on that score."

"Mebbe not, but it still ain't ours," Guffy persisted.

A troubling thought hit Harry. "Can you go back, Freddie? Safely, I mean. Will Miami be safe for you now?"

"I'm not goin' back," Freddie said. "Safe or not, I'm not goin' back. Made up my mind comin' here on the boat. First off, I thought a goin' back an' evenin' the score. Then I thought, that's stupid. Wouldn't do Mr. Chambers no good, wouldn't do me no good. With Mr. Chambers gone, there's nothin' left for me in South Florida, so I ain't goin' back. I'll see to it Morton's family gets his cut."

"So what do we do with the money?" said Harry. "Apart from Guffy's and Morton's shares, we still got over half a million dollars to dispose of."

It took Sally until lunchtime to clean up the wreckage of the pool hall. Eighteen cases of empty liquor bottles she stacked by the door, along with twenty cases of Beck's Beer bottles, twelve of Pauli Girl, and the zinc washtub piled with the Algerian red and pink champagne-type empties.

Not just a memorable party, an historic one. Hungover late risers drifted in from time to time, walking carefully and painfully. Sally opened a bottle of gin that had miraculously survived the carnage and offered each the traditional hair of the dog. Some accepted and drank their shot with trembling gratitude. Others closed their eyes and said no thanks, but they could sure use a cold beer. When Sally told them she had no beer, cold or otherwise, they got stiffly up from their barstools and made their suffering way to the next bar down the road.

Sally ate a bowl of cold conch chowder and four dried-out barbecued ribs that had been overlooked. Then she dragged the cases of empties and the washtub of wine bottles into the street and piled up cans and bags of garbage next to them.

Next, she tidied up the terrible living room and bedroom, throwing out old clothes of hers and everything that belonged to Bob. These she stuffed into two green garbage bags and pinned notes to the bags that said "For the Mission."

She washed, brushed her hair, dressed in fresh underclothes, her one good blouse and her best jeans, bundled up her other clean clothes and stuffed them in a small suitcase. From a hiding place under the closet floor, Sally took out her "trouble money," $345 she'd assembled. Every night, before she went to bed, Sally had tucked away a single one-dollar bill. This money Sally put in her purse along with her passport and birth certificate, slung the purse over her shoulder, picked up her bag, marched out through the poolroom without looking back, and walked, head high, down the Queen's Highway toward Pollack's Air Service. She'd forgotten if the afternoon plane went to Nassau or to Miami, but it didn't matter. Wherever it went, she was going to be on it.

Harry and Freddie and Guffy still sat in their rattan chairs, their meeting to decide what to do with the money stalemated.

"So, what do we do with the balance?" asked Harry "Half of it—six hundred thousand. What do we do with it?"

"There's always charities," said Guffy, laughing to show he wasn't really serious.

Freddie flapped a hand in disgust. "Rackets, most of 'em, an' I've just come to the conclusion that charity begins at home, so I'm changin' my mind about my share. Count me in with Guffy and Morton."

Harry sat silent, disquieting thoughts battling it out in those unpredictable and little understood parts of the brain and intelligence that deal with conscience and greed, right and wrong, virtue and the more primitive, baser emotion. Three hundred thousand dollars of dirty money. Money earned through crime. Money that had already been responsible for five deaths he personally knew of. Money accumulated through graft, fraud, extortion, and murder. And there he sat, contemplating sharing in this sordid, illicit, blood-stained profit.

A wave of revulsion rose like gall in his throat. He couldn't spend a penny of the tainted money without telling himself he was no better than the men who'd cynically and mercilessly assembled it. But he could put it to good use. He could justify taking it so long as he didn't keep any for himself. A while ago, Guffy had said, half-jokingly, that they could give it to charity.

And why not? Here was a chance to square his conscience and do good at the same time. A perfect way out of his dilemma.

That's what he'd do: divide it up between a dozen deserving and above-board charities and missions. Anonymously, of course. The poor, the homeless, the desperate, had no cause or reason to question the slimy origins of the benefits they would receive. In total, it wouldn't go far in solving the miseries of the world, but it would help. By God, it would help.

None of this would he attempt to explain to Guffy and Freddie. As far as they were concerned he would simply be taking what was due to him—collecting his share of the reward for the drama and dangers they'd been through, dividing the jackpot they'd won in a grimly bizarre lottery. No philosophizing at this point. No rationalizing or ponderous self-justification. Keep it simple. Take the money and shut up.

He pounded on the table, a chairman bringing the meeting to order. "You're right," Harry said to Guffy, "and you're right too, Freddie. I've just declared us all a charitable organization, and we're going to fund ourselves with a sizable endowment, so get the money."

Guffy clapped his hands in delight. "You two had me worried back there. Glad you finally got your thinkin' straight."

Freddie dragged the two cartons of money from under the bed.

"You go out on the verandah, Guffy," said Harry. "Anybody comes up the path, let us know."

Guffy went out and sat on the verandah. He had a clear view of the path and could also watch through the window of the bungalow as Harry and Freddie divided up the money.

"Four piles," said Harry, and in four piles they stacked equal bundles of dollars, francs, marks, and pounds. When they had finished, they put each share in a canvas duffel or a suitcase and closed the bags. Harry called Guffy in. "Take your pick." They each chose a bag, and the fourth bag Harry put by Morton's belongings. "You'll look after Morton's?" he asked Freddie.

"Yeah, I'll get it to his family."

"He got a big family?"

"Yeah, wife, kids, brothers, sisters, in-laws. This'll give 'em somethin' to fight over."

As Sally passed the police station, Sergeant Welsh came out with the handcuffed Bob and Mike and loaded them into the Jeep. Sally kept walking, determined not to look at Bob, but as the Jeep drove past her she stopped, put down her bag and watched until the Jeep disappeared round the curve by the ice-cream parlor. Bob didn't look back. Sally picked up her bag and continued down the road.

Harry and Freddie and Guffy sat in the bungalow, each with his bag of money. Freddie made the first move. "There's a plane to Nassau this afternoon, isn't there?"

Harry checked the time. "Leaves in about twenty minutes, if you're planning to be on it. You going to Nassau?"

"Yeah. That way I don' have any hassles with customs, not like I would if I went back to the U.S.A. Once I'm in Nassau, it'll be a snap to get the money transferred. I got friends in Nassau, they'll launder it for me." Freddie packed his change of clothing, folded Morton's things into the big carry-all that held Morton's share of the loot. "Be seein' you," he said.

"Take care." He grabbed his and Morton's bags and carried them through the door that Guffy held open for him.

"Freddie's okay," said Guffy.

"I wonder what he's going to do?" said Harry. "No wife, no Mr. Chambers to look after."

Guffy shrugged. "He's got three hundred grand."

"I hope he lives to enjoy it," Harry said.

Sergeant Welsh pulled the Jeep into Pollack's and parked in the shade of a stubby palm tree.

"Out you get," he said, and led the handcuffed pair across the concrete, up the six aluminum steps, and into the plane. "Sit at the back." Bob and Mike sat together in one pair of seats, the sergeant in the aisle seat opposite them.

Two tourists boarded. The woman saw the hand-cuffs, whispered something to her husband, and the couple went to the very front of the plane, as if distance lent security.

Sally got to Pollack's, bought her ticket, and sat on the wooden bench outside the office, determined not to board the plane until the last minute.

Freddie arrived in a cab. Sally wondered what was taking this sad, weary old man in the windbreaker and workboots to Nassau, and she decided that in spite of the fact he was such a big, ugly old man, he was probably very nice and wouldn't hurt a fly.

The pilot came out of the office and Sally followed him and the big old man to the plane. She had to pass Bob and Mike to get to a seat. Bob looked out of the window, but Sally knew he'd seen her.

Harry and Guffy heard the plane take off.

"'Bout time I went home to Lucy," said Guffy, picking up his bag of money.

"Think I'll wander down and see Sally," said Harry.

"None a my bizness, but what you plannin' to do about Sally?"

"I'm going to say good-bye to her, tell her I'm going fishing, and I don't know when I'll be back."

"You goin' fishin'?" said Guffy. "How long you goin' for? Where you goin?"

"I'm going to complete the charter," said Harry. "I'm going to get myself a mate, one of the guys you recommended, and I'm going down the Islands and across to Haiti, just the way we originally planned."

"You are?" said Guffy. "Well, I'll tell you. Now we ain't got people after us all the time, shootin' and carryin' on, I might jus' change my mind an' come with you."

"No," said Harry. "I've got to get off the Island before sundown. Sergeant's orders. I'm now an undesirable, remember? I can't involve you. Keep your nose clean, the sergeant told you, so keep out of trouble from here on."

"Guess you're right," Guffy said reluctantly. "Wish you hadn't told me 'bout goin' on that fishin' trip. Will I see you again before you go?"

"No. I'm just going up to Sally's, then I'm coming back here, packing my stuff, and taking off. Buy you a beer at Sally's, though."

They walked together up the Queen's Highway in the heat and dust and glare of the afternoon. When they got to the pool hall, Harry said, "Coming in for a beer?"

"Reckon I'll head on home," said Guffy. "You don't want me hangin' around when you're sayin' your good-byes. Good luck to you, Harry."

"Good luck to you, Guffy. Thanks for everything."

The two men shook hands, a little self-consciously. Guffy headed home, Harry pushed open the door of the pool hall. The long room was empty, swept clean. No pool players. No one at the bar. No sign of Sally. Harry called her name, and when there was no reply, went into the living room, and then the bedroom. The bed had been stripped, the sheets folded at the bottom of the bed. The curtained alcove that served as a closet was stripped bare. The drawers of the chest were empty. Two green garbage bags, packed with rolled-up clothes, bore notes, "For the Mission." Sally had gone.

Harry stowed his stuff in the *Rimshot*. He gave a dollar to a kid fishing off the dock to help him with the boat's lines. A familiar Jeep turned onto the dock and pulled up by the *Rimshot*. Constable Mathews was driving.

"Sergeant had to go to Nassau with the prisoners," he said. "Told me to make sure you off Hog Cay by sundown."

"I'll be gone," said Harry. "Give my regards to Sergeant Welsh when he returns."

"Will do," said Mathews.

Harry fired up the *Rimshot*'s engines. The boy pitched the last line into the stern and went back to his fishing pole. Harry eased the *Rimshot* away from the Club dock, out through the channel and past the reef.

If he didn't screw around, he could make Chub Cay before dark, first leg of his marvelous fishing trip. On the other hand, if he didn't screw around, he could make it back to Florida before dark, back to Balmy Breezes. He'd only been gone five days; Martin Pomeroy couldn't have gotten into too much trouble in that time.

The fishing trip wouldn't be the same without Guffy. Maybe he wouldn't like either of these two men Guffy had recommended. Hell of a thing to be cooped up for two weeks at least with someone you didn't get on with. He should have called Martin Pomeroy from the Club before he left, put his mind at ease . . . or learn the worst.

Make the decision, Harry. Wheel hard over left for Chub Cay . . . hard over right for Balmy Breezes.

"Oh hell," said Harry, as he spun the *Rimshot*'s wheel to the right, "One of these days I really am going to take off some time and go fishing."

He slammed the throttles full open. No screwing around. He was going to make it home before dark.

THE BEST IN SUSPENSE

BESTSELLING BOOKS FROM TOR